IMMORTAL ME

WINDED

EMMA SHELFORD

This is a work of fiction. Names, characters, places, and incidents either are the product of the author's imagination or are used factitiously, and any resemblance to any persons, living or dead, business establishments, events, or locales is entirely coincidental.

WINDED

Kinglet Books
Victoria BC, Canada

Cover design by Deranged Doctor Designs

ISBN: 978-1989677148 (print)
ISBN: 978-1989677056 (ebook)

www.emmashelford.com

First edition: May 2017

DEDICATION

For Oliver

CHAPTER I

The scent of hot fat and powdered sugar permeates the air. Punishing sunlight beats down on the crowd milling over black tarmac, and excited screams from carnival riders fill my ears. If I half-shut my eyes and breathe deeply, I can almost pretend that I'm at a market of my past. Perhaps in Bavaria—in what is now Germany—to trade silver for a new comb for my wife Gretchen.

But it's many hundreds of years later across an ocean and a continent, in Vancouver, Canada, and there are no combs to buy. And I'm not with my ninth wife but with Jennifer Chan, my current friend. There are worse places to be.

"I remember as a kid I wanted to win one of those stupid arcade games so badly. Those huge stuffed animals were beyond tantalizing." Jen gazes wistfully at the long row of game stalls, bright-colored and tawdry in the dusty heat. Discordant music fights with clangs and beeps, assaulting our ears along with the shouts of carnies. Prizes sway above our heads, cheap and fluorescent. I glance at Jen, whose nostalgia is written across her face as longing.

"Oh, come on, then," I say with mock resignation. "I'll win you one." I walk down the row, scouting for a game I can win with ease. A shiny gray lauvan floats across my vision, unattached to any source. Only I can see lauvan, the threads that swirl around each living person and object that has energy. I look around to find the source, but no one with gray lauvan is in sight. Jen catches up with me, her own gold-colored strands wrapped around her torso and shimmering in her wake.

"They're all rigged, Merry. Thanks for the thought, truly, but you don't need to waste your money."

"Oh, ye of little faith." I stop in front of a stall and consider the possibilities. It's an archery game—hit a bull's eye three times, win the largest prize. The bow has never been my favorite weapon, as hand-to-hand combat offers far more opportunity for lauvan manipulation, but fifteen centuries has afforded me more than enough experience to beat this contest. I dig into my pocket and pass the carnie a five-dollar bill, which he accepts with grimy fingers and a lopsided grin.

"Feeling lucky?" he says. "Pick your weapon. You get three shots." He hands me three arrows.

I examine the bow. I have never seen anything so cheaply made. I'm not confident the plastic will withstand the bending it is made to do, and when I pluck the string experimentally, there is hardly any give. The arrows are no better—two of them are bent and the third's feathers are almost completely stripped. I carefully inspect them all to learn how I must shoot for accuracy. Jen bites her lip next to me, her face a war between pity and an attempt to stifle laughter.

"Choose your favorite prize," I say to her. "This won't take long." Jen purses her lips and raises her eyebrows in skepticism at my words. "And also, promise me you'll put this thing to good use."

"What do you mean?"

"I don't know, perhaps frighten your roommate with it. Put it in her bed before she wakes up. And then toss it in the nearest bin—these stuffed things have been hanging here for who knows how long. They're disgusting."

"Let's cross that bridge when we come to it, shall we?"

"Promise me."

"Fine! I promise. Now let's see your amazing shot, Robin Hood."

I wasn't in England during the reign of King John, so I never found out if Robin Hood was a real person. It's often difficult to identify which noteworthy characters will become legends that stand the test of time. Some incredible souls are lost to memory forever and other mediocre people are immortalized. It's a mystery to me.

Without further words, I set one of the bent arrows to the bow and pull back to align my sights with the bull's eye. I aim to the left and a hair's breadth down to account for the arrow's bend. I breathe out and release.

The arrow leaves the bow with a dull twang and pierces the target with a thud, right in the center of the bull's eye.

Jen laughs incredulously and the carnie whistles.

"You won a prize," he says, waving a plastic figurine that I don't bother looking at.

"Keep it. I'm going for the grand prize."

"Maybe you should quit while you're ahead," Jen says.

"What sort of attitude is that?" I notch the other bent arrow in the string and sight, then release. It slots in snugly against the first arrow. Jen gasps.

"I'm almost a believer. Convert me, Merry."

"Not a problem." The last arrow, the featherless one, will be tricky, but nothing I can't handle. With my released breath, it flies in a wobbling line to push aside the first two arrows and slide in smoothly between them. The other arrows end up at drunken angles against the target.

"Well?" I say to Jen after I place the bow carelessly on the counter and turn to gauge her reaction. She stares at me, a slow smile crawling over her expression of disbelief.

"That was incredible. When did you learn archery?"

I suppose "time beyond reckoning" isn't a helpful answer.

"Oh, a long time ago. What can I say? I'm talented."

"Yeah, and so modest, too. You know, you were born in the wrong century. If you'd lived a few hundred years ago, you would have been a very dangerous man."

"Indeed, very dangerous to my enemies, but excellent to my

friends. Choose your prize, my lady." I wave at the dangling animals, then address the carnie. "Which can she pick?"

"Any of the big ones," he says, examining the target with its three arrows as if looking for a trick. "Congrats, mister. I've never seen anyone shoot like that."

Jen peers up, and then points to a dusty stuffed bear in the corner.

"That one, please."

I follow her gaze as the carnie grabs a pole and unhooks the bear from the rafters. It's quite hideous, with fluorescent blue and green fur and beady black eyes atop a too-wide grin. My jaw drops.

"You have to be joking. That's the ugliest mockery of an animal I've ever laid eyes on."

"I think it's cute. And you told me to choose."

"Only because I thought you had better taste than that."

Jen thanks the carnie and we walk away. When we are out of earshot, Jen clucks at me.

"Did you do that using your—you know, the lauvan thing?"

"What? No!" I protest vehemently, briefly annoyed that she thought I had to rely on lauvan manipulation instead of my own physical skills. Then I kick myself—that would have been a perfect excuse for my archery proficiency.

"When did you pick up competitive archery? Seriously, Merry, that was ridiculously good. Especially with that cheap equipment from the forties."

"I'm a man of mystery and multitudinous talents." A cop-out, but also true.

"I'm surprised, but I shouldn't be. That's exactly something I could see you being good at. It matches your neo-pagan tattoo job." She grabs my arm and flips it over to expose the blue oak leaf on my inner forearm then drops it again. "Are you going to tell me you can ride a horse, now?"

"Can't everyone?"

Jen laughs and pushes my arm playfully.

"I think we've done the fair. Let's head back and grab a drink. My treat for you winning me the bear."

As we turn for the exit, a single unattached strand floats across my vision, not an arm-span distant. It's the gray lauvan again, shiny and gleaming in the intense summer sun. I look around but no one nearby has strands of that description. Free-floating lauvan without a visible source? It can mean someone is hiding while feeling anxious, fearful, or vengeful, and that emotion causes strands to shed with enough frequency that I can spot them. And if I keep seeing the same source-less lauvan, it's possible that someone is following me.

Few people follow me with goodwill in their hearts. I should stay vigilant.

Jen swishes her straw against the ice in her cup, rattling the frozen chunks together loudly.

"I don't know how you're drinking hot coffee," she says. She shakes her head at me and fans her face to make her point. "It's only a thousand degrees out here."

"Poor northern girl. It's an unseasonal twenty-eight, max." I take a sip of my espresso. It's warm out, sure, but I'm flexible within reason. Jen, on the other hand, is visibly glistening. She holds her icy cup against her cheek and hisses through her teeth when the cold touches her skin.

"Who are you calling a northern girl? You said you were born in Wales."

She doesn't miss a trick, this one.

"I've lived all over since then. And speaking of heat," I say, putting my cup down in its petite saucer. "I'm leaving town for a few days."

"Oh, yeah? Where to?"

"You remember I told you about my friend who lives in Costa Rica?" Not that I told her much—I have known Braulio for well over seven decades, which is difficult to explain to Jen. "Well, it turns out he's not living there anymore." I trace the saucer's edge with my finger and track the movement with my eyes. "Let me rephrase that—he's not living, anymore. His funeral is on Tuesday."

Jen draws in her breath quickly.

"Oh, Merry. I'm so sorry." She grabs my fidgeting hand and clasps it between both of her own. "What happened?"

"Nothing unexpected." I raise my eyes to meet hers which are filled with compassion. I look down again quickly before she can elicit too much of a response from me. I don't want to travel that road at the moment—it's the only path I have wandered for the past week and a half. "Thanks, Jen." I let her hold on for a moment longer, then I give her hands a squeeze and take my own back. "It'll only be overnight. I'm going for the funeral and coming straight back. No need for sightseeing—I've seen that region before." And it's too soon to visit there again without Braulio by my side.

I look at Jen and smile. She returns the smile uncertainly, her eyes still concerned, but she seems willing to follow my lead. Ever since the incident at the volcano two weeks ago and her introduction to the world of lauvan, she seems reluctant to push me too much. It works for me.

A tinkling noise from Jen's purse that squats like a great misshapen toad on the table saves me from thinking of something to say. Jen digs through the plentiful mess within and extracts her phone.

"Oh, it's Cecil," she says offhandedly, then all her strands freeze as if she realizes she let something slip.

Naturally, I'm intrigued.

"And who is Cecil, might I ask?" I take another sip of my espresso while I wait for Jen's answer.

"Didn't I tell you? I met this guy at a friend's party last month." Jen shrugs nonchalantly, but her strands fidget around her body. She is nervous, for some reason. Does she really like him, or is she still deciding and so doesn't want to talk about him yet with others?

Or does she not want to tell me?

If so, it's high time for Jen to face her fears. It's good for her, with an excellent side effect of amusing me.

"What did Cecil say? What a name. I thought it had mercifully expired last century."

"He was named after his grandfather," Jen says, a touch defensively. "He was wondering when I was free."

"No time like the present." Quicker than Jen can react, I lean forward and snatch the phone from her unsuspecting fingers. One hand types a reply while the other fends off Jen's half-hearted attempts to grab her phone.

"Hi, Cecil," I say aloud slowly as I thumb-type. "I'm at the coffee shop at Fourth and Alma. I'd love to see you." I press send.

"You did not just do that!"

"Oh, come on. That was positively restrained. I was very tempted to put 'xoxo.' I think I ought to be commended."

Jen half-stands and take the phone out of my unresisting fingers.

"You're so annoying sometimes, you know that, right?" Her phone tinkles, and she quickly scans the new message. "Damn it, he's just around the corner. He'll be here in three."

"What I want to know is, are you embarrassed of him or of me?" I smile impishly at Jen and she huffs dramatically.

"Oh, neither. I just—this is very new, and I don't even know him much yet…"

"Still, a month of testing—he can't be that bad."

Jen laughs incredulously.

"Well, yeah, if we evaluate based on your track record. That girl in February, did you manage a whole month?"

"Five weeks with Andrea, thank you very much. And over two months with—damn, I forgot her name."

"Exactly my point. A month for me is still new. So, be nice."

"I'll try," I say dubiously. "But it's not my default mode. And no guarantee I'll try very hard."

"There he is," Jen hisses. She composes her face into a cheerful expression and waves behind me.

I don't bother turning around. He will come to us soon enough and I don't want to appear too interested, like a jealous boyfriend. I think I will go the big brother route instead. That could be fun.

"Cecil, hi," Jen says. She hovers on the edge of her seat as if unsure whether to stand and greet the newcomer or stay seated as he arrives. I chuckle to myself. Etiquette is not very well defined in this era and changes all the time.

Cecil rounds the corner into my line of view. I take a slow sip of my coffee—the last sip, unfortunately, I would have liked it as a prop—and raise my eyes to examine the stranger. He is tall, almost gangly, but decently built despite that. I get the sense that he has worked hard to put some substance on his lanky frame. His face is strong-featured, topped with sandy blond hair cut in a carefully decided style. His eyes are an intense, piercing blue, and overall, I can see why Jen is attracted to him. He's not a bad specimen, all in all.

That gives me even more reason to check his motivations with respect to Jen.

"Merry, this is Cecil," Jen says brightly. Only I can see that her strands are tense and jittery. "Cecil, this is my friend Merry."

I stand with a languid motion and extend my hand.

"Pleasure to meet you, Cecil."

"You—you too." He eyes me uncertainly. "I was expecting a Mary. M-A-R-Y."

I smile widely, showing my teeth.

"M-E-R-R-Y, actually. Fair enough mistake. Here," I pull a chair from a nearby table closer. "Have a seat." Cecil nods his thanks and sits down. I raise my eyebrows at Jen as if to say *See? I can be nice*, and she hides a smile behind her iced coffee.

"Did you have a good time at the fair?" Cecil asks Jen after a second of awkward pause.

"Oh, yes," Jen replies immediately as if happy to latch onto an easy topic. She starts to prattle about the motocross show and the food vendors. I tune out the audible conversation and watch the silent one. It's quite sweet, actually. Thin tendrils of Jen's golden lauvan cautiously twist and snake their way slowly toward Cecil, whose own russet strands are performing a similar tentative dance. Every so often, the ends of their lauvan touch and they explore each other gently before jolting back like nervous colts.

It would bring warmth to my jaded old heart if I didn't notice that Jen's lauvan are much more hesitant than Cecil's are. Once or twice, Cecil's strands wrap their ends around Jen's, attempting to capture them. Jen's twist away every time, only responding positively to Cecil's gentler overtures. I frown. This one might bear watching. There is more attraction on his side than on hers, and his lauvan methods don't bode well for how he might act in the physical world.

I tune back into the conversation when I hear my name.

"And then Merry won me this bear at the archery stall. Isn't it cute?"

Cecil looks at the grinning mockery of a teddy bear and grimaces.

"I think you have a very generous definition of cute," he says dubiously. Hah. I like him better already. I cut in.

"Of course it's not cute—it's a monstrosity hiding a belly full of moldering sawdust under its maniacal grin. I only won it for you because you promised to frighten your roommate with it and then toss its plague-ridden corpse into the dumpster at the first opportunity."

Cecil snorts and Jen pats the bear's head.

"There, there, he didn't mean it," she says consolingly to the bear. "So, what were you thinking for this afternoon?" This is directed at Cecil.

"Oh, um," Cecil briefly glances at me then back to Jen. "There's a festival on, down by the beach. There's a play at four. I thought you might be interested."

"Sounds great," Jen says at once. "We'd better get moving. I'll pay and we can head out." Jen jumps to her feet and hefts her purse to her shoulder.

"Don't throw your back out with that thing," I say, and she wrinkles her nose at me as she leaves. I turn to Cecil once she is safely inside.

"All right, Cecil." I lean forward to rest my weight on my forearms and gaze at him calmly. "What's the deal with you and Jen?"

Cecil sputters incoherently until he finally pushes out, "What do you mean 'deal?'"

"Awkward, indecisive response. Noted." I nod as if completing an internal checklist. "What was the name of your last girlfriend?"

"What?" Cecil looks nonplussed. "I don't see how that's any of your business."

"Hmm. Either hiding something or still a virgin."

"What?" Cecil yelps.

"Don't resist me, Cecil. I only want to know you better. Jen doesn't have an older brother, so feel free to slot me in that role." I note with satisfaction that Cecil's eyes are wide and uncertain, the anger that was forming not overtaking him yet. I'm having too much fun to stop now, so I continue while Jen is gone and I have the chance. "You seem like a decent guy, Cecil, despite the unfortunate moniker, so I'll give you a friendly warning—mess with Jen, and I'll be waiting for you on the other side." I flash him a smile that is calculated to be too wide and too calm for comfort. "You understand, I'm sure."

Cecil looks at me, alarm not at all hidden under a careful expression of neutrality. I try not to laugh and decide to lay off. Jen did ask me to be nice, after all. I lean back.

"Good call on the play, by the way. Definitely up Jen's alley."

Cecil breathes easier at my statement, although his strands stay tensed.

"Yeah? Okay, good. She seems the type, but you can never be sure."

Jen bustles back, her lauvan visibly calmer than before. She must not have overheard my conversation with Cecil.

"All paid up. Thanks for getting me out to the fair today, Merry."

"Anytime. Thanks for the coffee." I turn to Cecil. "Jen's a thoroughly modern woman, so she may insist on paying for half." I flash her a smile when she rolls her eyes. "But perhaps she makes a special dispensation for dating."

"Umm," Cecil stammers.

"Stop being a pain, Merry. Come on, Cecil." She gives me a wave and steps off the patio with her carnival bear. Cecil nods at me mutely and scuttles after Jen.

I'm not quite ready to leave the sunny patio with its happy clientele chattering around me. A light breeze swirls through an alder across the street, air lauvan dancing among the leaves. I let my mind go blank for a minute, not looking, not thinking, simply being.

Then I see it. To my left, just beyond a laughing patron's head, floats a shiny lauvan, the steely gray of a stormy sea. It's an untethered piece that drifts freely in the wind. I frown. It's the same lauvan I saw at the fair this morning when I sensed we were being followed.

I glance around surreptitiously as if looking for a waiter but don't see anyone out of the ordinary. Not that I would expect someone skulking in a trench coat and looking shifty—too clichéd, and it's too hot for coats—but I would recognize the strands if I saw similar ones surrounding a nearby body. I'm out of luck—nobody's lauvan in the vicinity even remotely approaches the steely gray of the floating threads.

I stand up, struck by an idea. Quickly but calmly, I push in my chair and stroll off the patio in the direction of the lauvan. It meanders down the sidewalk, pushed and pulled from the breeze created by strands of passersby.

I catch up to it at an intersection. My hand darts out as if I am waving to someone across the street, but instead I grasp the lauvan between my finger and thumb and draw it down to my side. I wait for the light to turn while I explore the strand, letting my own chocolate-brown threads tentatively prod and poke and wrap their tendrils around the gray strand. This is not a conscious move on my part—my lauvan would act this way toward any foreign threads.

Immediately, I receive a sense of the person who produced this lauvan. Nothing as clear as a vision of a face—even gender is unlikely. No, I'm restricted to a sense of personality or attitude, which can still be enlightening.

This lauvan has a strong signature of anger, with undertones of vengeance and a large dose of fear and desperation. My mouth tightens. That is a potent combination for someone who may or may not be following me for purposes unknown. I release the lauvan and it drifts away in currents no one can sense. I will have to be vigilant. I don't know who the person is, or why they're interested in me, but I do know one thing.

They are not getting the upper hand over Merlin.

CHAPTER II

Dreaming

We are lucky with the weather today. This time three years ago, when we hammered out a truce with Framric's Saxon army on our borders, it rained until the river broke its banks. Today dawned brilliant sunshine, cool but bright and spring-like. It's a perfect day for the festivities.

There is a clang when sword parries sword and a gasp from the crowd. The two combatants step back and circle each other to look for an opening. I'm on the edge of my bench, engrossed in the fight. One fighter lunges in a clumsy maneuver and misses his target who dances away.

"No, Balin!" I shout in exasperation with the crowd's collective groan. Balin is a fine swordsman in Arthur's service, but he's not showing his talent this afternoon. "You can move faster than that!"

Perhaps goaded by my taunt, Balin swings his sword up over his head to release a mighty blow. His opponent, the son of an Irish lord settled in eastern Brycheiniog, moves to block the downward stroke. Balin deftly changes his angle and cuts in from the side under the other's sword. The blow to the man's ribcage causes him to crumple, winded and bruised but alive. They fight with blunted weapons.

The crowd cheers and Balin raises his arm in triumph before he offers it to his vanquished opponent, who takes it gratefully.

I sit back on the bench. Guinevere claps politely for a moment. She hides her boredom well, but I can see more than most. It's a long morning of contests if one has no interest in them.

"Only a few more bouts before the meal," I reassure her. Guinevere nods gratefully at me. Arthur looks at us, his boyish face flushed and eyes bright from excitement. His expression turns to concern at my words.

"Are you weary of the games, Guinevere? I did not think to ask. Would you like to leave early?"

Guinevere smiles and pats Arthur's knee.

"Thank you, my lord," she says in her stilted Brythonic. "No, I stay. These fights are important. Saxons and your people together. People see me leave, what do they think?"

"True enough," I say. "These games, the festival, you did start it to celebrate the truce. Guinevere is an important part of that truce, and the people need to see her support."

"I could tell you what's going on," says Arthur, taking Guinevere's hand. "What each man is trying to do, good attacks, bad defenses. Would you like that?"

Guinevere leans against her husband, looking pleased.

"Yes, my lord."

"Wait a minute." Arthur looks my way. "Why haven't you taken your place in the sparring grounds, Merlin? I had my contest ages ago."

"You won almost," Guinevere says consolingly.

"It was close, but the better man won," says Arthur. "But Merlin has been unusually still and quiet all morning."

"Not quiet, loud," Guinevere murmurs with a smile at me.

"I would have thought the answer was obvious, Arthur. I fight to win, and I use every means at my disposal. Even the more unorthodox. I have an unfair advantage in a friendly contest, so I withdrew from the competition. Rather good of me, I thought."

"Oh, indeed. So kind of you to give us lesser folk the opportunity to shine," Arthur teases. "Why don't you try a fight without lauvan?"

"It's hard to separate lauvan and sword work—I only ever use both together."

"I think you're afraid you won't win without it."

"Oh, hush," Guinevere says, but I laugh.

"If you're trying to goad me into a fight, you succeeded. Boy," I beckon to a nearby servant. "Bring me my jerkin. Guinevere, where does your father sit?"

Guinevere scans the crowd, then points to a large blond man close by.

"There."

"Excellent. Don't wish me luck—I won't need it."

I stand and stride over to Framric, Guinevere's father and the chieftain of the Saxons with whom we have allied. I hail him in a loud voice in his own tongue.

"Lord Framric! Who is your fiercest warrior? I wish to challenge him." I repeat the declaration in Brythonic for the benefit of the crowd that watches me with interest and roars its approval at my words. Framric looks surprised but willing and confers with a man sitting three down from him. The man nods and Framric leans back.

"Your challenge will be met, Merlin. Meet Osgar, a warrior unparalleled."

The other man rises in place. I recognize him from an earlier bout. He is huge, at least a head or so taller than me, with braided hair and a grim brow. Muscles bulge beneath his sleeveless tunic and I wonder what I have landed myself in. He won his last fight handily—the other man still hasn't appeared from the healers' tent.

We greet each other with nods and a firm grasp of each other's forearms.

"You'll regret your brash challenge," Osgar says in Saxon.

"There are many who would contradict you," I say with a wicked grin. "But all of those are dead in battle and cannot talk."

Osgar grunts in return.

We break apart and I allow the serving boy to help me with my leather jerkin. Osgar pulls on a thick leather coat and accepts a blunt spear from an attendant. The blunted two-handed sword the attendant gives me is longer and heavier than my usual sharpened *spatha.* Sweat gathers on my brow as I consider my disadvantages. Huge opponent. Unfamiliar weapon. No lauvan. Why did I let Arthur get under my skin? This was a much better idea on the bench.

When we are prepared, we march to the center of the straw-strewn sparring ground. The crowd cheers. I eye Osgar, looking for potential weak points. He is depressingly fit and holds a sturdy round shield. He sustained one injury from his previous match, visible to me as a knot of lauvan on the lower right side of his ribcage. I promised Arthur I wouldn't manipulate lauvan to win, but I can't stop myself from seeing them. And once I see the knot, how can I ignore my advantage?

A drum pounds once, and Osgar and I begin to circle. I like to keep fights fast and my opponents on their toes, so I don't wait for long before striking first. I feint to the right with a real slice to the left thigh before I dance out of range. Osgar winces but is otherwise unmoved. He lunges forward with his spear which I dodge nimbly by sidestepping, but it was a ploy for him to get close enough to grasp my arm and pull me in.

Oh, no. Grappling with an overlarge opponent with no lauvan allowed? I have a few moves but I'm clearly at the disadvantage here. Better get out while I can and put a sword-distance between us.

I try to ignore the lauvan swirling tantalizingly in front of my eyes. Osgar throws me over his back in a move designed to stun me, but I twist halfway through and roll gracelessly but safely a distance away. I regain my footing just before a disturbance of air lauvan alerts me to an incoming missile. I dodge it narrowly and Osgar's spear thuds into the ground beside me, shaking with the force of impact.

That's it. This fight is not going my way and I need to change the tide fast. I charge Osgar with a whirlwind of blows designed to overwhelm. He backs away, around in a circle. Too late, I realize his goal and shout in frustration, but he yanks his spear out of the ground and uses it to block further blows.

Neither of us has the advantage now, until by chance I slip inside his defense. I seize my opportunity and press my blade to Osgar's throat. My victorious grin barely has time to cross my lips before the cold iron of Osgar's spear presses into my own neck.

We are still for a long moment, silence between us and in the crowd beyond. I break it by starting to laugh. I take my sword away and step back but hold out my arm in friendship.

"Well fought, my friend. A win for both parties?"

Osgar's broad face splits in a grin to match mine and he grasps my arm heartily.

"A win for both! Come brother, let us drink together. I'll bet I can drink you under the table."

"That's a challenge I'll gladly accept."

The crowd cheers.

CHAPTER III

The next day, I'm walking in the cool under a row of trees on campus when I hear my name.

"Merry! Hold up."

I turn to see Wayne Gibson striding behind me. He's just shy of forty, his balding head gleaming in the dappled sun. His short but well-built body and beginnings of a tan contrast against the white and doughy physique of many who work here. He's a good man, and one I should probably get to know better, if I recall Braulio's advice to open up. I have been reserved during our casual lunches and hallway conversations thus far.

"Wayne. Heading to your office?"

"Yes, marking awaits. On a day like today, you don't know how tempted I am to hand out random letter grades and escape to the beach instead."

"I hear you, loud and clear."

"What are you teaching this term?" Wayne's forehead glistens in the persistent heat.

"Currently? A condensed course on Shakespearean tragedies and another on Chaucer and his contemporaries. In a few weeks I'll start one on medieval French literature for the French department—they want me to fill in for an instructor on maternity leave."

"French, hey? Better you than me. I'm up for politics of the Italian Renaissance over the next few weeks." Wayne waves at a passing colleague and then winces. I glance pointedly at the livid purple bruise that peeks out from under his sleeve.

"What a shiner. I hope the other guy looks worse." I say it in jest, but Wayne nods.

"He does." At my bemused expression, he elaborates. "I've taken up MMA, mixed martial arts. The gym I go to offered training, so I thought I'd try it."

"That cage-fighting business, where anything goes?"

Wayne grins. "That's the one."

"Remind me not to get on your bad side." On reflection, Wayne's revelation doesn't surprise me. He has never struck me as a mild-mannered professorial type. But then, that doesn't describe me either—perhaps that's why we get along.

"Speaking of bad sides, did you hear that someone was looking for you at the office? I was passing by, and heard the guy asking for your schedule and the room numbers. He seemed a little dodgy, but the admin assistant told him anyway."

"That doesn't surprise me. The admin and I don't see eye to eye. Did you get a look at the guy?"

"Brown hair, short, a little older than you, maybe. Do you know him?"

"Not as such." I scan the lawn full of students basking in the shade of sweeping trees. Wayne's inquisitive eyes are on me and I debate what to tell him. Answers will lead to more questions, but I grow weary of hiding everything. Braulio did tell me to open up, after all. And I have known Wayne for over a year—at some point, I have to take the leap. "I think I'm being followed."

"What? Why?"

"I interrupted someone's plans and they didn't take it well." Wayne's lauvan are dancing with curiosity, and already I regret telling him anything. "I'd better get going—I have a flight to catch. I'll be back in a few days. Let me know if you see the man again, will you?"

"Sure thing. You should come along for some MMA training. Might come in handy."

I pat him on the shoulder and turn to leave. "Perhaps I'll keep you around as my bodyguard instead."

Fighting is my strong suit—I wouldn't have lasted this long

without it. But how do I fight someone who hides in the shadows?

I tuck my satchel under the aisle seat and slide in smoothly, unhampered by the suitcases everyone finds essential. I cannot count how many journeys I have set forth on with nothing but the shirt on my back, and once or twice not even that. Granted, I see no reason to exclude a few luxuries—a toothbrush and comb are prominent in my satchel—but the sheer volume of "necessities" that travelers require staggers me.

Oh, well. It's also a mildly amusing way to pass the time, as I watch an older woman attempt to wrestle a behemoth bag into the overhead compartment. She rams it repeatedly, not realizing that another suitcase impedes her way. She keeps trying, providing a case study of insanity—doing the same thing while expecting different results.

I'm mildly absorbed by the insane woman five rows up that I'm startled when a voice says, "Excuse me."

A young woman, perhaps Jen's age, gestures at the window seat past me and smiles. Her smooth black hair ends in a short braid which flips up underneath truly enormous hoop earrings that frame her soft-featured face. Her bronze skin glows with the healthy radiance of youth.

"Of course." I stand and squeeze into the aisle behind her. She murmurs thank yous and apologies as her arm brushes my stomach.

When we are both settled again, she glances at me and smiles. Taking my cue, I say, "Looks like it'll be a full plane." It's an inane comment, but small talk has to start somewhere, and I don't have much to go on with this woman yet.

"Yes, a long flight too. I'm connecting from Calgary." She sighs then adds, "But then I'll be home with my family, so it's worth it." She looks at me again and a small crease furrows her brow. "Have we met before? You look familiar."

It's doubtful. I have a very good memory for faces and places and this woman is pretty enough for her features to stick.

"I would have remembered you," I say with a grin. I hold out my hand. "My name is Merlo." I decided to stick with my name as "Merlo Nuanez" for this trip, as a tribute to Braulio. It's how he always knew me.

I don't expect the reaction I get from the woman. Her eyes widen to their fullest extent and it takes a moment before she extends a tentative hand to grasp mine.

Just then I hear "Excuse me," from my left and I turn. Waiting to slot into the seat between us is an enormous man, built like a bull with the shoulders to match. I sigh inwardly and am grateful for the aisle seat to lean into.

My conversation with the woman is cut short by the man's arrival, so I'm left on my own to contemplate the meaning of her reaction. Upon reflection, I decide the name Merlo must mean something to her, a favorite uncle who died tragically, perhaps. I put her reaction from my mind, along with the vanquished hope that this flight could have passed much more pleasantly with her conversation.

I spend most of the flight in one of my trances and forget about the woman and her reaction until we disembark. In the terminal, I crane my neck to look for her, but she has disappeared. I sigh and resolve to find a taxi and hotel room.

The little Catholic church is packed. Vaulted ceilings soar

to the sky, painted a brilliant white and edged with gold paint. The red-carpeted aisle bursts with Fernandez family members, while carved wooden saints in ornate wall sconces gaze down serenely at the multitudes. I position myself at the back and wait for the funeral mass to begin. There are so many people that no one takes a second glance at me.

Braulio had three sons and four daughters with his wife Juliana, and each of those had their own children, not including the families of Braulio's siblings, likely here also. In front of me, two women greet each other with kisses on the cheek and their men hug briefly. What must it feel like to be part of a family so large and connected? I certainly would not have this many at my funeral if I ever died. The only family I ever cared about was my mother, and it has been many centuries since I laid her to rest in the cold earth, along with my wives and lovers. And children—well, that never worked out.

A small boy skips in front of me, unaware of the solemnity required at a funeral. I smile, sure that Braulio would have too. I'm happy for Braulio. A little envious, but mostly happy, that he created this life for himself. That he took life by the scruff and made it his.

Mass is long but familiar. I have been to plenty in my time, although hearing the service in Spanish instead of Latin is a new twist. I follow the responses automatically while my mind wanders through Braulio's life. After the final blessing, the priest paces down the aisle, trailed by the deacon and other ministers. I follow the chattering crowd processing three blocks to Braulio's old home, now the abode of his eldest son. I wasn't invited, strictly speaking, although if Braulio had told anyone about me, I would have been. But I'm hungry and curious to see the place Braulio called home for many years. I know it only by description.

The house stands behind a sturdy metal fence, too tall to

scale easily, as do many in crime-ridden San Jose. The green-tiled roof is sharp against freshly painted white walls inset with arched windows. It's a modest but quietly prosperous-looking house. The gate is open and a steady stream of Fernandez family members file through. I slip in unnoticed and enter the tiled lobby which is blissfully cool after the blazing sun outside.

The living room is already crowded, so I squeeze between a large potted rubber tree and an even larger older lady to enter the dining room. It's filled with far too many chairs and an enormous mahogany table that is laid out with a splendid assortment of sweets, and my stomach rumbles assertively. I swipe a cookie and gaze at a collage on the nearest wall. It's of Braulio's family, and I recognize him in many of the photos.

An older man enters the room, perhaps mid-fifties, stout but with Braulio's nose and mouth.

"Excuse me," he says to me in Spanish. "Are you Merlo Nuanez?"

I'm taken aback. How does he know my name?

"Yes," I answer cautiously. "I wanted to pay my respects to Braulio's family. I knew him."

"Thank you, Señor. I'm sure my father would have been pleased that you are here. He left a sealed package with instructions to give it to a man matching your description, with your name."

"I'm intrigued."

"It's in the study. Follow me."

The study is lit by a bank of windows looking out on a small graveled courtyard. Inside are stacks of papers and books piled on bookshelves and the nearby tiled floor. It's an organized chaos—each sheaf of papers is rubber band-bound with a handwritten label, and the stacks are neatly arranged.

"Father hadn't lived here for a few years, but he insisted on keeping his study intact for his occasional visits. I'll have to clear it out now, I suppose." Braulio's son points at the desk, on which sits a plastic grocery bag tied with string. An envelope tucked in the string is inscribed in shaky letters with, "Merlo Nuanez."

"I'll leave you to have a look. Please, come back and eat when you are done."

The man leaves, and I sit at the desk to tear open the surprisingly bulky envelope. When I lift the flap, a few lauvan of Braulio's terracotta color sneak out. I pour the contents of the envelope into my hand with interest. It's a watch, Braulio's watch that he owned for decades. Its heavy gold face ticks quietly in my palm, surrounded by reddish-brown threads. My throat closes briefly. A tag attached to the watch strap reads, "For Merlo, the man to whom time means everything and nothing."

I fasten the watch on my wrist, where my brown lauvan entwine carefully with the fragile lauvan surrounding the watch. There's also a letter, written in English.

Dear Merlo,

If you are reading this, I'm sorry my weak mortal body couldn't keep up with you. I tried. We had a good run. I'm counting on you to remember me, so my legacy will live forever.

Keep this book safe. It is the culmination of my research and the tireless workings of my immense intellect. I'm confident you'll need it one day, because now we both know that the spirit world is real. Did I remember to say I told you so?

You'll be fine, anciano. *You're a survivor. Remember to trust, and for god's sake, find yourself a woman. A good one, another Josephine. Someone needs to keep you in line.*

Your friend,

Braulio

I'm chuckling with moist eyes by the end of Braulio's letter. It's his voice, speaking to me from beyond the grave. I'm curious about the contents of the bag, now. What has Braulio left me?

The plastic bag slithers off to uncover a bound notebook. Its brown leather cover and spine reveal nothing about its contents.

A title graces the first page, carefully inscribed in Braulio's recognizable hand. The lettering is strong and sure, unlike the wavering script of the letter. Braulio must have written the notebook some years ago.

Of the Elementals, Pertaining to Their Characteristics, Function, and Connection to the Physical World.

Braulio is right, again. This could be very useful. I flip through the pages for a sense of the contents. I have to brush away Braulio's old lauvan to see the pages. This book is everything Braulio worked on and believed in deeply, and so it collected his lauvan as precious objects are inclined to do. Inside are paragraphs, notes, sketches, maps, all organized by element. I read a random line.

The Iroquois believe that there are separate deities to rule each of the cardinal directions (e.g. Da-jo-ji, spirit of the west wind). This belief corresponds well with the ancient Greek Anemoi. Therefore, in addition to evidence presented earlier, we can conclude that multiple elemental spirits are instrumental in the control of the element of air.

This is brilliant. I know what I will be reading on the plane home.

I shiver with a deep crawling sensation that starts at my shoulders and rolls up and down my back. At the same time, my lauvan twitch in synchrony. Odd. Braulio's study has no air conditioning and through the open window flows a punishingly warm, humid breeze. Sweat beads on my forehead despite the lauvan-barrier I half-heartedly constructed upon stepping off the airplane into the hot, soupy air. I have been too long in northern climes to enjoy the heat on first flush, despite my teasing of Jen.

It could be Braulio's spirit come to haunt me. I smile at that. It's unlikely. I'm certainly the last person to know if there is an afterlife and what form it might take, but I can guarantee that Braulio would have better things to do than follow me around. Reunite with Juliana, his wife of fifty years. Or float down to the beach and watch bikini-clad women sunbathing. Either possibility would be much more likely than haunting me.

Perhaps the heat is getting to me. I bend over the table, intending to slide the notebook into its plastic shopping bag. The sound of a clearing throat stops me short. I thought I was alone. My head swivels to inspect the new arrival.

A young man hovers in the doorframe, clearly wanting to enter but fearful of intruding. His straight black hair sweeps over a high, broad forehead above lively brown eyes. I would guess his age to be around twenty-five but his round cheeks and short nose attempt to disguise him as much younger. I don't know him, but I do recognize Braulio's strong jawline, prone to stubbornness. This must be one of Braulio's offshoots.

"Señor Nuanez?" The young man says quickly in Spanish when he has my attention. "I thought you might like a drink. It's very hot today." He brandishes the beer bottle in his right hand at me while keeping a tight grip on another in his left. His dark green lauvan are twitchy, as if he is nervous. I can't think why. He knows nothing about me and has no reason for fear. But now that I look closer, it's not fear but excitement and apprehension that drive his jumpy strands. I wonder what he is expecting.

"Thank you. That was kind of you." I take the offered bottle—blissfully cool, condensing in running droplets of water down the sides—and take a swig, leaving an opening for the man to speak.

"My cousin Manuela says you're from Canada," he says in perfect English, his accent strong but entirely understandable. "She was on the plane with you." He sticks out his hand with boyish enthusiasm. "My name is Alejandro Fernandez. I'm Braulio's grandson."

I take his hand, trying not to grin at the vigor of the handshake, and answer in English.

"Nice to meet you, Alejandro. Can I say your English is very impressive?"

"As is your Spanish, for someone from Canada."

"Touché. I spent a lot of years in Central America."

"I studied in America. My grandfather picked his two favorites, Manuela and me, and paid for our university educations."

"That sounds like him—never shy about expressing his opinions."

"You knew my grandfather well," Alejandro says. His lauvan grow still and tense. He is getting to the real reason he brought me my beer. "He told Manuela and me stories, incredible stories, of his youth and travels. He spoke especially about you."

I don't answer or give him anything in my face or bearing that he can latch onto as confirmation or denial of his words. I simply gaze at him evenly while the beer cools my palm. It was always my impression that Braulio never spoke of me to his family. What does Alejandro think he knows?

"For a long time, we thought you were one of crazy old grandfather's stories, like his research into spirits that grandmother couldn't stand." Juliana's staunch Catholicism clashed with Braulio's liberal spiritual leanings, and I remember Braulio telling me she never asked about his research trips, and he didn't offer to tell. Alejandro continued, "But the more time we spent with grandfather in our late teens, helping him before he moved to his care home, the more he told us, and showed us. His research was persuasive, especially the way grandfather told it. But what really convinced me, convinced us, were the pictures."

My face is still but my mind whirls. What pictures could he possibly be talking about?

"Grandfather loved photography, right from his youth."

I can't disagree. He bought a camera as soon as he could afford it. Nineteen forty-seven, I believe it was. He took pictures of anything that would stay still for long enough. I made it clear to him that I was off-limits. It's been my policy ever since photography began—avoiding being painted or sketched is fairly simple, and few artists are talented enough that a likeness between images would be remarked upon. But photographs—the images are too clear, too obvious. I don't need evidence of my existence throughout the ages. If ever found, it could lead to some awkward questions.

For example, this conversation with Alejandro.

"Grandfather kept all the photos he ever took. You should see the boxes and boxes of them—it gives my father a headache trying to decide what to do with them all. But there are a few he kept separate, and he showed Manuela and me. They're all of you." From his back pocket, Alejandro pulls out a thin envelope, yellowed with age. He passes it to me. Braulio's sharp penmanship is on the front. There's only one word.

Anciano.

Dammit, Braulio. What have you done? And why are you not here now to help me solve this mess you created?

My lauvan tremble with uncertainty, but outwardly I am calm. I flip open the back flap of the envelope and slide out the photographs. There are only four, after all. The topmost one is unremarkable in composition. It's a street scene, only a few blocks from where we now stand. I'm shading my eyes with my hand, but the angle of the shot allows the features of my face to stand out clear and unmistakable. Behind me is a partially constructed building which I noticed today is now a department store. I recognize the scene—I visited Braulio five years ago and took him out for lunch at his favorite grill. He wasn't in a wheelchair yet, but he needed as much support walking as I could give him.

The second photo is quite different. The subject is me again, but this time I'm talking with a thin Japanese man holding what appear to be tickets. I'm wearing wide-legged pants and a tight shirt. Behind us rises a large sign, emblazoned with the words "Expo '70" in English and Japanese. I remember that trip—Braulio wanted to study the Shinto animism of the Japanese and I accompanied him as I often did. I greatly improved my lauvan-cable map for Japan while I was there.

The next photo gives me a pang. I'm on the steps of a tiny white church, dressed in a double-breasted suit with vest. I'm beaming, happy in a way I rarely see in the mirror these days. Linked through my left arm in a boat-necked dress with a tightly cinched waist is Josephine. Her glow shines through the grainy black and white as clearly as it did on the day of our wedding. We gaze at each other, our interest in the world outside our own sphere of joy plainly minimal.

I spend a moment on that photo, but I can't look for long. It stirs up too many feelings I don't want to have right now—not in front of Alejandro, who is intently gauging my reactions to the photos—so I flip quickly to the next and last photo. It's a very old picture, taken on a beach with palm trees hanging over the sand. I'm in close-fitting swim shorts from the forties with my arms around two giggling girls, both in high-waisted halter-top bikinis. Even through the black-and-white image my tan is almost dark enough to match the bronzed skin of the girls. I'm laughing, my mouth open and teeth white against my dark skin.

One of the girls looks up at me and the other holds her arm out to the camera as if in invitation.

I calmly slide the photos back into their envelope and hold it. I meet Alejandro's eyes. They are expectant and beyond curious. I suppose it's time to say something.

"So? What do you think you know?"

Alejandro frowns.

"Grandfather told us everything. How you have lived for hundreds and hundreds of years, never aging. How you can see things no one else can."

I don't know what Braulio was playing at, but I now have an unintended initiate. Hooray. I rub my eyes.

"Who else knows? You and your cousin, the one from the plane, I presume. Anyone else?"

"No, no one else. Grandfather told us how important it was to keep it a secret."

"And Braulio thought you two could be trusted." I sigh. "I hope he was right. I don't have much of a choice, now."

"You can. We would never tell, ever." Alejandro leans forward in his eagerness for emphasis.

"And where is our other confidante? Manuela, you said? Why isn't she here for the big reveal?"

Alejandro looks discomfited.

"She was never comfortable with the idea of you, and meeting you on the plane, in reality—she'd rather stay a distant secret-keeper. I'm sorry."

"No need. It's an entirely expected reaction. Trust me, she isn't the first."

"She won't tell, though. Not ever."

"Well, it's not like anyone would believe her without the pictures." I wave them in the air and watch Alejandro's eyes track the envelope. I should destroy them, but I don't want to lose that picture of Josephine. Perhaps I will tuck the photos in my sketchbook. "And now they're mine. So, that solves that loose end."

"Yes, Señor. They are yours now. And I know grandfather loved you like a brother, so if there is anything you need, you only have to ask." Alejandro's strands twitch nervously but then straighten with determination. He is afraid of what I might ask of him, but courageous enough to offer anyway. I'm starting to like him. He seems to have the Fernandez backbone.

"Thank you, Alejandro. I'll keep that in mind." I shove the envelope into the plastic bag with Braulio's notes. "But for future reference, call me Merlo. 'Señor' makes me feel ancient."

"But Merlo, you are ancient."

I raise my eyebrow and let out a bark of laughter.

"Cheeky bastard. That's your grandfather in you."

Alejandro smiles then, and as he does so his eyes light up with the adventurous twinkle that Braulio always had. Damn. I'm going to miss Braulio.

"Merlo? Grandfather left me money in his will. I'm going to use some of it to travel. Can I—could I—is it too much to ask if I can visit you in Vancouver?"

"Really? We've just established that I'm immortal with otherworldly powers, and you want to stay as a houseguest?"

Alejandro fidgets and backtracks.

"No, I understand you wouldn't want—it's fine, I just thought I'd ask—"

I look at him, bemused.

"Well, of course you can stay. I simply don't understand why you're all right with this."

"Grandfather trusted you. That's good enough for me," Alejandro says clearly without his previous hesitancy.

So much trust, unearned in this generation. I don't understand Alejandro yet but I'm starting to respect him. He is an odd mix of diffidence and bravery, of unknown and familiar. I'm curious to know him better.

I dig out my wallet and give him my card. It only has my name and phone number on it, all the better to remain anonymous.

"Here. Call me when you know you're coming."

"Are you free this Saturday? I may have already booked my ticket. I can change it, of course."

"Wow. You really felt comfortable about me, didn't you? Saturday it is."

Alejandro takes the card and frowns when he reads the name.

"Merry Lie-tone," he pronounces slowly. "Is that your name now?"

"Merry Lih-ton," I correct him. "And yes, I have to change it every so often so I can't be tracked." I check my watch. "I should go—my plane leaves in a few hours."

"Of course. I will call a taxi." Alejandro turns to go, then looks back. "Thank you, Merlo, for letting me visit."

I shrug and smile.

"Don't expect anything too exciting. I'm a simple university instructor in a one-bedroom apartment, nothing glamorous these days."

He smiles back and exits, leaving me a little windblown with the developments of the past half-hour. Strangely enough, a single thread of his dark green lauvan is connected to my center. The color is strongest near my body and fades to transparency an arm-span away, as all connections do. That was oddly quick. I hardly know him. I reflect briefly, then smack my forehead with my palm.

"Braulio, you old dog. This was your plan all along." Braulio knew I hadn't told anyone else about my past, and he didn't trust me to take care of it myself. So, in his typical take-charge fashion, he set up two new acolytes to take his place. Time will tell whether Alejandro is a worthy successor of his grandfather. I find myself eager to know him better, to talk about what I can't with anyone else, and to share my experiences with someone who won't shy away.

CHAPTER IV

Dreaming

Braulio puffs up the slope, his face red and sweaty.

"What I do for you, Merlo."

"You're a true friend," I say absently and push on to the summit of the small hill we are attempting to crest. "But so am I. Look at this as a wonderful opportunity to get fit."

"Fit?" Braulio huffs. "I'm in fine form. As fit as the day I met you."

"Then pick up the pace. You know what the problem is? Juliana feeds you too well. Ever since you married her, your belt size has increased steadily."

A stick wallops me on the back of my calves and I grin. Teasing Braulio is always easy, especially about his looks. In truth, he is still a fine specimen at forty. He hasn't lost his youthful vigor and he's vain enough to stay trim.

"Perhaps if I had immortality, I too could stay young forever," he says with a grumble. "I've had to start watching what I eat." This last is said in a high-pitched nag, which I presume is in imitation of his wife. "Imagine that."

I don't answer, because we have reached the top of the hill. A glorious vista spreads before us of jagged snowy peaks surrounding an intensely blue lake. A ribbon of silvery brown descends from a mountain and trails around the perimeter of the lake before it vanishes through a cleft between two peaks.

"There it is," I say with satisfaction. We have hiked all day to find this lauvan cable. "It's right where I expected it to be." I pull out a piece of thick paper from my backpack and trace the path of the cable over the topography of my map.

"Have you given much thought to the purpose of the lauvan

cables?" Braulio says but doesn't wait for a reply. "I'm sure they have great importance in the spirit plane. Far too many cultures speak of them. I wonder if they act as a conduit, or a way elementals can interact with the physical plane. Are you listening, Merlo?"

"Not really. You were jabbering on about spirits again."

"You'll see, one day," Braulio says darkly. "I'm entirely certain I'm correct, and one day you'll know I'm right."

It's a long road from Powys, not all of it smoothed by frequent traffic. Arthur's villa is less than an hour's ride from here, and I am eager for a hot meal and a warm fire. Drizzling rain hasn't penetrated my cloak, but I am damp from the moisture-laden air, nonetheless.

A rider canters toward me over a hill from the direction of the villa. It's a fast pace—unexpected for long-distance travel—and I wonder where he goes in such a hurry. Perhaps he carries important news.

The traveler approaches and I recognize Lancelot, one of Arthur's warriors. He is the son of a local lord and was fostered across the sea for a time, where he learned Saxon and grew into a fearsome swordsman.

He is too pompous for my liking but his dearth of humor makes him easy to tease, which redeems him in my eyes. I hail him and he slows his horse. His face is wary.

"Lancelot. I didn't expect to see you on the road. Didn't Arthur charge you to keep the villa and his wife safe while he is in the east?"

Lancelot's lauvan flinch at the mention of Guinevere but he gives no other sign.

"Yes, while my leg healed. But Arthur has returned, and my wound is much better. He gave me an important message to give to Pellinore."

"What is it?"

"You'd best speak to him about it," he says and kicks his horse into a trot. "I've no time to lose. Farewell, Merlin." He encourages his horse into a canter and disappears down the road.

That's strange. I can think of no reason to contact Pellinore. I wonder how the most recent campaign went while I was stuck negotiating in the north. I push my own horse into a trot, eager to discover the meaning of Lancelot's haste.

I approach the villa to find it in an uproar. Horse boys and kitchen slaves huddle together, chattering and gesticulating excitedly. Indecipherable shouting travels through the open villa door, through which a maid runs out to join a nearby group. I stop her.

"Wait, girl. What's happening here?"

"My lord Merlin!" Her eyes are wide—she wasn't expecting me. "Thank goodness you're here. My lady has locked herself in her chamber and won't open the door for anyone."

That's strange news. In the few months I have known her, Guinevere has always struck me as a sweet, mild-mannered woman. What the rest of the house sees as reserved and cold, I see as shy and painfully aware of her lack of Brythonic language. Perhaps she has more fire than I was aware of.

"That's ridiculous," I say firmly, then raise my voice. "And did Arthur give you all permission to congregate here like gossiping old women? Return to your duties at once."

They scurry in all directions and leave me to stride through the door toward Guinevere's chamber. Arthur sits, slumped, against the wall with head in hands. He looks up at the sound of my boots on the tiles. His face is awash in misery, tempered only slightly by relief at my presence.

"Merlin. You're here."

I squat to speak to Arthur more closely.

"Tell me what happened."

Arthur closes his eyes and holds the bridge of his nose as if his fingers are the only thing that keep him from disintegrating.

"I came home from the campaign this morning—decisive victory, by the way—and went immediately to greet my wife." This final word is said with more vehemence than I am used to hearing from Arthur. "Lancelot stumbled out in a panic as I approached, without a shirt and holding up his trousers. He was obviously trying to escape when he heard our horses. I was in shock, at first, but then I grew angry. So, so angry." He leans against the wall with his eyes still closed. "I couldn't move for a moment—should I chase after Lancelot or confront Guinevere?—but while I dithered, Guinevere ran to the door and slammed it shut. Lancelot got away and I've been outside this door ever since."

He finally opens his eyes and stares at me with pain. "What do I do, Merlin? How did this happen?"

I stand.

"Nothing will get sorted when the two of you are on opposite sides of a door. I assume you aren't planning any violent retribution on Guinevere, otherwise you would have broken down the door already."

"No, of course not. She won't open the door, though."

"She won't open it for you, you mean. Stand back for a moment." Arthur gets up and walks down the hall to lean against a pillar, facing the central courtyard. I rap smartly on the door and say in Saxon, her native tongue, "Guinevere, it's Merlin. May I come in?"

There is a moment's pause, then there is the sound of

furniture sliding across the floor, and the door opens a crack. Guinevere's frightened eye peers out to confirm my identity, then she flings open the door for me to enter. She swiftly pushes a wooden trunk back against the door once I am within.

"I can't believe you're here," she bursts forth in rapid Saxon. "It's just what I've been praying for. You're the only one I can talk to." She paces back and forth across the room like a caged wolf, then stops to look me in the eye. "Is Arthur furious? I didn't dare open the door to his shouting. I didn't understand a word, and I don't want to be beaten. But I can't make him see—how can I explain when I don't speak Brythonic?" She wrings her hands feverishly.

"Guinevere." I take her shoulders and steer her to sit on the unmade bed, whose blankets are strewn haphazardly across the foot. "Calm yourself and tell me what happened. You slept with Lancelot? Was it the first time?"

"The second," she murmurs to the floor. "He's been teaching me Brythonic while you were away. Then with Arthur gone, he was very attentive and kind. And he was the only one with whom I could have a real conversation." She rubs her feet together like a penitent child, which isn't far from the truth. I sigh.

"You didn't flee with Lancelot today. Why?"

She meets my eyes with outraged pride. Not such a child, then.

"I would never do that. Arthur is my husband, and my people depend on me for the peace to hold. I've done wrong, and now it's up to me to try and make things right."

"Many men would kill their adulterous wife," I say in a detached tone. To my surprise, Guinevere lifts her chin and answers in a strong voice.

"I will face the consequence of my actions."

I regard her for a moment, this proud daughter of a Saxon

king. She gazes back, undeterred.

"As it happens, Arthur has no desire to hurt you. I gather he's more bewildered than angry, and he's not sure what to do. Let's bring him in and I can translate."

Guinevere fidgets with her fingers, but nods. I open the door. Arthur leans against a pillar, looking drained.

"Arthur, come speak with Guinevere," I say in Brythonic. "She wants to explain herself. I'll act as translator."

"Should I, Merlin? Is there anything she can say that will help?"

I shake my head.

"I'm the last person to dole out marriage advice, but I think you need to hear her out. Come in."

Arthur rights himself as if his shoulders weigh far more than they should and moves slowly into Guinevere's chamber. Guinevere stands by the bedpost, gripping the wood with white fingers.

"My lord, I am so sorry." She pauses for my translation. "I betrayed you for a moment's respite from my solitude. I will make any amends you desire, anything at all. But for the sake of both our peoples, please let me try again to be a good wife to you."

Arthur looks into Guinevere's eyes until I stop speaking, then he moves his gaze to the window while his jaw works. There is a long silence.

"I too want peace." Arthur's voice is hoarse. "As for amends, you will not see Lancelot alone again. And if solitude is the problem, you will continue your Brythonic lessons with Merlin, as often as he can spare the time."

Arthur turns abruptly and leaves the room. Guinevere sinks onto the bed and covers her face with her hands. I squeeze her shoulder then follow Arthur down the corridor until he enters his own chamber.

"I think that was wise, Arthur. Difficult, but wise."

He throws himself into a chair and groans.

"I've only just won over the key warlords with my battle strategies. How will they respect a cuckold? And how can I ever trust Guinevere again?"

"Did you trust her before? Trust must be earned over time. You need to know your wife better first. And for that, I recommend you learn some Saxon from me."

"I don't feel that I should be the one to put in the effort after Guinevere's actions."

"Then you will never have a successful marriage," I say sharply. "Give and get, push and pull. You get out what you put in."

"Are you saying it's my fault Guinevere slept with Lancelot?" Arthur says hotly.

"In some part, yes. You left your new wife alone and friendless in a strange land, among people who speak a foreign tongue. Small wonder she turned elsewhere for solace, especially since she hardly knew you at all."

Arthur's shoulders droop and he rubs his face in his hands. I continue in a softer tone.

"Don't misunderstand me—Guinevere is not blameless. But give her a second chance, and she might become the friend, lover, and ally you hope for. As for the warlords, let me help. They want peace as much as you do—they'll support you once they understand your position. One last thing. What do you want to do about Lancelot?"

Arthur's face hardens.

"I want to slide my sword deep into his gut and let him writhe in agony until he dies."

"Right. Well, I'll back you in whatever you want to do." Privately, I wonder if Arthur would get the chance. He's an accomplished fighter with passionate vengeance on his side, but

Lancelot is almost unparalleled on the battlefield.

The light of anger dies in Arthur's eyes, and he looks older and tired.

"I can't do that. He's too valuable to lose. We'll have to send word that I forgive him, ask him back."

"How can you be so fair-minded? The man rutted your wife."

Arthur's face spasms.

"It doesn't matter. We need him. I can't afford to let my personal grievances get in the way of our victories. But he will be posted in the furthest reaches of Gwent, far from here. I don't need to see his treacherous face more often than I must."

CHAPTER V

I finish the last pages of Braulio's notebook the morning after I arrive home from San Jose, the hot sun streaming in my window. It's truly fascinating, especially since I now know the information is of crucial importance rather than the cryptic ramblings of an obsessed man. Braulio spent years researching, and it shows. Everything is meticulously referenced, and the conclusions drawn are considered and reasonable.

But when I put the book down on my coffee table, I'm not sure how to use the information. Everything is so theoretical, and I can't imagine how to apply my new knowledge. Still, anything I can learn about the spirit world is better than the scant nothing I know now.

Perhaps I will text Jen and let her know I'm back. I pull out my phone. Normally I would call, but it's early. My desire for connection shouldn't supersede Jen's sleep.

I'm back. Lunch soon? How is loverboy?

The phone buzzes seconds later. Jen is up.

Good to hear. If you mean CECIL, he's fine. Coming on strong, though. Too strong?

Hmm, I wonder what that means. Another buzz shakes my phone.

Lunch on Friday? Text me later.

Deal.

So, Cecil's lauvan antics are translating into real-world actions. I wonder what he did. Jen didn't seem interested enough to tolerate too much pushing, but we'll see. Cecil bears watching.

Dr. Dilleck stands when I enter her office until I take a seat on the couch opposite her.

"Good morning, Merry. How are you today?"

She looks tired. There is a fine sheen of navy-blue lauvan over her eyes, which she has had ever since our first meeting. It's a common feature and generally indicates self-deceit. Often, it's a philandering spouse that the significant other doesn't want to know about. A glance at Dr. Dilleck's hand reveals a bare ring finger. No husband, then.

Still, I'd bet that whatever she's trying to hide from herself is what's keeping her up at night, especially since the strands over her eyes appear to be thinner than before. Something is coming to a head. Perhaps I should offer my shrink skills to her in exchange. A therapy circle, as it were.

We dabble in small talk, then she gets down to business.

"Is there anything in particular you'd like to discuss today?"

"Why don't you pick a topic? You probably have a better idea than me of what is worth discussing." I grin at her. Her lips twitch in a small smile, revealing a dimple on her left cheek.

"All right. Since you seem to be feeling better after your bad news, let's try a different topic. Last time, you mentioned a casual romantic encounter with a woman you met in—" She checks her notes, tucks a strand of silky hair behind her ear. "Wallerton. What made you initiate that relationship? Lead me through your thought process."

I laugh.

"What do you expect me to say? I was alone in a strange town. I was bored—Wallerton isn't known for its nightlife. I wanted female companionship. She was beautiful, interested in me, and I didn't want to go back to my lonely hotel room by myself."

She coughs delicately.

"That was—comprehensive. Thank you for sharing, Merry. Your last relationship, how long was it?"

"Mmm, about five weeks."

"And before that?"

"One hook-up, and a two-month stint before that."

She folds her hands over her notepad and leans forward slightly. Her narrow face, framed by the hair that has slipped away from her ear, is intent.

"Have you had a long-term relationship with anyone since your wife passed away? Longer than a few months?"

"No."

"What's keeping you from being in a long-term relationship?"

I shrug, feigning indifference, although it's obvious in my opinion.

"I suppose I don't want to fall in love and have to lose again." And again. "I don't have the stamina for that. It's easier to not go down that road."

Dr. Dilleck steeples her fingers.

"So, you feel that you are protecting yourself from future hurt." I nod, and she looks at her fingers. "It's an entirely understandable reaction to the sort of loss you've encountered." She puts her hands on her knees and pierces me with her sea-blue eyes, bright even through the haze of her lauvan. "But I hear you say the words 'lonely' and 'alone' repeatedly. Have you considered that you might be searching?"

"Searching?" I repeat blankly.

"Do you believe in soulmates?"

I think of all my wives and lovers, each one of whom I loved passionately, unreservedly, with all my heart.

"No. Not at all."

"Then perhaps you could do yourself a favor. Can you

consider not closing your heart off forever? You can give yourself time to heal, that's necessary and wise, but can you keep yourself open to the possibility of new love?"

I gaze into her earnest eyes. Such a mixture of naivety and wisdom—she reminds me of my very first love, Nimue.

"I'll consider it," I say finally.

I walk out of her office at the end of our session and think how much simpler this would be if I told Dr. Dilleck everything. She doesn't know what she's asking of me.

CHAPTER VI

Dreaming

Silver water gleams dully through the trees under a sullen sky. Finally, water. My horse, who has been breathing heavily for the past half hour, tosses his head and begins to trot. We are both in need of a long drink after the passage through the western hills. It's a long and arduous path to the sea where I hope to meet Irish ships, come to support Arthur against the newest Saxon wave of militant invaders. That is, if they have come. We could use their help. If they are here, I can board and lead them up the river to Arthur's stronghold.

But the horse and I won't get far without water. I urge my beast toward the lake, which is tantalizingly close. The trees end suddenly at the edge of a stony shore where tiny wavelets lap quietly against the pebbles. It's only a little lake, after all, but pleasingly clear of weeds and treefalls.

My horse trots forward eagerly and dips his nose into the water. I slide off and grope in my saddlebag for my water skin. A voice interrupts me.

"This lake is sacred. Those who desecrate the waters must pay the price."

I whirl around. On a fallen log above me stands a young woman. She wears a woolen dress of soft blue and a solemn expression. Her clear gray eyes are cool below raven-black hair braided around her head, and sky-blue lauvan swirl around her torso. She is beautiful, but in an untouchable way.

"I'm sorry," I say. My mouth is dry from thirst, but I don't dare disobey, not until I know who else may be with her. "I didn't know. Sacred to whom?"

"Why, the Lady of the Lake, of course. And to the goddess

she serves." She looks imperiously at me for a moment, then her face collapses into laughter. Where before she was a cool beauty, now she is full of life, pretty and radiantly so. "I'm only joking. What sort of goddess would object to a horse and rider quenching their thirst?" I must look taken aback, because she adds hastily, "Please, forgive me my little joke, traveler. I see few people, as a rule, and I could not resist." She smiles at me tentatively, her eyes bright and hopeful. I laugh.

"No harm done. I was trying to imagine what penalty you could possibly make my poor horse pay."

She laughs, then says, "Would you care for some ale instead? I was about to have my midday meal. You're welcome to join me."

"How could I refuse? I'd be happy to accept." I look dubiously at the sky, whose threatening clouds are now accompanied by a gusty breeze. "Is there somewhere out of the wind?"

"This way. Your horse is finished? Good, follow me."

She leads us along the shore to a rocky outcrop and nimbly picks her way around it. The horse and I follow more slowly, bracing ourselves against a stiff wind that funnels down the lake. We might be stopped here for a while, if the threat of those clouds is made good.

There is a small thatched shelter on the side of the rock. It's hardly more than a cow byre, with one side open to a partial view of the lake. An overhang of rock affords some shelter for my poor beast, who looks resigned when I lead him under it and unstrap my bag from the saddle. I join the young woman in the shelter as the first raindrops arrive.

"Whew! Just in time." She collapses onto a coarsely woven blanket spread over the bare earthen floor. "Make yourself comfortable. It's not much, but at least it's dry."

"Lucky I met you when I did. I wonder how long the rain

will last."

"Until sunset," she says at once. When I look at her with a raised eyebrow, she shrugs. "I'm the Lady of the Lake, after all. I have special insight into all things water."

"Really." I'm interested. What does she mean? Does she have abilities like mine? "What form does your insight take?"

"You don't believe me, do you? That's all right. There are only a few of us of the old ways left on this coast."

In answer, I hold up my arms to show the Druidic oak leaves tattooed on my inner wrists. Her eyes widen.

"Oh! Are you from Eire? I've met only a very few acolytes of the Druids, and none by chance. Where have you been hiding?"

"I've hardly been hiding. I was born in the north, near Caernarfon, but took a ship to Eire when I was sixteen. Sorry to say, I didn't have the discipline to see my training through. Now, I'm an adviser to the warlord Arthur in Gwent." I lean back on the blanket and stretch my legs. "Now, your turn. What's your name? How are you connected to water? And where is the ale you lured me here with?"

She giggles and her eyes light up entrancingly. She twists to pry out an earthen jug wedged in a corner of the shelter.

"I won't answer those in order. Here is the ale." She untwists a wad of leather from the jug's mouth and passes me the ale. I drink greedily, my thirst getting the better of me. She pulls out a couple of apples from last autumn's crop, offers me one, and takes a bite of the other. "My name is Nimue. I was selected from those families on the coast who are left who still follow the old ways. I was chosen because I can sense the ways of water. It's nothing I can see or touch—more of a feeling, or thoughts that come unbidden into my head."

"I'm Merlin. I wondered." I have a sudden, intense urge to tell this strange girl about my powers. And why not? What would it matter? It's not as if she will tell anyone I know, out here in the wilderness. "I have my own abilities, so I wondered what yours looked like." I describe the lauvan and how I can manipulate them. Nimue's eyes grow wide and when I demonstrate by changing the color of my shirt from red to black and back again, she claps her hands with delight.

"Oh, that's marvelous. I wish my gifts were that dramatic."

"You called yourself the Lady of the Lake. What does that mean?"

"This lake is particularly sacred to the goddess. It's fed by three springs, and the river Romney flows directly to the sea from here. I'm tasked with protecting the lake, making the appropriate offerings, performing ceremonies with the other ladies—"

"Others?"

"There are four of us. Me, Arden is Lady of the Wind, Lady of the Grove is Idelisa, and—well, the previous Lady of the Hearth deserted her duties, so we're in search of a new one. They all have some abilities with their elements. Mine is the strongest, although Arden isn't far behind. We work to keep the goddess honored in this land." She sighs and tosses her apple core into the rain. "Although I think it's a losing battle. There are so few of us. And I expect the goddess can take care of herself." She glances at me, her face furtive and guilty. "You must think me blasphemous."

"Hardly. Only one leaf on my wrists, remember? I quit my training early." I rest my head on my hand and listen to the roar of the rain on the lake and in the trees. My horse whickers contentedly under his roof behind our wall, happy to rest.

With a sigh of contentment, Nimue pulls off her boots and woolen stockings to wiggle her toes in the darkening afternoon. The peace and tranquility of this place are calming me. It's a world apart from the hustle and worry of life at Arthur's side. I can hardly believe I told Nimue about the lauvan, but something about her—her open guilelessness, her bright eyes, the excited wonderment of her smile—makes her hard to resist. It felt natural for her to know everything.

This strange, lovely girl in the wilderness has me entranced.

"Water," Nimue says musingly, out of the silence. "The nice thing about it is its constancy. You know what to expect from water. But look at that." She waves at the lake, where wind pushes great sheets of rain across the turbulent surface of the lake. "Air is unpredictable. It's quick and changeable. It can be a gentle breeze on your cheek one moment, and a gust to push you down the next. If there's anything I've learned, Merlin, it's to be wary of wind."

After I awaken, my heart races as if I am meeting Nimue for the first time. Memories flash through my mind's eye, unguarded as I am at the cusp of sleep: the longing to hear the music of her laugh once more; trips through the hills on my trusty horse to her quiet lake; the ever-thickening bond of our connected lauvan, sky-blue and chocolate brown. How can it be that my emotions do not dull over the years, but somehow grow even more acute?

CHAPTER VII

I lean against a wall and watch a steady stream of travelers issue from the frosted double doors of Vancouver's airport. Waiting at arrivals are a line of welcomers: excited children clinging to parents' legs, bored sign-holders, eager lovers. Some travelers look around anxiously until they spot their party, but others look ahead, tired or indifferent or feigning indifference at their lack of a warm welcome.

I'm more impatient than I expected for Alejandro's arrival. Since Braulio's death I have felt my friend's loss keenly, painfully aware of the absence in my life of the last person who truly knew me. It was a shock to find out that Alejandro and his cousin Manuela know my secrets, but the more I think of it, the more I appreciate Braulio taking charge. He was meddlesome but wise.

This batch of arrivals has almost petered out by the time Alejandro steps through the doorway. He clutches a black duffel bag over his shoulder and gazes around with an air of bemusement. The stub of a plane ticket is clenched in his fist, tightly wrapped in his dark green lauvan. He must have been looking forward to this trip. I make no motion, but when he spies me his face breaks open in an excited grin, and I smile in return. The lauvan that inexplicably connect us twang with Alejandro's relief. A strange otherworldly breeze, that peculiar hair-raising sensation I felt when I first met Alejandro in Braulio's study, ripples down my spine. How odd.

I push myself off the wall and saunter over to greet my guest.

"Welcome to Vancouver, Alejandro. Good flight?"

"*Hola*, Merlo! It was great. Wonderful view coming down. What a beautiful city!" He stops abruptly, as if remembering where he is and who he's talking to, afraid of showing his natural enthusiasm. I laugh in response.

"I was going to ask if you wanted to go home and rest or do a little sightseeing. But I think I have my answer."

He grins again, genuine and now uninhibited.

"Where are we going?"

"You'll see. Come on, the car's this way."

Alejandro stretches his arms out to encompass the glittering ocean and gleaming cityscape.

"Look at the view! It's so beautiful. I understand why you chose to live here, Merlo."

We are on top of Grouse Mountain, directly above the city. On a cloudless day like today, it's a particularly spectacular introduction to Vancouver. Clear mountain air fills my lungs, and the heat of the sun is tempered by a gentle breeze.

"It will do for now. I've lived in worse places."

"How long will you stay?"

I shade my eyes to watch a tanker steam into the city's harbor. It looks like a toy from here.

"I can usually manage fifteen years before people question my unchanging features. Longer, if I want to put in the daily effort to add a few wrinkles by knotting my lauvan. I only do that if I have a good reason to stay."

"Fifteen years isn't so bad." Alejandro frowns and shrugs apologetically. "It must be very short to you."

"I'm used to it. Wandering has always been in my blood. But I won't deny that staying put is becoming more appealing as the centuries pass."

Alejandro joins my appraisal of the ships.

"We live for such a short time. You must think we're so young—babies, almost."

"I do have more experience to draw on, and I've forgotten more than you'll every know." Alejandro gives me a look, and I laugh. "It's true. But none of that really matters. There is something deeper, in some people at least, a more complete understanding of the world and how it works, that is independent of knowledge. When I find those people, I hold on, because they are worth knowing. Even for the short time they're allowed."

"Do I have it?"

I give him an appraising look, although I'm almost certain I know the answer.

"I'll let you know. You're on probation—your trial run is underway."

Alejandro looks out to sea, pensive. Past his head, an unattached strand floats. It's steely gray, again. How curious. Before I can reach out to pluck it from the air, my phone rings.

"Hello?"

"Merry Lytton?"

"Speaking."

"This is Bethany Venter, from Westerly Gifts in Steveston. You asked me to call if I heard about that Drew fellow."

"Yes." I listen intently. Bethany knows about my abilities since her niece Sylvana helped me out a few weeks ago during the volcano fiasco. A man named Drew contacted Bethany with the hope that she would help Potestas, the organisation behind the eruption. Beside Anna, location unknown, Drew is my only link to Potestas.

"Two things. A friend of mine was told his last name when he visited her. It's Mordecai. Drew Mordecai."

"That's excellent. Much more to work with. And the other thing?"

"I found a pair of leather gloves behind the counter. Sylvana must have put them there, but I remember Drew wearing them when he visited the first time. I know it's not much, but you did say…"

"No, it's perfect. I'll be there shortly." It's a long shot, but a personal item like that may have traces of lauvan that could tell me something.

With my phone back in my pocket, I turn to Alejandro.

"Seen enough views? Ready for another stop?"

"Can we take the gondola?"

"Unless you want to hike down."

"Then yes, I'm ready."

❧

We pull up a few blocks away from Bethany's shop. A pharmacy is across from us, and as I slam the door Dr. Dilleck hurries across the road. When she reaches our sidewalk, she pulls out a pill bottle from the paper bag she carries. The bottle slips out of her hands and rolls to a stop against my right foot. When I pick the bottle up, the label under my thumb shows the word diazepam.

Dr. Dilleck holds out her hand with a smile of thanks. Her eyes widen when she recognizes me.

"Merry! Hello, hi. I—uh, hi."

Interesting. She's not as calm and collected outside of her office.

"Good morning. It's a fine day to run some errands in Steveston."

"Yes. Yes. Well, it was great seeing you, Merry. I won't keep you."

"See you Thursday."

"Yes, of course. See you Thursday." She beats a hasty retreat down the sidewalk. I'm left baffled.

"Who was that, Merlo?" Alejandro says. "She was very nervous. I think she likes you."

"You think she—? She's not a teenager, Alejandro. And besides, she's my therapist."

"Your what?"

"My psychologist, shrink—I tell her what's in my head."

"Surely not everything?" Alejandro looks horrified.

"Not everything."

"Good. Her brain might explode if she wasn't sufficiently prepared."

I laugh.

"Indeed. I've no idea why she was acting so oddly." I glance at the pharmacy then pull out my phone. "Let's find out what pills she was popping."

"You saw the name?" Alejandro looks down the street, but Dr. Dilleck is nowhere in sight. "That seems a little personal."

"I lost my inhibitions a few centuries ago. Ah ha, here it is. Diazepam, common brand name of Valium, a common anti-anxiety medication. Well, that's interesting. I thought she was looking peaky."

"Funny to have your therapist on anxiety drugs."

I feel myself bristle on Dr. Dilleck's behalf. What an odd reaction on my part, especially since Alejandro is correct. I try to soften my tone when I speak.

"No one is without their own demons. Come on, let's find out what Bethany has to say."

As we walk toward Westerly Gifts, I'm left with an anxious feeling in my stomach. The lauvan that inexplicably connect me to Dr. Dilleck tingle uneasily. What's happening to Dr. Dilleck? Why did she act so strangely in my presence? And why do I care?

ꝭ

The door to the occult shop bangs open to the accompaniment of wind chimes. I close it behind Alejandro with a familiar shove of my hip against the resisting frame. A tall figure with long silver hair rises in a swirl of scarves.

"Afternoon, Bethany," I say. Bethany smiles warmly.

"Merry Lytton. How lovely to see you. Please, come in."

"This is my friend Alejandro. He knows all my secrets, so you may speak freely."

Alejandro reddens with shy pride, and Bethany nods gravely.

"Of course. Here are the gloves that Drew left. Do you think they'll help?" Bethany brings out a pair of soft leather gloves and lays them carefully on the counter. A faint humming starts in my ears and I shake my head to ignore it. There are no obvious lauvan on the gloves. I will need a closer look.

"I hope so. I'm looking for a trace of Drew's presence on the gloves. Someone has been following me, and I think it might be Potestas, the organization he works for. He's my only lead so far, so…" I lift the right glove up gently and peer inside. No matter which way I twist the hole toward the light, no errant strands emerge. I lay it down on the counter, my hope rapidly fading.

"Nothing?" Alejandro asks.

"It's been so long, especially for a mundane object like a glove. I shouldn't have expected anything. I suppose I'm back to square one." I pick up the left glove and peek in. Is there a glimmer in the thumbhole? "Wait, I might have something." I reach into the glove and carefully feel around with my thumb and index finger. Both Bethany and Alejandro stare at me in expectation. Alejandro might even be holding his breath. Closer and closer, until—a muted zing thrills up my arm and it takes all my self-control not to twitch my hand away.

"I have it," I say, barely breathing myself. This thread is infused with a powerful sensation, just like the gray lauvan shed from whoever has been following me. Sure enough, when I carefully extract the fragile strand, it is faded and wispy but undeniably gray. There is a faint iridescent sheen on the end of the lauvan, as if it has been dipped in an oil slick. Odd. But otherwise, there is no doubt.

"Well?" Alejandro says. "What is it?"

They both look at me, waiting. I forget sometimes that no one else can see what is obvious to me.

"Proof that Drew is my shadow. Potestas is after me."

"Oh dear." Bethany looks woeful. "I wish there was something I could do to help."

"Keep your ear to the ground. I appreciate you calling me about this, Bethany. You stay safe." I beckon to Alejandro and turn to the door.

"You too, Merry."

Alejandro finally starts to droop when we leave Bethany's shop.

"So, you do have a limit. I was beginning to think your energy was boundless."

"I'm okay. Where are we going next?"

"Home, for a well-earned rest. Shower, dinner. We can pick up some beer on the way."

Alejandro sighs in contentment.

"Yes, please."

We walk around a corner to the back alley where my car waits for us. The blue of my Lotus appears from behind a red minivan, then a steely gray strand floats by my face.

Drew's lauvan again, without a doubt. He is persistent. I wonder with growing unease what his purpose is. I pluck the strand from the air and snatch my hand back reflexively at the sensation.

"What happened?" Alejandro peers into the space where the lauvan writhes.

"Another lauvan from Drew. There's so much anger and agitation pent up in the strand—it shocked me."

"He's here? Why would he follow you, do you think?"

"I don't know," I say, pensive. "He must have a deeper purpose than simple curiosity or fear to send him across the city. I suppose we'll find out sooner or later."

A crack like a gunshot rents the still air. Time slows as lauvan in the air twist, buffeted this way and that by the passage of a tiny projectile.

It is a gunshot. And the bullet flies directly at my heart.

CHAPTER VIII

There is no time to think, hardly any time to move, only enough time to lunge sideways and twitch my fingers around the closest lauvan I can find. My questing fingertips grasp my own flowing strands, and I pull in a desperate maneuver to harden a shell of lauvan around my body as a defense. These are the tricks that have kept me alive for all these years—this is not the first bullet I have had winging in my direction. The shell works to deflect projectiles, allowing them to bounce harmlessly off.

But my fingers encounter tremendous resistance and my own lauvan are unresponsive. There is no time for second chances. The bullet slams into my body like a punch, tearing deep into my shoulder and forcing through the other side with a terrible burning sensation. My quick lunge prevented it from piercing my heart. I should be grateful, but the pain overwhelms every other feeling. My back wound is on fire and blood gushes down my shirt in front. I drop to my knees and slump over my damaged shoulder, gritting my teeth. Dimly I hear Alejandro shouting my name. I need to pull myself together. I need to know who shot me.

Slowly, so slowly, I squint. My vision blurs, in and out of focus. Down the alley, tires squeal. A gray compact peels out of a line of vehicles and races to the road. It leaves a cloud of glossy gray strands in its wake.

Too late, I think of the license plate number and the information it could have provided. Damn. But I don't have any more concentration to devote to Drew. People are running our way and one is filming me on her smartphone. Double damn.

Alejandro kneels before me, his terrified face bobbing in my sight.

"Merlo, Merlo! What happened?" He blanches when he looks at my shoulder and breaks into rapid Spanish. "Oh god, there's so much blood. Where's it coming from? What can I do?"

"Help me get away." I take a shallow breath and wish I hadn't. I need a chance to heal myself out of sight of prying eyes. "Too many people."

The growing crowd chatters in excitement. Someone babbles into their phone.

"Where can we go?" Alejandro's eyes dart around frantically. "Can you make it to the car?"

I have done more on worse injuries, but just because it's happened before doesn't make this time any easier.

I sit up straight and nearly scream from the stabbing pain. The car feels a thousand leagues away, and exertion increases the steady gush of blood from my wound.

"Stop! Stay still. The blood..." Alejandro grips my uninjured arm tightly to prevent movement. He needn't worry—I have no intention of recreating that particular sensation.

A faint siren builds in volume. Someone in the growing crowd must have called an ambulance. I resign myself to a trip to the hospital and focus instead on breathing.

The ambulance is a nightmare. The attendant never leaves my side for a moment, checking blood pressure and pulse and bandages. Alejandro holds onto a handrail, white-faced, his eyes darting back and forth from me to the attendant and back again. I grit my teeth and take shallow, steady breaths to manage the pain. Blood seeps through the bandage and the attendant looks worried.

If I don't untangle my lauvan soon, it might be too late. I will have to risk it. Not yet, but soon. The little I managed before the ambulance arrived was not nearly enough. A wave of pain throbs across my shoulder and chest and I lose concentration.

"Are we almost there?" Alejandro peers through the front windshield.

"Nearly," the driver replies. The siren howls above us, drowning out his words, wailing over the pulse of blood in my ears.

At the hospital, the attendants slide me quickly but efficiently from the ambulance stretcher onto a gurney. They are smooth, but the slight motion almost makes me pass out. I could more easily handle the pain if I had something to do, some reason for distraction. My wound is more dire than I thought. I need to fix my strands while I'm still conscious. I reach my right hand up to my injured shoulder.

"Best if you don't touch." The attendant firmly presses my hand back to my side. "Let the doctor see it first."

No doctor will be as effective as me. Damn it, how can I be alone?

A nurse rushes over.

"Gunshot to the shoulder," the attendant says without preamble. "Exit wound. Fair bit of blood loss."

"We'll take him straight to the trauma room. And what is *he* doing here?" The nurse points at Alejandro with a frown. "You know the protocol for suspicious injuries—he shouldn't have been in the ambulance." She turns to a fellow nurse and says, "Get security to watch this patient—in case the attacker comes back."

The attendant looks sheepish and I interject.

"It's fine. Alejandro's with me. And the security won't be

necessary."

"Standard protocol. You can take it up with the police later."

They push me to a large room with over-bright lights and wheeled tables filled with medical equipment. Before I disappear from Alejandro's sight, I give him a beseeching look. *Time*, I mouth. I need a chance to stop the bleeding.

Nurses and a surgeon gather around my gurney. The lights dim slightly, and it's not from someone hitting the light switch. I need to stop the bleeding *now*.

CRASH.

The nurses gathered around me look up in surprise. I seize my opportunity and bury my fingers in the mess of lauvan above my shoulder. It won't take much to staunch the blood, just a few strands in place will do…

"*Lo siento*, sorry, so sorry. I am clumsy. Let me help. Oh! Sorry!"

A grin flits across my face despite the pain. It sounds like Alejandro has upset a cart of supplies and is pretending to help tidy. The nurses start to turn back, but Alejandro bursts into the room, falling head over heels.

"Sorry, so sorry! I fell, so sorry!"

One of the nurses runs forward to usher him out of the trauma room. The others look scandalized, then turn back to me. One shakes her head and tears my hand away from my shoulder.

"No touching. Let's have a look at that wound."

She gently lifts off the bloody compress that covers my injury. The surgeon leans in and her brow furrows.

"You were shot in the shoulder a few minutes ago, isn't that correct?"

I look down at my shoulder, smeared with fresh and drying blood. The wound itself is little more than a scratch, perhaps what might happen if I cut myself lightly with a knife. Damn and double damn. I healed the skin over the wound to stop the blood but went too far. I had no time for finesse.

"Yes, but I don't know if it went in. Perhaps it glanced off? You know, I'm feeling quite a bit better now."

The surgeon looks skeptical. It's not a convincing explanation, but the evidence speaks for itself.

"I was told there was an exit wound. Can you sit up?" She helps me raise my torso into an upright position. I hide my grimace as fresh waves of pain roll down my chest. I didn't heal enough for that.

"There's only a scar on the upper shoulder. Have you recently recovered from a wound to that area?" She presses the healed exit wound, and I attempt to keep my face impassive while a searing jolt of pain lances through my flesh.

"Yes, last month I fell on a sharp corner. I'm feeling better. Can I go home now?"

The surgeon shakes her head in bewilderment, not denial.

"We'll clean the area first and prescribe you some antibiotics along with instructions for dressing the wound properly. Follow the instructions and check in with your own doctor in a few days to make sure it's healing nicely."

The surgeon leaves, still with a puzzled expression on her face. The nurses bandage me and help me into a hospital gown—my shirt is ruined after the blood and the ambulance attendants cutting it away—and transfer me to a wheelchair to take me back to the exit. Alejandro meets us at the door and puts my good arm over his shoulders.

"Now where?" He looks exhausted.

"Home. Let's find a cab. I need to finish healing myself."

Alejandro ushers me into my apartment and helps me lower onto my bed. I wince with the motion.

"What can I do?"

"I'm fine." I grin weakly at Alejandro, who appears unconvinced. "Honestly. I need some time to untangle my lauvan, then I'll be as right as rain."

"Untangle?"

"It's a wound, and my lauvan are snarled above it. If I remove the knots, I can heal the wound."

"Nice trick." Alejandro yawns. I point toward the living room.

"You're on the couch. Sheets and blankets should be there. Help yourself to anything in the fridge. Sorry this evening wasn't quite what we envisioned."

"Your life is more exciting than you said, Merlo."

I lay back and sigh in discomfort.

"Lucky me."

Alejandro leaves me alone to ready himself for sleep. I pull off the hospital gown to reveal bare skin and position a mirror for a better view of my shoulder to begin the lengthy process of untangling. I removed some of the knots in the hospital, but there is plenty to do. I resign myself to the task. It's tedious, but pain is worse.

After three quarters of an hour, my brown lauvan are free flowing once more, and my mind turns to stickier problems. Why the hell did Drew shoot me? And how can I find the bastard to strike back?

I sink into my pillows and prop my phone against bent legs. Let's see what the all-knowing Internet can show me. I have a last name now, thanks to Bethany, so I'm searching for a needle in a much smaller haystack. I type in "Drew Mordecai."

There are no pictures of interest—none are of the same

person and I can discount the ones that don't match Sylvana's previous description of a brown-haired man in his thirties. I return to the links. There is one for Facebook, a White Pages ad, and some blogger from Minnesota, all of which I ignore after a quick view. Below those, however, are some businesses. In the text preview for each link, "Drew Mordecai" appears next to a list of other names. But when I search the sites themselves, there is no trace of his name on any page.

I'm flummoxed. Someone with Drew's name has connections with these businesses, but not in a public capacity. Unfortunately, I have reached the limit of my technological skills. I try to keep current, but there is only so much I can do.

I can visit in person, though, since I can see much more than most. The addresses of the four businesses with Drew's name are all local, none of them very far away. Tomorrow I will visit each and see if I can sniff out my attacker. I'm itching to meet him face to face and show him my appreciation for his gun work.

CHAPTER IX

Dreaming

Celeste takes a sip of her coffee from its tiny, dainty cup. A sip at a time is all one can handle of the bitter brew Café de Foy serves. The tiny cups it's served in protect our tongues as much as our purses. Celeste sits up straight and waves to a figure striding under sweeping chestnut trees in front of the café. I turn when the man approaches our table.

"Monsieur Fragonard," Celeste says and pats her shawl in place. "How are you?"

"Madame Linne, Merle, good afternoon," says Jean-Honoré Fragonard, a promising Rococo painter and a friend of ours. "I would be better if I hadn't run out of Prussian blue. And my usual color man has none! Now I must wait until I go to Montmartre tomorrow to buy some. Bah!"

"What are you painting, Monsieur?" Celeste asks. She loves Jean-Honoré's work and has sat as a model for him a few times in the past. He carefully positions her so her fire-ravaged right cheek is not visible, leaving only the smooth skin and high color of her left cheek. For my part, I love both her sides and have sketched her entire face in my book, to Celeste's consternation.

"A great tableau of a picnic by a river. I've put you in, Madame, and your beauty glows far beyond what paint can achieve."

Celeste smiles with pleasure even as she bends her neck in an instinctive gesture to hide her cheek.

"Are you meeting the marquis this afternoon?" I nod at a table on the far side of the room where a young man in a high powdered wig sips coffee with an older portly gentleman. They are both a cut above most of the bourgeoisie who frequent this café.

"Yes. I have to eat somehow, and he loves my *Happy Accidents of the Swing*."

"Who doesn't? He looks in a good mood today, so best of luck. Come to our apartment later for a drink if you've a mind to celebrate or commiserate."

"A kingly offer. I will see you tonight, Merle. Madame." He bows to Celeste then walks smartly to the marquis.

"Oh, Merle. I'm so happy right now."

"For what reason? You like the coffee? You're with me? Or you're now a woman of leisure instead of a lady of the evening?"

"There are worse ways to make a living. I was a very high-class courtesan, if you recall. Only the richest gentlemen could afford me." She places her cup down with careful precision on the table. A fleeting expression of fear is followed by a wry smile. "Well, not all of them were gentlemen, were they?"

"Not that last one with the torch, no." I match Celeste's light, playful tone, but the memory of our first meeting boils in my gut as angrily as it did when it first occurred. Screams from down the hall in the hotel near the Palais Royal. My bursting in at the scent of burned flesh. Celeste's slumped form on the crumpled sheets. My fingers ripping at the man's lauvan as he flailed helplessly. My instant lauvan bond with the unconscious Celeste as I laid her gently on my own unused bed. Burns are difficult for me to heal, and with the extent of damage she was lucky to live. I did the best I could with her strands, but she will carry the scars for the rest of her life.

"Celeste, *ma cherie*, we don't have to decide now, but I have only a few more years before people start to question my unchanging face. Have you given any thought to our next steps? I could give myself wrinkles and gray hair if you wish to stay in Paris—it's not easy, but it can be done."

Celeste brushes back my hair with a smile.

"No wrinkles, please. Why mar this handsome face when you have no need to? No, I'm almost ready for a change. I love Paris—conversations, friends, the life humming at all hours—but I've been here for many years now. Is there somewhere new to you? Where haven't you been?"

"I've been everywhere, that's the problem."

"Oh, you." She slaps my arm playfully. "Now you're just being difficult. Is there somewhere you haven't been for a long time?"

"Hmm. What do you think of Russia? The upper classes speak decent French these days, and I could fill in a few holes in my lauvan cable maps."

Celeste thinks for a moment, and an adventurous glint kindles in her eyes.

"In a few years, yes. Take me to Russia."

My mind fills with thoughts of Russia, a region I haven't visited since the fourteenth century, when Ivan the Great was king and Moscow lay in the territory of Muscovy. Celeste idly swirls her coffee, lost in thought.

"Merle," she says dreamily. "Why are there no air lauvan cables, up in the sky? Why only earth cables?"

"As far as I can tell, the Earth is much like a human body, with its own lauvan network and centers. What would the sky be doing with a cable? What would support it? Air lauvan are so fragile."

"You're such an earth snob. I'll bet there are air cables, way up high where you can't see them."

"Even when I fly?"

"Even then. Oh, what a beautiful thought—what if rainbows were air cables? How lovely."

I laugh and cover her hand with my own.

"I love your imagination, Celeste. Never let go of that whimsy."

Winter storms have kept us bound within the walls of the villa for days. Guinevere sews a new cloak for Arthur by the flickering light of the fire that billows smoke into the room with the worst gusts. Arthur is stoic about his incarceration by the weather, and alternates between looking at maps to plan for the summer campaign and mending his scabbard. I am not so occupied.

"Merlin, please sit down," Guinevere says. "You make me anxious. So many steps, back, forth."

"I'm so bored." I fling myself onto a bench by the fire. My fingers drum against the wood. Arthur looks up from his map.

"You could help me plan for next summer."

"We've already discussed tactics a thousand times. I don't know what else you expect to find on that parchment."

"What about some more music?" Guinevere says. She eyes my harp, which stands in the corner. Its oiled wood gleams invitingly in the firelight, but I shake my head.

"My fingers ache from playing all morning."

At that moment, the winds die. The shutters stop their ceaseless banging and clattering and the whistling through the tiles on the roof quiets. I leap up.

"Finally. I'm off for a deer-run. Don't expect me anytime soon."

Before the others can say anything in return, I grab my cloak and move to the front door. A loud knocking gives me pause. Who would be foolish enough to venture out in this weather, aside from me?

Arthur stands in readiness.

"Open up, Merlin. Let us see who needs a warm fire."

I slide the bolt and pull the carved door slowly toward me. A woman wrapped in a long gray cloak stands on the stones before the door. She is tall and stately, perhaps forty, with clear gray eyes and a high forehead.

"Greetings. I look for a man named Merlin. Is he within? It's a matter of some urgency."

"I am he," I say, bewildered. I have never seen this woman before. She studies me with an appraising eye.

"Let her in," Arthur calls out. "And shut the door before we freeze to death."

I usher the woman in. One last glance before I swing the door shut affords me a curious sight. Trees in the distance toss and sway under the influence of a mighty wind. But here, the most I feel is a gentle breeze.

The woman accepts a chair graciously from Arthur and allows Guinevere to take her sodden cloak and call a slave for some warm wine. I wait until she is settled in front of the fire before I speak.

"You said you had urgent news? And what is your name? I haven't met you before."

"You haven't met me, but you are very close with my sister of the elements. I am Arden, Lady of the Wind."

She is one of the four ladies honoring the old goddess, of whom Nimue is Lady of the Lake. But what urgent news would the Lady of the Wind have for me? Unless… I slide onto the bench near her with fear in my heart.

"Nimue. Is she all right?"

Arthur and Guinevere exchange curious glances, but all that matters are Arden's next words.

"She is why I am here. Nimue is gravely injured. She asked for you, saying you could help. I find it hard to believe, but she was insistent."

"What sort of injury?" Not everything can be fixed with lauvan. I hold my breath to wait for Arden's answer.

"A terrible leg wound—it's broken in many places. If she survives, I doubt she'll ever walk again."

"Any inflammation?"

"Not when I left. There were only a few scrapes. Most of the injury is internal. She was climbing a hillside and the rocky scree loosened under her feet. Her leg caught in a tree root on the way down."

I breathe a sigh of relief and lean back, painfully aware of the hammering of my heart. There is still time. Bones, I can mend. Inflammation is trickier but can be remedied if caught early. If I hurry, I can heal Nimue.

"Let's go. I can help, but sooner will be easier than later." I stand and both Guinevere and Arthur look at me in surprise.

"Hold on, Merlin," Arthur says. "Who is this Nimue that you would instantly run to her side? In the worst storm we've seen all year, no less?"

I sway back and forth, deciding what to tell two of my closest friends. I have never mentioned Nimue to them. Some might think it odd but in all my years, forty in total, I have never considered myself in love until Nimue appeared. Even now, I wonder at the extent of my feeling. It's a foreign, albeit pleasurable sensation, but it always felt odd to bring up Nimue to Arthur and Guinevere in conversation. My trips to her lake were not remarked upon, as I often come and go without warning.

"Merlin, you have a love? I did not know." Guinevere smiles at me. "I am glad. What is she like?"

"What?" Arthur is half-laughing, half incredulous. "I never expected this from you. Have you finally found a woman who can melt your iron heart? I didn't think it possible. And to not tell us?"

"Because I knew you would react like this," I mutter, although I'm pleased they now know. Secrets are tricky. And now I can speak to them of Nimue, something I hadn't realized how much I wanted to do. I turn to Arden. "Are you ready to travel, or shall I go on ahead?"

"I am ready," she says. She eyes her sodden cloak. "Ready enough."

"I can fix that." I stride over to her cloak and pull long strands of water lauvan off the material. Water follows, and drips onto the floor when I release the threads. When I finish, I hand the cloak to Arden who takes it with an appreciative look.

"That's an excellent trick. Many thanks, Merlin."

"You've told Nimue about the lauvan?" Arthur shakes his head in amazement. "It must be serious. When are we to meet her?"

"She doesn't often leave her home." It's uncomfortable to imagine my two worlds together under one roof. "Perhaps one day."

"Go quickly and make her well once again," Arthur says. "But hurry back—we'll want to know she's safe." He gets up and holds out a hand for Arden. She stands with his help then clutches his arm, her eyes wide and unseeing. Her pale gray lauvan writhe with intensity around her head and wrap around Arthur's arm below her grasping fingers.

"Arthur Pendragon," she says in a hoarse voice. "You are connected to others in ways you cannot fathom. You will last far beyond the grave and will return again when you are needed." Arden closes her eyes, then begins to cough. Arthur helps her back to the bench until she is recovered. When her coughing fit subsides, she looks up with interest.

"What did I say? I'm prone to prophesy. A few have even come to pass."

Arthur glances at me, baffled. I shrug in reply and fasten my cloak in preparation for our departure. Normally I wouldn't give much credence to tales of prophesy, but these ladies are different. Nimue always knows exactly when the rain will stop or where a stream can be found. Could Arden have really said the truth? And what does it mean, to last beyond the grave?

CHAPTER X

In the morning, I hand Alejandro a bus schedule and a map on which I have circled main attractions.

"I have to fetch my car then follow up on some leads on my shooter. If you'd like to meet for a late lunch, make your way here by two o'clock." I point to a circle on the map.

"What if the shooter comes back for you?"

"I'll be watching out for him. Don't bother locking the door when you leave." I slide open the balcony door and step out. "See you later."

"What are you doing?"

I grin.

"Just watch."

I gather the necessary lauvan and pull hard.

My body dissolves and reforms as a merlin falcon, the form I take when I want to travel at speed. My feathers ruffle in the wind and I look up at Alejandro's face, every hair follicle on his slack-jawed chin visible to my raptorial eyes. It never gets old, that trick.

My taloned feet push off with a thrust of powerful wings. As I soar away, I release a shriek for Alejandro's benefit. Oh, the beauty of flight. Not much comes close to the freedom of the open air, the unfiltered sun warming my feathers, the muffled roar of the city spread below me.

It's not far to where I parked my car in Steveston, not as the merlin flies. The neighborhood lies on a sharp corner of land, the sea on either side. A long causeway above a dyke that holds the ocean back from the delta lowlands points me in the right direction.

I'm nearly there when I spot a disturbance in the air to my left, coming from inland. It's a writhing cluster of air lauvan, like the ones that flow through my feathers. There is nothing calm about these. The huge mass rolling my way in midair reminds me irresistibly of a minnow ball in a defensive maneuver against seals.

It's coming fast, directly toward me. I flap harder and catch an updraft to gain some height, but the lauvan ball also rises. A chill passes over me. There is nothing natural about this wind.

My car is so close, but not close enough. I fold my wings and plummet in a dive that would normally fill me with exhilaration. All I feel now is dread at the ball of lauvan that drops from above. It's close enough now for me to hear a shrill whistling, growing louder and louder. If I can make it to the ground and regain my human, much heavier, form…

I'm swept into a whirling frenzy of wind. Roaring and whistling fill my ears and my little feathered body is buffeted in every direction. I don't know where the ground is, which is a problem because I wasn't very far away to begin with. Round and round, this way and that—I shriek my dismay and desperately try to regain my balance. My beak snaps at the strands but I can't easily grasp one for balance.

I catch a glimpse of the ground, far too close now. With a gargantuan effort, I thrust my wings out stiffly and, in the slight pause this affords me, clasp a bundle of frenetically dancing lauvan in my beak.

The winds still for an instant, and I flap my way out of the melee and to the ground as fast as my wings will carry me. As soon as I land on a patch of asphalt behind a parked car, I revert to my normal form and sit on the ground, breathing heavily.

So, flying in bird form is no longer a viable mode of transport. Wind does not act in that manner naturally. Is this another scheme of Potestas? If so, my enemy has power over the wind itself, incredible power that I can only dream of. How is this possible? I may have met my match, and more. Why the winds died when I grasped the lauvan in my beak, I can only guess. Perhaps they were not expecting my meddling.

When I stand and dust off my jeans, I recognize the street. My car is only a few blocks away. Good. I will feel better with a ton of steel around me. I haven't felt that shaken up in the air since I flew through a rain of arrows during the battle of Agincourt in 1415.

The car is right where I left it, miraculously untowed. I check the map on my phone when I slide into the driver's seat. Wilson and Jones, a law office potentially connected to Drew, is only a few minutes away.

There's a space out front in which I manage to squeeze my Lotus. Frosted glass etched with the firm's name informs me I'm in the correct location. My eyes rake critically over my too-casual jeans. I will spruce up before entering—it pays to make a good impression. A quick glance up and down the sidewalk to make sure no one is paying attention, a few quick twists of lauvan, and I'm dressed in business slacks and an open-necked button-up shirt. One last look around reveals a little girl staring open-mouthed at me. I wink at her and step into the blissfully air-conditioned lawyer's office.

"Good morning," says a receptionist smoothly. Her shiny brown hair is coiled neatly in a bun, with nary a strand out of place. The office is tastefully decorated in dark green and wood with a glossy book of aerial photos on a glass coffee table in the waiting room. There is nothing out of place, no untethered lauvan to see, no hint of anything untoward.

"Good morning. I was told I'd find Drew Mordecai here. Is he available?" No point in dancing around. If she's heard of him I'll see a reaction, no matter what her verbal answer might be.

To my annoyance, her strands of light pink show no motion whatsoever.

"I'm sorry, there's no one here by that name. Do you have

an appointment?" She moves her computer mouse to check her calendar. I wave to stop her.

"No, no, it's fine. I must have the wrong place. Sorry to bother you." Before I turn to go, a flicker catches my eye. A free-floating strand clings to a file folder above the receptionist's head. It's a deep purple that looks familiar, although I can't place it at the moment.

"Have a good day." The receptionist dismisses me and returns to her computer. I let myself out.

The insurance broker and the credit union are equally bland and unhelpful and it's with very little hope that I enter the cupcake shop, Sweet Thing, after texting Jen to invite her to lunch with Alejandro. The girl behind the counter greets me.

"Good afternoon! What can I get for you?" She is very chipper with a neon green apron and a wide smile. I don't think I could muster up that much enthusiasm for every customer, but I'm a jaded old soul.

"Nothing for me, thanks. I'm looking for Drew Mordecai. Is he in?"

A flicker of uncertainty passes over her face. Could I have found something at last? She turns to her colleague behind her, who pipes icing on fresh cupcakes.

"Carly, what's the name of our new dishwasher?"

"Peter, isn't it?"

"That's right." She turns back to me. "Sorry, no one here named Drew."

"Thanks anyway." I must look despondent because she holds up a tray of mini cupcakes.

"Cheer up. Have a sample."

I can't help but smile and reach for one.

"Thanks."

I walk to the door and reach for the handle then stop. On the doorjamb, almost faded beyond recognition, is a free-floating lauvan. It's the gray of a stormy sea.

Bingo. I carefully pinch the strand between finger and thumb and exit the store. Once outside, I examine my finding. The faint echo of fear and anger lingers, and that strange oil slick coloration is present on the end. Drew was here before. Unless he is simply partial to miniature pastries, Drew has a connection to Sweet Thing. I need to find out what it is.

CHAPTER XI

The sun is relentless, and even I am glad for the umbrella over our restaurant table on the balcony. Alejandro and I are waiting for Jen at one of my favorite spots overlooking the water—the combination of dazzling sea, moody mountains, and glittering city is hard to beat. At least, within a quick car ride from my apartment.

"That was amazing, earlier," Alejandro says. "With the bird thing. You know." He wiggles his eyebrows, trying to communicate his thoughts without the nearest patrons overhearing.

"Yes, I do know to what you're referring. And thank you. I honed that particular skill many years ago, but it's a complex one that took me a great while to master. It's too handy to not have in my arsenal."

"It must be incredible to fly. Did you feel trapped in the airplane? Wait, why did you take the airplane?"

"It's too far to Costa Rica. I don't have the stamina for that. But yes, flying is like nothing else."

Alejandro sighs wistfully.

"I wish I could try it. I know your life must be a burden sometimes, but there are serious perks."

"I could take you up. It's been a long while since I've changed another, but it can be done."

Alejandro sits up very straight and clutches the table with both hands.

"What? You could do that? When? Are you free this afternoon?"

I laugh and take a sip of beer.

"Easy, there. We'll go up before you leave, I promise. You're a brave soul—I've had many who flinch at the thought."

"I'd like nothing better. Can I choose the type of bird? What are you, some kind of hawk?"

"A merlin falcon, naturally."

Alejandro's face widens in a smile.

"Of course. I think I'd make a good eagle. Not one of the bald ones, a golden eagle. Big, graceful, sharp talons."

"Really? I was notching you down as a pigeon, myself." My teasing brings out a huff of disgust from Alejandro.

"Merlo. I hope I can prove to you one day that I am not a pigeon man."

I have ordered nachos and beer to share, and the platter arrives a few moments before Jen does. The server is between Jen and Alejandro when I greet Jen. The server moves, and Alejandro sees Jen for the first time.

The reaction of their lauvan is electric. One moment, the two are surrounded by their own lazily swirling strands. The next, every lauvan points toward the other. It lasts only a moment, but it is intense. Strangely, neither Jen nor Alejandro appears to notice.

"Jen. There you are," I say. "No Cecil today?"

"He's working, so it's just me. He'll swing by later."

"Jen, this is Alejandro Fernandez, my friend's nephew from Costa Rica." I introduce him as Braulio's nephew, not grandson, to make my friendship with Braulio more plausible. "Alejandro, this is my friend, Jennifer Chan."

Alejandro sticks out his hand eagerly with an infectious smile that Jen can't help but return. Their lauvan immediately intertwine at their joined hands and a single strand from each remains connected after they release. That's interesting. It's very unusual to make a connection that quickly with a total stranger. I'm curious to see what happens between them in the coming weeks.

"Merry! Wake up. I was asking Alejandro if you've taken

him to the aquarium yet and he said no. What kind of host misses that?"

"He's only been here one night. You do expect a lot. And we were rather busy. Alejandro kindly accompanied me to the emergency room after I'd been shot."

"What?" Jen clutches the table. "Merry! Are you okay?"

"Fine now. Powers, remember?" I say. Jen glances at Alejandro with a stricken look on her face. I alleviate her fears. "Alejandro knows. His uncle told him, typical meddlesome man that he was. But the salient point is, I have an enemy with a serious mission. You remember Potestas, that organization behind the Mt. Linnigan shenanigans a few weeks ago? It looks like they're after my head, and they don't have it yet. And I have no clues to track them down, only a name that leads to dead ends."

"Should you be outside? Are you safe here?" Jen glances around furtively as if to spot a sniper lurking in the bushes.

"It's a crowded restaurant, not a back alley. No one will do anything." I debate whether to tell Jen about the resistance in the lauvan I felt while I dodged the bullet, or the lauvan ball that came from nowhere. Jen's anxious face convinces me not to. Until I understand how they are related, there is no need to worry her unnecessarily.

"Okay, what's the name? Maybe I can help." Jen looks determined. "You're not safe until we figure this out."

I gaze at her, and my throat tightens slightly with emotion. Braulio was right—I need people who know me. When you don't have anyone, it's easy to forget how good it feels to have someone on your side. I clear my throat. "His name is Drew Mordecai. Brown hair, short, thirty-something. But I couldn't find much, so don't waste too much time. Hopefully, he'll make a mistake soon and I'll catch him at it." I pick up a cheesy nacho and pop it in my mouth. "Eat, drink, you two. And relax. Jen, tell Alejandro everything he's missing as a result of my poor hosting skills."

Jen begins to chatter and Alejandro hangs onto every word. Both their lauvan dance with excitement and joy. What a reaction—I haven't seen its like in quite some time.

A pair of women saunters by. They are embracing our unusual heat streak with open and welcoming arms. Both wear sandals and tank tops in the spirit of minimalism. Best of all, both are dressed in short, blousy skirts showing off generous lengths of well-shaped legs. I have seen shorts that are shorter, but there's something delicious about a skirt.

I watch them approvingly as they swing past. The modern world is filled with miraculous inventions that I use daily but on occasions like this, one of my favorites is sunglasses. How much simpler it is to surreptitiously look at a woman without embarrassing her and acting like a fool yourself.

"Merry. You're ogling those girls and ignoring us," Jen says. Damn it. Sometimes women are unhelpfully intuitive.

"I am not 'ogling.' Honestly. What do you take me for, some lusty teenager?"

"Not far off sometimes." Jen shakes her head and grins. An unexpected gust of wind sweeps along the street. It takes the walking girls by surprise and their chatting is instantly replaced by shrieks as the wind lifts their skirts and flutters them about, exposing a healthy view of be-thonged bottom.

I grin widely and Alejandro's jaw drops as he looks at the girls. Jen punches my arm hard.

"You big jerk! You totally did that."

"What?" I'm taken aback until I realize what she means. She thinks I used lauvan to push the wind about. I say loftily, "I can't believe you would think that. I would never abuse my powers for so frivolous a purpose." Alejandro snorts and Jen looks skeptical. I amend, "I would only rarely abuse my powers for so frivolous a purpose. And I'd do a much better job, too."

Alejandro laughs and says, "That sounds more like the stories Braulio told me."

"Oh yeah?" Jen says, propping her chin on her hand. "Like what? Tell me more." She grins at me. "What sort of hijinks did Merry and your uncle get up to?"

"Apparently, Braulio and Merlo here went to a dance," Alejandro says. I listen, amused, curious to hear what Braulio told Alejandro, eager to hear my memories come from somewhere beside my own head. Alejandro continues, "And Merlo decided to try a new dance move on his partner. He told her to prepare herself for the 'Russian rise.' She had no idea, of course, but when they did the move, she ended up high in the air, legs apart and skirt flying."

Jen laughs hard enough for neighboring tables to glance at us curiously. I roll my eyes.

"Your uncle, I'm afraid, was excessively prone to manipulating the story if it made the tale reflect better on him. What he neglected to pass on was that he taught me the move and dared me to use it." I laugh. "Typical Braulio."

I subside, with the remembrance that Braulio will never again tell a story, misremembered or not. My smile turns wry and sad and I look across the water to the distant mountains, clear in the bright heat.

Jen and Alejandro exchange glances at the edge of my vision, and Jen says, "Are you two free tonight? I'm going clubbing downtown with Cecil and my roommate Amanda. It'd be great if you want to join us. It'd be fun for Alejandro to experience Vancouver nightlife, such as it is."

Alejandro brightens, then looks at me for confirmation. I waffle for a minute for appearances' sake.

"Clubbing? I'm sure Alejandro wants to go, but aren't I getting a little long in the tooth for that?"

"You're not even thirty yet," Jen says. Alejandro coughs. I studiously ignore him. "Besides, don't give me that line. I know you go out. And we're heading to that club on the east end—it's more of a professional crowd." Suddenly her face falls. "Although maybe you shouldn't be downtown at night."

"Why not?" I'm truly mystified. Jen leans forward and whispers one word.

"Potestas."

I sigh and rake my hand through my hair.

"I can't hide in my apartment forever because some lunatic is after my head." Jen looks at me in complete disagreement. I say, "Besides, there'll be plenty of people in the club, and downtown is always packed. Alejandro and I were in a deserted alley when I was shot. I'll be there." Jen takes a breath as if to dissuade me, so I turn to Alejandro instead. "Are you interested?"

"Oh, yes," he says at once. His eyes flicker to Jen when he replies, and most of his lauvan are still oriented in her direction. Jen's lauvan are reciprocating, twisting toward Alejandro. Jen shows nothing in her bearing or demeanor that indicates an attraction to Alejandro beyond her usual cheerful welcome of a new acquaintance. The fragile russet and gold lauvan that connect her to Cecil are still present, alongside the lauvan now connected to Alejandro.

"Well then, it's decided," I say with finality. "Thanks for the invite."

"Hi, Cecil!" Jen waves behind me. I turn to where Cecil climbs the steps of the balcony. His blond hair gleams in the sun, and Jen's lauvan squirm a little. I take a bite of the last of the nachos to hide my smile.

"Is it time already?" Jen says, busying herself with her purse. "Cecil, this is Merry's friend Alejandro. He's visiting from Costa Rica."

"Welcome to Vancouver," Cecil says, extending his hand to Alejandro. Alejandro shakes it heartily. Their lauvan, however, tell a different story. Their strands refuse to touch, and twist around each other warily, defensively, on edge. What an odd reaction between strangers. It can happen when people take an instant dislike to each other, but it's rare. And if I hadn't seen the lauvan I would never have guessed. Alejandro and Cecil look perfectly amicable on the surface.

"I invited these two out dancing tonight," Jen says to Cecil.

"I meant to tell you—I can't make it." Cecil looks slightly annoyed, but the expression quickly morphs into disappointment. "Sorry, babe."

Jen looks taken aback at the familiar moniker, but otherwise ignores it. Alejandro's lauvan dance with agitation. The silent story is so fascinating, I could watch it all day.

Not long after, we pay up and leave. Jen's comment about Potestas, as much as I brushed off her concerns, is certainly valid. I'm still no closer to knowing who Drew Mordecai is and when he will strike again. It's unlikely that he will start a shooting spree in a club with so many innocents in the way. But then, what do I know? Potestas was willing to erupt a volcano over an entire town before. Still, I'm not one to cower in the shadows. I would rather face my foes head-on, or at least live my life unhampered by fear.

We stroll through throngs of people streaming along the sidewalk in the warm, dusky air. Alejandro saunters casually, but I can tell he is bursting with excitement and pride as an international traveler, living the big-city life. The problem with living so long is that I have done everything before, but I can live vicariously through my friends.

"What are you smiling at, Merlo?"

"It's a pleasant night. Ah, there's the club."

"Oh," Alejandro says with a hint of despondency. "There's a very long line."

There is no way I'm waiting. The line stretches the block and disappears around the corner. Halfway down the line, a hand waves frantically at us, and Jen emerges from behind a leggy blonde. I direct my steps in her direction. Jen's dressed in a tight-fitting blue dress with large, sparkling earrings, and Alejandro's eyes widen slightly.

"Hi, guys. We've been waiting for ages, and we're still not in. Amanda," she points at her roommate, whose brown hair is pulled back in a high ponytail above a shiny purple top and tight black pants. "This is Alejandro, and you've met Merry. Alejandro, meet Amanda."

I cut across their greetings.

"Come on, I'm not in the mood to wait. Follow me."

"But if we lose our spot, it will take forever to get back!"

"A little trust, please." I stride off without looking behind me, and after a moment the clicking of the girls' heels follow. At the door I beckon to the bouncer, an oversized man with a good-natured face despite an attempt at solemnity.

"A word, please," I say to him. The man leans forward.

"You'll need to line up with everyone else."

"About that." I reach toward his nearest lauvan and twist it around my index finger. My own lauvan twirl around it and I concentrate on my intent. "I believe we were invited by the owner."

The bouncer's face grows curiously blank. He nods slowly.

"If you'd kindly unlatch the barrier," I say pleasantly. "We'll be on our way."

He nods again and fumbles with a hook fastening a velvet

cord to the silver pole keeping the crowds at bay.

"Good man." I pat his shoulder to release his lauvan from my own and walk past him. "Come on, the rest of you. The music awaits."

The girls' heels click-clack behind me as I stride down the open hallway toward thumping music ahead. Once we are out of earshot of the bouncer, Jen grabs my elbow.

"How did you do that? And why did you let me stand in line for so long?"

I laugh at her expression, equal parts indignation and admiration.

"I have a few tricks up my sleeve, you should know that. Although I do apologize for not giving you advance warning."

"I don't know what you said, but I'm glad you're convincing. Thanks, Merry." Amanda pats her hair and adjusts her top. "You should have been with us last week. Remember Underground Nightclub, Jen? We must've waited an hour and a half."

"I admire your dedication," I say. "I don't have nearly that amount of patience."

"How can you live for so long, yet not have patience, *anciano*?" Alejandro mutters to me in Spanish.

"What do you mean?" Jen answers in Spanish. In English, she says, "I do speak Spanish, you know. Why did you call him 'anciano?' He's not that old."

Alejandro's lauvan flare and flutter with exhilaration at the revelation of Jen's language abilities. My nails dig into my palms, but my voice is calm.

"Just a nickname his uncle had for me. A little joke. Now, what can I get everyone to drink?"

I escape to the bar while the others find a table. Alejandro's apologetic face bobs in the wake of the two girls. I want to smack Alejandro upside the head. This is what happens when you put your trust in someone without knowing them well. I have been preparing Jen for ages, and she still only knows about the lauvan, but here is Alejandro with the whole story and only a few days of visiting. I hope he can be trusted.

The club is loud and dark. Music pumps from the disc jockey on a dais above the dance floor, where sweaty bodies gyrate and twist to the pulse of bass. This club actively discourages the younger set, those who are drunk on life and their first legal alcohol binge, so the clientele is a little classier. But when people get together to drink and dance, decorum tends to fly out the window no matter the era. We are only human, after all.

There's a lull at the bar when I arrive, and I place my order easily. A woman with sleek blond locks and cheeks warm from dancing slides up. She smiles at me, then turns to the bartender.

"Red wine, please."

"Put that one on my bill," I say to the server. To the woman, I say, "You look thirsty."

"You don't need to buy me a drink." She looks flustered and glances around as if searching for an escape.

"No strings. I'm feeling generous tonight—just enjoy." I put a few dollars in the tip jar and collect my drinks then grin at the woman and make my exit. She wears a half-smile as she watches me go.

When I arrive at our table and pass around drinks, Alejandro looks settled in his chair. Amanda is already on the dance floor, and Jen is on the edge of her seat, talking to Alejandro.

"Are you sure you don't want to dance?"

"Oh, you have to dance," I reply immediately.

"Why?" Alejandro asks, a touch defensively.

"Dancing's important. You can tell a lot about a man by how he dances. Let me rephrase that—women evaluate men on how they dance."

Jen tsks at me and rolls her eyes.

"Don't listen to him, Alejandro. We do no such thing."

"Oh, perhaps not consciously. But most dancing is a prelude to the main act." Alejandro stares at me blankly. I raise an eyebrow and clarify. "The horizontal tango? The dance between the sheets?"

Alejandro sputters and Jen laughs incredulously.

"Come on, Merry. Where do you come up with this stuff?" She turns and scans the writhing dance floor. "Okay, tell me who's the best in bed. Go on. I want to hear this."

I cross my arms and lean back, surveying the crowd. I spot a couple of likely candidates but decide to analyze a few of the men for Alejandro's education and Jen's amusement. My first target is a wildly dancing man with a laughing partner and a pocket of space around him as people avoid his flying elbows.

"The guy in the red shirt. He has no idea what he's doing, but damn it if he isn't having a great time doing it. Clumsy but enthusiastic. And with a partner willing to go along with it, they'll likely have a fun time. Now, cowboy hat over there," I point to a very inebriated young man clamped onto the back of a pretty girl. "He's practically grinding her right on the dance floor. He's interested in getting what he wants, and that's it. Three minutes, roll over and done, I'd guess. See her face? She's only barely tolerating him."

"What about that guy?" Jen points at a man in a buttoned shirt half-heartedly moving to the beat. "He's hardly doing anything—not much for you to analyze." Jen looks smug as if she has stumped me. Nice try, Jen.

"Au contraire. Doing little says a lot. He has one move—the hip sway. I'm betting he's a missionary man. Too timid to try anything else. Now, blue shirt on the left, he knows what he's doing. And," I nod at the woman dancing with him, large hoop earrings swaying to the rhythm of her movements. "She knows that he knows. She'll have a good time tonight."

"Oh, come on. You're saying that she'll take him home? Really?"

In reply, I nod again at the couple. The woman laughs, leans toward the man's ear, and says something that makes the man smile. She laces her fingers through his and leads him off the dance floor, toward the exit. I laugh and take a swig of my beer.

"Now I can't dance," says Alejandro. "You'll both be sitting here, judging me."

"Have your drink. You'll change your tune soon enough." I sip my beer, then look up at a gentle touch on my shoulder.

"Would you like to dance?"

It's the woman from the bar, the one for whom I bought a drink. I smile broadly and stand in one swift motion.

"Absolutely." I turn to Alejandro. "Watch and learn, my young friend."

A very long lifetime of music has given me a finely honed sense of rhythm, and enough practice dancing will turn anyone into Vaslav Nijinsky. My partner melts into my rhythm effortlessly. There are many other types of dance I prefer, but the primal urgency of modern club beats is satisfying in its own way. I'm enjoying the closeness of my partner as our lauvan brush each other's, and the thrum of the music.

Then, I see it. A lauvan floats beyond my partner's ear. It's a distinctive glossy gray, visible even in the poor lighting of the dance floor.

I'm instantly woken from my warm focus on the woman in front of me to a cold alertness of my surroundings. Drew is here, following me once again. Would he try something in the club, or will he be waiting for me down a dark alley? Downtown is crawling with revelers—surely, he wouldn't be stupid enough to blast a gun within earshot of hundreds of people? I remember the desperation emanating from his lauvan and suddenly I don't know what he's capable of.

I'm not in the mood for dancing anymore. As soon as the music morphs into a new song I leave my partner, who looks bewildered by my exit. Sorry, lovely, but you don't want to be near me tonight. Not with a crazed gunman after my blood.

Jen and Alejandro are still at our table, heads close together and looking cozy. I slide into a seat.

"Sorry to interrupt your tête-à-tête, but I might have a problem. Drew is here."

"What? You saw him?" Jen looks horrified.

"His lauvan. I don't know if he'll try something in the club or wait until I'm outside."

"What does he look like? I can walk around and look," Alejandro says.

"That's the problem, I've never seen him. I only have a description, myself. I'll have to keep an eye out for his lauvan. I think I'm done dancing tonight, though. Too vulnerable on the floor."

"Cecil and I are going to Whistler tomorrow with a few friends. I just asked Alejandro to join us. Do you want to come too? Get out of Vancouver for a night?"

"Thanks, but I teach tomorrow afternoon."

"Maybe I should stay too," Alejandro says.

"No, I feel much better with you and Jen out of harm's way. I don't want stray bullets finding you. No, go and enjoy the mountains."

Alejandro doesn't look convinced, but the lauvan waving in Jen's direction are likely stopping him from protesting further. He seems to have taken to Jen, and Jen's lauvan are reciprocating. I would love to see what happens with Cecil in the room.

In fact, I might leave them alone a little longer. I'm curious to see how this plays out.

"Bathroom. Keep your eyes open for brown-haired, average-looking, thirtyish men."

"That certainly narrows it down." Jen purses her lips and gazes around at the many specimens who fit that description.

The bathroom is on the far side of the club and I weave through the crowded edge of the dance floor, between cramped tables surrounded by laughing, drunken people on their Friday night. Replace the flashing lights with torches, and sequins with silks, and I could be any time in history. The bathroom is a nice addition, though. I do love plumbing.

It's empty except for one man splashing his face in the sink and looking distinctly unwell. I head to the urinal. Before I have a chance to unzip, a sharp hissing cuts over the muffled throb of the music. I glance up to the source, which appears to be a vent in the ceiling. A sickly green smoke shoots into our small, enclosed space directly above the other man. I hardly have a chance to react before he begins to cough uncontrollably, and a noxious smell assails my nostrils with acrid fumes. I hastily assemble a barrier of my own lauvan to block out the stench. Through my streaming eyes, I watch the other man collapse on the floor, retching. I stumble over and drag his convulsing body toward the door. My foot connects and kicks it open, and we fall out of the bathroom. The door slams shut behind us and we are left gasping for air.

"I hear you had terrible gas in the bathroom, Merlo."

"Har, har."

We are standing outside after being ushered out of the club. After the incident in the bathroom, they cleared the building to inspect the duct system. They were very accommodating to the other man from the bathroom, but I snuck out before they could start on me. I have no intent of claiming damages or whatever they are worried about. I know who the real culprit is.

"You think Drew did this?" Jen's tone is part skeptical, part worried.

"I saw no evidence, but who else sent in noxious gas? And right when I entered the bathroom? Although how he did it is beyond me." The lauvan ball that attacked me this morning rolls through my mind. Is Drew the one controlling the air? "No, this stinks of a sloppy attempted murder."

"Stinks. Heh."

"Take Alejandro home, Merry," Jen says. "He's had a lot to drink. Watch your back, and text me when you get there."

The quiet of my apartment at two in the morning is a welcome peace after the turmoil of the club. Alejandro sags against the elevator wall, looking drained. I'm the opposite—I'm wired and alert, evaluating my surroundings for new threats. It's what has kept me alive all this time and after the club, I feel justified. But the silence in the hallway outside my door is a good sign, and suddenly I long for bed, and sleep, even if it brings the inevitable dreams.

Alejandro opens his mouth in a jaw-cracking yawn as I open the door and nods gratefully when I usher him across the threshold first. His tired shamble stops abruptly once inside. I am immediately on my guard.

"Merlo? Did someone come by while we were out?"

"No. Why? What's wrong?"

"Never mind. Something didn't feel right. I probably drank

too much."

I stalk inside, gently push Alejandro closer to the open door, and proceed to look in every dark corner of my little apartment. It doesn't take long. No one is hiding, ready to pounce. There is, however, plenty of evidence of who visited my humble abode late at night. I'm certain it wasn't a social call.

"Drew was here," I say grimly. Alejandro grows pale.

"What? How?"

"It's not difficult—I never lock my door." It drives Jen crazy, but I figure if someone wants to get in, a flimsy door lock won't stop them for long. Besides, I don't have much worth stealing and what I do treasure has no value to a thief.

"Maybe you should start." He closes the door and flops onto the couch. I run my fingers along the nearest gray lauvan that floats with its many brethren throughout my apartment. The influx of fear and hatred that I receive is overpowering. There is still murder in this man's heart. No wonder there are so many free-floating threads. Drew must be shedding them like a moulting duck. What was he planning for tonight? Did he accomplish his task? A hint of regret and self-loathing underpinning the stronger emotions tells me that he did not.

"Merlo, I think the things on your bookshelf have moved." Alejandro points across the room, his brow furrowed. I follow his gaze. My harp sits at an unusual angle, and my shrunken head from Ecuador is pushed to lean against my sketchbook. I pace over to examine the one item that I can't see well through a fresh covering of lauvan. It's my roll of Tibetan prayer flags. They always have a dense covering of multicolored lauvan from the prayers of believers, but now there is a new layer.

There are a few steely gray strands, but the majority are a fine, nearly invisible silver. The same silvery threads dance on the air in a breeze and fill the sky with effervescent clouds during a storm.

Curious. How did they come to be wrapped around my prayer flags, when their place is in the sky? Air lauvan are as ephemeral as they come. They never last for long and they rarely wrap around objects.

"What is it?" says Alejandro from the couch.

"Somehow, Drew has harnessed the wind and bound it to these flags." As I say it, questions spring immediately to my mind. I answer the first by throwing the prayer flags to the floor.

Instantly, a terrific gust of wind whips through the living room. Drapes flail, windows fly open, and paintings fall off the wall.

As soon as it starts, the wind dies. We are left in awestruck silence, me clutching the dining room table and Alejandro covering his head on the couch. I shake my head in amazement and continue to talk as if a maelstrom had not recently erupted in my apartment.

"As I said, he has somehow harnessed the wind. In all my long years, I have never seen that. That means that either Potestas is handing out some powerful new tools, or Drew is like me."

I say it, but I don't dare to hope. Too many years of searching for others like me, with too few leads, have left me cynical that anyone else exists. What can I say? I'm one of a kind. If Drew can harness the wind, can I? I have made half-hearted attempts in the past, but I have never seen the point, until now. Drew has just shown me it is possible, and effective.

"Really? That's frightening. Then why did he try to shoot you? Couldn't he have pulled some lauvan instead?"

"Why bring lauvan to a gun fight? Guns are quick, easy, and long-range. But yes, I'll have to be extra vigilant. I might have met my match in Drew. We'll see."

"I don't like leaving tomorrow, after all this. Are you sure you'll be okay by yourself?"

I try hard not to laugh. What does Alejandro think he can do that I can't? I have survived for this long on my own—I can handle one more night. It's a kind thought, though, and I give my answer the grace it deserves.

"Thanks, Alejandro, but I'll be fine. Look, I even promise I'll lock my door in the evening."

"Okay, if you're sure."

While I pull out my phone to text Jen about our safe arrival, Alejandro opens his duffel bag. He hastily unzips the mesh of the inner pouch of his bag.

"Merlo, my ticket stub! It's gone!"

"Are you sure?"

"Yes, yes, it never leaves that pocket. Did Drew go through my bag?" Alejandro looks disgusted and rummages through the rest of his belongings to check for lost items.

"Why would he take your plane ticket stub? It was already used, it had no value anymore." But as I ask the question aloud, an answer forms in my head. That ticket stub was covered in Alejandro's lauvan. Now that I know Drew has lauvan abilities, I fear what his purpose is with the strands shed by my young friend. Suddenly, I'm grateful Alejandro is leaving town tomorrow, if only for a night.

CHAPTER XII

Dreaming

It's Imbolc, and Uther's household has traveled to a neighboring lord's villa for the festivities. It's early enough in the year that the Saxons haven't made an advance yet, and we can count on peace for at least a few more weeks.

I'm out for an early morning stroll to clear my head. I would have changed into my deer form, except for the hunters preparing for tonight's feast. I would rather not be the main course. It's too bad—I would have liked a good run through the surrounding woods of budding aspens and craggy oaks. I'm restless and ready to travel after a long winter tutoring Arthur. I need to move, to see new things, to talk to someone besides a teenaged boy and a grizzled warrior. Now that Morgan is married and gone, there isn't even the diversion of a female point of view. Although it was strained at the end between us, so I can't say I wasn't glad to see her go.

Lord Lot's villa is on a narrow, meandering river, adjacent to a hamlet of twenty or so thatched houses belonging to his farm laborers. Arthur is friendly with Lot's son, Gawaine. I'm partial to him myself—it's not hard to warm to his easy good humor and sharp wit. He is built like a mountain, which is good practice for Arthur when they spar. He isn't among the festival attendees yet. His father has him running a message to Ergyng, closer to the eastern border of Gwent. Hopefully, he will be back soon. Arthur was disappointed to miss him and spent most of last evening sulking in a corner of the hall.

By the time I walk past the palisades surrounding the villa toward a small meadow in the forest where today's festival is taking place, the party is well underway. Laughter and the clunk of wooden tankards float on the still morning air. I grin broadly and quicken my pace. We all need this. After a long, cold winter, it's time to celebrate spring at last, even if the ground is still so wet that my boots squelch in the mud.

The trees give way to a clearing in the woods, where most of the nearby peasants and all the closest nobles are gathered around a bonfire. Everyone is on equal footing today because all are happy to see winter leave. Ale is also a wonderful equalizer. I see a few stumbling already, early as it is.

Arthur stands with a few village boys, young men really, but comes to my side when he sees me. He is my height now but still skinny with a mop of hair that curls no matter how closely he has it trimmed. He holds a tankard out to me, brimming full of ale.

"Here, Merlin. Mother Gwawl from the village says this is her best brew of the year, and it was going fast, so I saved some for you."

"Excellent. Time enough for swill when we don't care anymore." I bang my cup against Arthur's so the liquid sloshes out and runs down my hand, then I drink deeply. It's decent, but not the best I've ever had. I wonder how the bad batch will go down.

"Not as good as your cook's," I say. "I'll miss her brews this summer."

"Must you go?" Arthur must realize he sounds too petulant for fifteen, because he adds quickly, "It will be dull here without you, that's all."

"I'll be back before the winter storms, you know that. And there's plenty to do in the summer. Arms practice, hunting, preparing your father for battles. You could visit your sister, ride to see Gawaine."

"You promise you won't die out there?" Arthur asks in jest, but I can sense the sincerity in his voice and in his coiled lauvan.

I pat him on the back.

"I'm a survivor. Don't worry, I'll be around for a good long time."

"Why don't you visit Morgan with me before you go?"

"Arthur, surely you're old enough to realize that isn't a good idea. I didn't treat her as well as I should have. Women don't forget, and I doubt Morgan will forgive."

"Pity. We could have been brothers." Arthur sighs. "I don't understand girls at all."

"High time you learned. We've been neglecting that part of your education. In fact, we'll start today."

"What?"

"Yes. By supper tonight, you will have chosen a girl to speak with, and discovered her favorite color, her pet name, and the sweet treat she likes most."

Arthur looks nervous but relieved.

"I thought you'd have me kiss one. Talking isn't so bad." He gulps and looks around. "I think."

"Lesson number one: only kiss a woman when she wants it. A forced embrace will never taste as sweet as one you've earned."

"Earned?"

"Speak with her, learn about her. Sooner or later, if it's right, a fire will spark. Then you can make your move."

"That's very vague."

"Let's practice, then." I toss my head in an imitation of coquettishness and lay a hand on Arthur's forearm. "Hello, Arthur. Enjoying the festival?"

Arthur shakes my hand off, equal parts embarrassed and amused.

"Stop it, Merlin. People will see."

"You'll have to dive in yourself if you don't want help. Remember: color, pet name, sweets." I drain my cup. "I'm off to find more ale. Good luck with your mission."

I leave him looking grumpy and wrong-footed. Poor Arthur. He has lived a sheltered life, far different than me at his age. I had been scrambling to live, fighting tooth and nail against starvation for a year, using strength and wit and charm, anything to buy me shelter and food for a night. Arthur will grow out of this awkwardness soon, but it doesn't hurt to be challenged. That's what I'm here for, after all.

I find more ale and speak with Uther's cronies for a while about new horses and campaign plans. When I glance back at Arthur sometime later, he is hovering near a group of giggling girls. He looks anxious and miserable, and I almost laugh aloud. A brilliant thought pops into my head, and I excuse myself from the men to saunter casually into the woods.

Once behind a tree, I think carefully about my goal then twist my lauvan appropriately. I have begun experimenting more frequently with changes in my appearance, subtler things than my deer form. The fewer changes I make, the easier they are to hold. My jaw softens, my nose shrinks, my hair grows long on my head, and stubble disappears from my chin. My shirt lengthens to a dress and tightens around newly formed breasts. If only I could see myself to check for inconsistencies. I look around and spy a puddle between two nearby trees. Luckily, it is a wet spring.

A dark-eyed beauty gazes back at me from the still water. Perfect. I laugh out loud and the woman in the puddle lets out a man's guffaw. Whoops. A quick twist of lauvan around my throat, and my mirth releases in a dainty titter. I'm ready.

I mince out of the woods and idly meander close to Arthur. We watch the bonfire for a moment. When he notices me, his eyes widen and snap back to the fire. I sigh inwardly, then take the initiative.

"I love Imbolc. The delicious apple cakes and fresh milk,

and this time of year is so precious, with the sweet little lambs being born. Don't you think?"

Arthur reddens at being addressed by me.

"Yes, it's very nice."

Is that it, Arthur? I prod for more.

"My father has promised me a new horse this year. I'm not sure what to call it. Perhaps Lady or Sweet Apple. What's your favorite?"

"I don't know." He glances at me quickly, then looks away and furrows his brow as if pretending to think. I'm growing exasperated and try one last tactic to get him to engage.

"Do you like my dress? I don't know if red really suits me."

He looks more carefully at me, catches sight of my breasts, and turns away, blushing.

"It's nice."

I smack him across the back of the head.

"Arthur Pendragon. If a woman asks you how she looks, you can do better than that. Flattery will get you a long way. I have a lot to teach you if that conversation is your best effort."

Arthur's stunned look is swiftly replaced by comprehension, followed by embarrassment and indignation. His cheeks flush again, but this time from anger.

"Merlin?"

"One and the same."

"That's a dirty trick."

I laugh.

"I was trying to give you some practice. You sorely need it." I twirl in front of him. "What do you think? Don't I make a fine woman?"

"I'm not going to answer that."

"You're right. Larger tits." I twist my lauvan and my temporary breasts swell. Arthur's mouth falls open and he covers his eyes with one hand as if he has a headache. I give a great belly laugh that turns heads. "All right, I'll leave you alone now. Don't forget: color, name, sweet. And remember to compliment her and say more than two words at a time."

I'm still chuckling when I retire to the privacy of the trees to change, although it emerges from my mouth as a quiet titter. Sometimes it's too easy to tease Arthur.

The road north is nearby, but I'm uncertain exactly where. It doesn't matter—everyone is at the gathering already. I close my eyes and release my lauvan with a sigh. They spring back with alacrity and a tingling, shifting sensation tells me I have returned to my true form.

A gasp erupts in front of me. My eyes pop open in horror.

"Merlin?"

Gawaine sits atop a gray charger, his mouth agape and eyes wide. Oh no. No one here knows except Arthur, and I hoped to keep it that way. Only a month ago, a woman was run out of her village by her fellows for witchcraft. Most of Uther's acquaintance laughed at the backward villagers, but if they see true powers before their eyes, they may not be so complacent.

"Gawaine! You're back." I don't know what to say and feel ill at ease. What does Gawaine think he saw? How can I ensure his silence?

Gawaine's round, honest face is fearful. He twists the reins in his hands and the leather creaks with the strain.

"Are you really Merlin, or one of the devils that the monks speak of?"

I debate briefly with myself which option would give me the advantage but decide on the truth.

"It's me, Gawaine. Truly."

"A devil would say that."

"Nothing I do will convince you otherwise if you believe that. Honestly, I'm human. I was born with unusual abilities, that's all."

"That's all?"

"Look, you know me. I mean no harm, I promise. I'm good-natured. Usually. When I feel like it."

This cracks a reluctant smile from Gawaine's worried visage.

"I'll admit, that does sound like you. How can you change your appearance at will?"

"Who knows? I was born with the ability. I've never found a satisfactory explanation. Don't you want to know why I looked like a woman?"

"I don't know, do I?"

I laugh and Gawaine's patient horse reaches down with its nose to graze.

"I was trying to give Arthur flirting practice. He's quite abysmal at it."

Gawaine throws back his head in laughter.

"I wish I'd seen his face. Poor Arthur—I'll see if I can help."

"I'm sure he'll be grateful." I tug at the horse's bridle to lead him toward the meadow. "What news from Ergyng? I didn't think you'd be back already."

"Not good." Gawaine's usually cheerful face sets into grim lines. "Uriens' stronghold was ransacked, and Uriens is dead. The Saxons are moving early this year."

My heart sinks. Uriens has kept the Saxons at bay for years. It's ominous news if even he is vanquished.

"Have they crossed the river yet?"

"No. They don't know where the ford is, and it's far too marshy this time of year. But if this fine weather holds, it won't be long." We enter the meadow, and I let go of the bridle when Gawaine swings down from the saddle. "I must give my father the news. Oh, and Merlin?" He turns to me and lowers his voice. "Your secret is safe with me."

He punches my shoulder genially, chuckles, then leads his horse away. I'm left unsure of the future. Another person knows of my strangeness—I hope Gawaine can contain the secret. And the Saxons are growing ever bolder. Can I leave these folk to their battles without my help?

Arthur kicks his horse into a trot.

"Come on, Merlin. We're almost there. Do you think Ban has any ale to spare?"

"For you? I expect so. After your victories last year, the lords all think the sun shines out of your ass. Perhaps you can convince him to give me some ale, too."

"They're not so sure of you, are they?"

"It's all right, I'm used to being an outsider. Besides, I'm a good enough fighter than no one wants to get rid of me for fear of losing. That's an agreeable validation."

We trot through a meadow of early spring wildflowers, yellow cowslips and violet pasque flowers, and splash through a tiny brook before skirting a copse of blackthorn. Arthur points at a group of figures past the trees.

"Isn't that Ban?"

I squint at the group. A pack of dogs yips and whines at the men's feet.

"A hunting party. Looks like your ale will have to wait."

"I was looking forward to that. Oh, well." Arthur urges his horse into a slow canter then hails the group. "Lord Ban! Good day!"

The men stop and turn, and the dogs start to bark. My horse snuffles uncertainly, but I prod him into a canter to keep up to Arthur. Ban disentangles himself from the men and dogs and strides forward.

"Arthur Pendragon, well met," he shouts across to us. We narrow the gap, and Arthur swings down from his horse to grasp Ban's arm in greeting.

"How is the hunt?" Arthur gestures at the waiting group.

"Only just begun," Ban says happily. "Slow to get started today. With any luck, we'll pull down a few rabbits, and perhaps a stag. Slim choice this time of year. What brings you to northern Gwent in the spring? Here, join us on our hunt."

"Gladly," Arthur says. He points at me. "You remember my adviser, Merlin?"

"Yes, of course. Well met, Merlin." Ban's reception is slightly cooler to me. I'm a foreign enigma to these southern lords, and they still haven't figured me out. Ban is all right, though, only a little wary.

"Lord Ban." I dismount and walk my horse beside Arthur's. The dogs streak ahead, and the men follow. There is a festive feeling in the air.

"We've heard rumors over the winter from the Saxons," Arthur says. He glances briefly at me. What he has heard is not a rumor—I infiltrated some Saxon settlements on the south coast with a disguise of blond hair and the Saxon tongue on my lips. My information is much better than rumor. "The Saxons have invaded, yes, but they are not necessarily looking for a fight."

"I've seen plenty of fight in them," Ban says amicably.

"Not all of them," Arthur corrects himself. "Some are fleeing persecution on the mainland and wish to settle peacefully here. Most of our men have known fighting all their lives. I'd like to send emissaries to the Saxons, see if they'll discuss a truce with us."

Ban waits a minute before he answers. The dogs begin to bark and set off in pursuit of a rabbit. Some of the men follow, shouting encouragement. Ban finally speaks.

"It's funny you should say that. It was only yesterday that I had another visitor speaking of the Saxons. But his message was much different. He urged me to show no mercy to the interlopers, to leave no one alive who dared trespass on our lands. His words, not mine. I must say, he was convincing. Why should we care what problems the Saxons have on the mainland? Let them stay there and work it out themselves."

"Was the man sent from Idris and Morgan?" Arthur asks quietly. When Ban nods, Arthur sighs. "My sister and her husband are single-minded in their quest. Tell me, Ban, even if you don't care about the Saxon plight or how their children are being slaughtered by savage hordes in their homeland, how do we benefit from ceaseless fighting?"

Ban shrugs. Arthur presses his point.

"And is our land overrun? Are we so inundated with farm workers after the plagues twenty years ago that we want to turn away able bodies? And tell me, Ban, what is a better defense against a wolf in the flock: a tame dog, or another wolf that follows your command?"

Ban chuckles.

"You have a point, there. I won't deny more fighters on our side would be welcome, even if they speak the Saxon tongue. You may be young, Arthur, but I see that head on your shoulders is a wise one. You can count on my support."

"Thank you, Ban. We'll leave you to your hunt. We're to call on Cador next."

"Good luck with him. A fiery one, but get him on your side and he'll follow you to death and beyond." Ban rubs the head of a dog who nudges his leg. "All right, all right. Look, even the dogs want me to hunt."

"Farewell, Ban," Arthur says, and we mount our horses and strike out to the west. I wait until we are out of earshot before

I speak.

"I'm impressed, Arthur. You are developing quite the silver tongue. Keep at it, and Idris and Morgan will have to follow your lead."

"I hope so. I truly believe this is the right path. We might finally have the advantage, find a peace of sorts—could you imagine?"

I nudge my horse into a trot.

"Come on, Cador won't convince himself."

CHAPTER XIII

After my morning class, I stop at Wayne's office. It's cramped, with packed bookshelves and a small window cracked open in a vain attempt to entice a breeze.

"Hi, Wayne. Need a break?" I hold up two coffees and pastries bought at a shop on the way. "Hope you like raspberry."

"Merry! Hey, thanks. Yes, I'm falling asleep here." He stands and stretches. "Sitting too long. Do you want to eat on the roof? I swiped a key from the office. There's an overhang to get out of the sun."

"Lead the way."

The roof is blazing hot, but the promised overhang protects two lawn chairs from the punishing sun and a steady breeze carries away the worst of the heat. I pass Wayne a coffee and pastry before we sit and stretch our legs out comfortably. Students mill below us on the lawn like sedentary rabbits.

"How's the fighting? Any new bruises lately?"

"Nowhere I'm willing to show you," Wayne says with a grin. "Naw, it's going well. My fights have been evenly matched so far. What about you? Any news on your stalker?"

Right. I forgot I had told Wayne about that. I suppose it's time to let him in a little more. He took my last news without blinking, after all. If I have read him right, he is worthy of letting in. I hope.

"He found me. More specifically, a bullet from his gun found my body."

"What?"

"Just a graze, thankfully." I don't need to tell Wayne more than that. "He tore off afterward and I've been on the hunt for him ever since."

"What did you do to piss him off so badly?"

"I did a good deed but got in his way. He's part of some criminal organization. It's called Potestas, have you heard of it?" Wayne shakes his head. "All I have to go on is his name, Drew Mordecai. His name is tangentially connected to a few businesses in town. Coast Bond, Wilson and Jones, Douglas Savings, Sweet Thing."

"Douglas Savings is a credit union, and isn't Sweet Thing that cupcake shop on Fourth Avenue? What are the others?"

"An insurance broker and a legal firm."

"What's the connection?"

"I don't know. They come up when I search for his name online. But when I click on the links, the pages can't be displayed." I spread my hands in a gesture of helplessness. "I'm a literature instructor, not a detective. I've visited each physical location, but they're all useless."

"By the way you're talking, I take it you aren't going to the police." He eyes me sideways, then shrugs. "You have a good reason, I hope. So, criminal organization, hey? I've never heard of anything fishy from those companies, but they could be good at hiding. You want me to help search for this Drew Mordecai? Sounds like I've got a few more skills in the technology department than you do." He grins at me.

"Researching secret criminal organizations never seemed like a relevant skill set to acquire. Who knew?" I shiver suddenly. The sun dims, hidden behind a thick bank of cloud rolling in from the north out of an otherwise cloudless blue sky. I stand in amazement at the edge of the roof.

"Where did that come from?" Wayne stands beside me and we watch the unseasonable fog bank move inexorably in our direction. Students below us point at the fog and hastily gather their belongings.

It could be a freak weather pattern brought on by conflicting air masses. But after the warning in my apartment, I'm wary.

This might be for me.

Within seconds, the fog is upon is. I have rarely seen fog this dense—Wayne is standing beside me, but I might as well be by myself. Am I still five floors up? Who knows?

"Let's go inside," says Wayne's disembodied voice. "It's pea soup out here."

"If we can find the door." I let go of the barrier, then wish I hadn't. Now I have no frame of reference.

A flapping sound dives past my ear and I duck instinctively. Another follows, and feathers brush my cheek. I yell and swat at my unseen avian attacker.

"What's going on?" Wayne shouts.

"Damn birds attacking me. Argh!" I duck again and flail my arms in the hope of grasping some loose lauvan, but no such luck. I whirl around when I hear approaching wingbeats behind me. The bird hits me straight in the face, a maelstrom of flapping wings and black feathers. Silver lauvan swirl frantically, almost unseen in the fog.

I can't keep my feet and stumble backward, but my legs hit the barrier and stop. My torso, however, swings forward. I let out a strangled cry when my top half whips around in an arc over the unseen void. My mind races over my options. Will I have time to transform into a hawk? How can I land to keep my arms and head protected to heal myself with lauvan?

A hand grabs my upper arm and pulls roughly, almost dislocating my shoulder. I'm flung onto the gravel of the roof, blood pounding deafeningly in my ears and gravel digging into my palms.

The light swiftly brightens when the unnatural mist blows away in tatters with the resumed breeze. Wayne holds onto the barrier a few feet from me, face pale under his tan.

"What the hell just happened?"

I shake my head wordlessly and stand, my legs shaky from

the aftermath of adrenaline. I rub my shoulder.

"Nice reflexes, Wayne. Thanks for saving my life. And know this—whatever you're doing at the gym, it's working."

Wayne laughs, a little wildly.

"Freak weather, rabid birds—I'm getting off this roof. Come on, I need a drink."

Wayne and I walk out of the campus pub, both at our ease. Beer went a long way toward dispelling any lingering adrenaline from our avian adventures on the roof. The sun is low in the sky, and the spaces between buildings are shadowy.

"It's stupid," Wayne says. "But ever since I started MMA, I've secretly wanted someone to jump out at me from a dark alley."

"You want to test yourself. That's not stupid at all. Although the someone in the alley probably has a knife." I look around, but the stretch of pavement we are on is empty. "Why don't you show me what you've got?"

"What?" Wayne laughs incredulously. "Here, now?"

"Why not? No one's around. Come over to the grass for a softer landing. I promise to avoid your face."

"But you haven't trained at all. I'll pummel you."

"I've done a few other things along the way. Trust me, I can handle myself. Come on, take me out. If you can."

Wayne raises an eyebrow.

"It's like that, is it? Okay, Merry, you asked for it. Don't say I didn't warn you."

He lifts his arms and bends his knees in a fighting stance. I grin widely and adopt my own position, natural as breathing. It has been a long time since I have had a chance to spar. I didn't realize how I've missed it. There is something so vital about a fight. Blood pounding in my ears, my muscles tense and ready for anything—I feel more alive than at any other time. Wayne's lauvan are tightly coiled yet still flowing. He is calm and sure of himself. He will try to go easy on me—for the first few seconds—until he realizes who he is fighting.

I dart out swiftly, without warning. My first punch, aimed at Wayne's shoulder, lands only a glancing blow from his quick side-stepping. He follows up immediately by grabbing my wrist. He wraps his arm around mine, twists toward me, and digs his shoulder into my torso to push me to the ground.

I twist mid-fall to put my hands out and use my momentum to spring away, but not for long. My arm hooks underneath Wayne's, and I grab his other wrist. I'm feeling risky and ready to have fun, so I tuck my leg between his calves and hook my other leg to flip him backward onto his bottom.

Wayne lands with a grunt but immediately leaps up. I'm right with him, and he puts both his hands around my neck to snap it down. When he lets go, I fling my head back up, but Wayne rams into my torso and bowls me over. Without thinking, I grasp two handfuls of his lauvan in an automatic reaction. Wayne doesn't pull away, which would have created some havoc and pain for him. Instead, he stays still for the brief moment it takes me to let go then straightens. How did he know? Before he can make another move, I hook my leg around his from my horizontal position and fell him easily.

Wayne rolls away, panting, and puts his hand up to stop. He starts to laugh.

"Where did you train? Or are you just a natural?"

"Oh, I picked up a few techniques here and there," I say airily. "But truly, you're incredibly quick. I thought you'd only been training for a short while?"

"What can I say? I'm a fast learner." Wayne straightens his

shirt. "Early class tomorrow, I'd better get home. Thanks for the drink and the fight, Merry—I'll say this, you're an interesting man to know."

By the time I leave Wayne, my car is lonely in the staff parking lot. I feel pleasantly inebriated and at peace with the world.

Whack.

Something hits my head with the force of a small rock at terminal velocity. I rub my scalp and look around for the missile.

Whack.

Another hits my head, then my elbow.

"What the hell?"

I spy the culprits—hailstones, the size of my knuckle, roll before my feet. I look up at the cloudless sky.

Suddenly, the air is filled with hail. It pings and patters on windows and over asphalt, falling faster and denser with every passing second. Each stone is large enough to hurt, and I hunch my shoulders and walk to my car.

I could swear they are getting bigger. I pick up my pace, but each hailstone that hits me does so almost hard enough to leave a bruise. This is ridiculous. Vancouver doesn't get hail like this. Especially from a cloudless sky…

Drew must be behind this. I glance furtively around but no one is in sight, at least not as far as I can see through the storm of ice balls. I pull a few of my lauvan to harden in a shell above my head, where they do a marginally decent job at softening the blows. Disturbed air lauvan dance between hailstones, and I'm beginning to get nervous. What is Drew capable of? Surely he won't best me?

A particularly large hailstone thumps into an unprotected area between my shoulder blades and knocks me forward. Only a few more steps to my car. My heart sinks, then flares with anger at the sight of my car. The now baseball-sized hailstones have pounded terrible dents in the hood and roof.

"Bastard!" I scream to my unseen opponent. Unbelievably, the hail falls even more furiously. I sprint the last few paces to my car. Before I pull the handle, a faint tingling in my lauvan makes me sidestep. Directly where I was standing, a hailstone the size of my head smashes into the asphalt. A chill runs down my spine and I attempt to pull open the driver's side door. It doesn't budge. It's not locked—I never lock my door—but upon closer inspection, it's apparent why I'm foiled. A gossamer sheen of air lauvan covers the door and holds it tightly shut.

I leap aside as another mammoth hailstone whizzes past my shoulder. I dig in with my fingernails, rip the lauvan sheet in two, dive into the car, and slam the door.

Instantly, the storm stops. All that is left is the muffled dripping of hail melting off the car in the May heat.

I groan aloud when I survey the damage to my car from the safety of my seat. It never had a chance. I tighten my jaw and add the pock-marked Lotus to my list of grievances against Drew. I'm looking forward to the day of reckoning.

I stretch my arms above my head languidly from my perch on the balcony and watch stars appear, twinkling as sunlight fades from the ever-deepening blue of the night sky. Days are long at this time of year. An errant breeze ruffles my hair and flaps my shirt. I peer to the left, where a pile of ominous storm clouds follows the wind to obscure my starlit night. I shiver from the cool air on my bare arms and step back into the apartment. Rain begins to pour shortly after. I suppose it's time for bed. Without Alejandro here, it's too quiet—what's the point of staying up any later?

The doorbell buzzes. Who would be ringing up at this time of night? I press the intercom.

"Yes?"

"Merry?" a female voice answers, followed by a gulping, choking noise. Is she crying?

"Who is this?"

"It's Anna. Anna Green." Another sob. "I need help. Everything's gone wrong and I don't know who to turn to. Can I come up?"

I lean my forehead against the wall, one finger lightly resting on the intercom button. Anna. Beautiful, fiery Anna. I'll-cover-my-hometown-in-volcanic-ash Anna. New-initiate-of-the-shadow-organization-Potestas Anna. She might have answers to my fruitless searching, or she might have a knife to stab in my back.

But, most importantly, I told her she could call me if she were in trouble and needed a friend.

"Come on up. Ninth floor."

A minute later, a quiet knock pushes my half-open door further ajar. I move into view. Anna stands on the threshold. Her long auburn curls hang damply and drip on the hall carpet. She wears only a dark blue sundress, which clings tightly to her curves. Her eyes are red and her shoulders shake.

"Oh, thank god you're okay." She passes a trembling hand over her eyes. "When I heard—I had to leave. But I didn't know where to go."

She steps forward and I reflexively open my arms. She falls

into them, sobbing. I kick the door closed with my foot and lead her to the living room. She sinks onto the couch and covers her face with one hand. I perch next to her.

"What happened?"

She takes a shuddering breath.

"When I heard you'd been shot—no, I wanted to leave before then, but I didn't have the courage until now. They're messing with forces that should be left alone. And murder? I knew I had to get away. I couldn't be a part of that." She looks at me then, her brown eyes glistening with waiting tears. "You have to believe me, I never wanted that."

Should I say it? What the hell.

"You were willing to let the volcano erupt over Wallerton."

"No one would have been hurt—" She pauses, swallows. "I see now how wrong that was. I can't believe I went along with it for so long." Her head droops, and she twists the hem of her wet sundress.

I examine her lauvan briefly. Should I take Anna at face value? Luckily, lauvan rarely lead me astray. Even the best liars give themselves away with contradictory lauvan. Anna's swirl tightly around her body, twitching occasionally with emotion, precisely the sort of movements I might expect from a distraught, nervous runaway. She is genuine.

I stroke her hair back behind her ear, and she closes her eyes.

"Come on, let's find you something dry."

"Tell me more about why you left," I say. We are comfortably ensconced on the couch, sipping wine and watching the rain fall from the darkened living room. It's a cozy scene, and not one I imagined ever sharing with Anna. She is perkier now—her curls have bounced back now they are drying, and she sips her wine calmly. Her feet are tucked up under the housecoat I lent her with an enticing amount of leg peeking through the opening.

"How could I stay? Drew tried to put a bullet through your heart. When I heard that, it was as if a fog had lifted from my brain, and I could think clearly again. I left as soon as I could." She reaches over and pops open the buttons of my shirt. Before I can ask what she's doing, she slides her hand across the bare skin of my chest. Her delicate touch is cool on my rapidly warming skin.

"What are you doing?"

"There's no wound. Did he miss you entirely?"

"Just a scratch." She lays her hand above my beating heart for a moment then withdraws it. I take a sip. "Nothing to worry about. You said Potestas was dabbling in things they shouldn't. What sort of things?"

Anna looks me in the eye for a long moment.

"Spirits," she says finally. "Elementals. Potestas wants to harness their power."

"But you knew this already. You told me in Wallerton."

"But I had no idea how strong the elementals are. We have no right to be meddling with that kind of power. We don't have the strength. I don't, anyway." She looks at me slantwise. "You might. I don't know what happened on Mt. Linnigan, but there is something special about you."

I continue to gaze at the rain, visible in front of streetlights in the distance despite the darkness. Anna laughs lightly.

"You can keep your secrets. You obviously know more than you're letting on, which is probably why you were smart enough to stay away from Potestas."

"I don't know much. In all honesty, I'd never seen spirits

until you called them out of your necklace."

"You can see them?" Anna sits upright and focuses her eyes on my face. "How? What do they look like?"

She may be genuine, but as a rule I don't discuss my abilities with just anyone, especially someone with Anna's checkered past.

"It doesn't matter. What's important is that you've left Potestas and can move on with your life."

She leans back into the couch swiftly and takes a sip of her wine.

"You're right. Here's to new beginnings." She raises her glass and I follow suit. After she drinks, she says, "I would love a glass of water."

"Of course."

When I return from the kitchen, glass in hand, we sit in comfortable silence and watch the rain fall. The lights are off in my apartment, but there is enough glow from the city to see clearly. I want more answers about Potestas and their nefarious goals, but at the moment I'm too mellow to ask. Anna's body next to mine radiates heat, and I wonder lazily where she plans to go from here.

Anna lays her hand gently on my thigh above the knee, each finger landing in sequence. She waits a moment, then begins to move her hand around in slow circles, her eyes on the motion. I don't say anything for a long while, letting her rub my leg as her hand moves higher and higher up my thigh. Finally, I speak.

"What are you doing, Anna?"

Her hand never pauses, but she looks into my face with a solemn expression.

"You've been good to me, Merry. I appreciate that."

I sigh hard.

"You know you don't owe me anything, right?"

"I know."

I lean my head back against the couch and stare at the ceiling.

"This is where I'm supposed to take your hand away, tell you you're upset and not acting yourself, to not do anything rash."

Silence from Anna, whose hand never stops stroking and getting closer and closer to her target. I look over at her.

"You know I'm not that kind of man, right?"

She smiles then, slowly, wickedly, as her hand deftly unbuttons my jeans and sneaks inside, making me sigh in a much different way. Before I lose myself in the sensations, I wonder briefly what Dr. Dilleck would make of this behavior. Anna leans close to my ear, her breath brushing my cheek.

"I'm counting on it."

I blink blearily awake. The clock spells out four o'clock, glowing an unrelenting red. Why am I up? Something is off. There is a hum I can only sense, not hear, as if I can detect frequencies beyond normal human capabilities.

Rolling over doesn't help. Anna's soft breathing is a counterpoint to traffic noise from the road below, neither of which lull me to sleep. Damn. What is it?

I sit up and Anna stirs from the motion.

"What's happening?" she says sleepily.

"Can you hear that hum? I think it's coming from the kitchen." I swing my legs over the side of the bed, but Anna snakes an arm around my midriff.

"I don't hear it. It's probably just the fridge. Come back to bed."

I dither for a moment, but the prospect of fumbling in the

dark for an unidentifiable noise is much less alluring than Anna's invitation.

Anna envelops me in warm sleepy movements when I lay back down. Her arms and legs slide around me, pliant and smooth, and she presses herself into me, her softness and curves filling in my edges and hardness. "Mmm," she murmurs in my ear, warm breath on my cheek. "Well, hello there, big boy." In the darkness I see the faint glow of her lauvan coiling rapidly and descending under the blankets. I grin invisibly, slide my hands to her hips, and cover her waiting mouth with mine.

CHAPTER XIV

Dreaming

We have had a stretch of rare quiet for the past few days. It's a temporary truce for both camps to regroup while we wait for the rains to slow. Arthur sent me across the river with a white flag a few days ago. He wants to speak to the leader of this Saxon band, a huge blond man named Framric with a ferocious beard. Framric did not dismiss me outright, as I feared he would. Instead, he asked for a few days of truce to think. I was quick to agree on Arthur's behalf—we all needed the rest.

Camp is wet and dismal, but many of the men have managed to find shelter in a series of caves nearby, so it could be worse. Arthur made it widely known among the men that we are engaging in peace talks. It's not a universally praised move but since he has the backing of the other lords, no one protests too loudly.

I rub my hands together and gaze aimlessly into the woods. I'm aching for a run but even my deer form would take shelter in this weather. The inaction makes me restless. I should join Arthur with his other advisers, discussing terms, but I can't be cooped up in the stuffy, smoky tent for another minute.

Two horses with their riders appear on the road out of the woods, a watery vision through the wet. They are cloaked and hooded against the rain, so their faces are not visible. I do, however, recognize the lavender lauvan swirling around the smaller figure.

I silently watch the riders approach without acknowledging them. They will arrive soon enough, and I doubt they come with news I want to hear.

They come to a halt before me, and their horses snort and whicker. The smaller rider lifts her hood off her head.

"Hello, Vivienne," I say. "I didn't expect to see you on the battlefield."

"I see no battle, only men huddled under tents trying to stay dry. Even so, I would not have bothered to come except that we carry an important message for Arthur Pendragon."

"From his sister, I presume. And what does Morgan want to meddle in this time? She can't still be singing the same tune?"

"The Saxons do not belong here, and it is our duty to drive them away." The other rider finally speaks and pushes his hood back from his face.

"And who are you?" I ask mildly. I'm not interested in debating with a mindless minion of Morgan who trots out her well-worn phrases.

"I am Mordred, cousin of Morgan and Arthur." He juts his chin out. He is very young, perhaps eighteen. It's a dangerous age—finally grown into the strength of manhood, with puffed ego and bristly pride that are easily wounded. His pale white lauvan stand stiffly out from his body.

"Cousin? I've never heard of you. But come in, I'm sure Arthur will receive you. He's a patient man."

I hold out my arms in an offer to lift Vivienne down from her horse, which she accepts. Her cloak slips around her body and exposes her abdomen, where a tiny lauvan cluster of palest pink curl tightly within her lavender strands over her still-flat stomach. I grin.

"I see congratulations are in order, Vivienne. And who is the father?"

Vivienne is flustered, and I can guess the father from Mordred's flabbergasted expression. I laugh.

"That can happen when you plow a woman. Welcome to

the real world, youngster," I say. Mordred's face is beet-red from embarrassment and anger at my teasing. He's not a humorous fellow, I gather. I lean toward Vivienne. "Going for the young ones, now? Did I ruin you for grown men?"

"Don't flatter yourself," she snaps. Mordred looks ready to throw a fit at my revelation of our relations. "And how did you know about the baby?"

"I have my ways." I wink at her, and her eyes widen. "Come, I'll take you to Arthur. Mordred looks like he's about to burst with his message, and I'd rather Arthur clean up."

I lead them to Arthur's tent, where he and the other lords speak endlessly of options and wait. Wait for sun, wait for answers from the Saxons.

My entry with two new faces clearly provides a welcome diversion to the men. I wave carelessly at the newcomers.

"Arthur, these are emissaries from your sister, Morgan. You remember Vivienne, and this is Mordred, who claims to be your cousin."

Predictably, Mordred bristles at the insinuation of a lie.

"My father, Agravaine, was your mother's brother. So, yes, I am indeed your cousin."

"Yes, Mordred," Arthur says slowly. "I recall. Agravaine took up with a slave girl, who bore him a bastard son."

"I'm as much Agravaine's son as anyone!" Mordred's voice is raised and some of the lords furrow their brows in disapproval. I cut in.

"Nothing wrong with a bastard, Mordred. You're in good company." I wiggle the fingers of my raised hand. Mordred looks unappeased, and Arthur changes the subject.

"You have a message from my sister?"

Vivienne answers quickly, latching onto the new topic.

"Yes. My lady has a simple message: cease the peace talks with the Saxons, or she will remove the men she has placed under your command. For good."

Arthur looks grave, as well he should. Morgan's not inconsiderable support of our campaigning has helped us win many battles. It would be a large blow, a substantial decrease in our manpower. She has let Arthur command them ever since her husband fell ill with a wasting sickness that he has yet to recover from. Now? I don't know how we would fare without her forces.

The lords look outraged and some sputter with indignation. Mordred finally looks at ease now that he holds the position of power, and Vivienne's chin is high.

Arthur turns to the men.

"What say you?"

"We are too close to a peace," says Gawaine. "Losing the troops now will make us look weak, but we need this truce."

"I agree," says Percival, a warrior from western Gwent. "A pause in the fighting would give our men a chance to work the fields. We are so close."

I take a wrinkled autumn apple out of my pocket and carve off a slice with my dagger, then pop the slice in my mouth with the blade and my thumb.

"Morgan's men are a full fifth of our army," says Gawaine's brother Gareth. "We would be very vulnerable without them. Too vulnerable, perhaps. And the peace is no sure thing. Why is Framric taking so long? Is he waiting for good weather to attack us unawares?"

There is some murmuring at this. Arthur listens carefully to all of them, while Mordred and Vivienne stand silent and I eat my apple.

"What do you say, Merlin?" Arthur says finally. "You know the Saxons better than anyone."

"Too well," Percival mutters. I stare at him levelly.

"Do you want to say that again, Percival?"

Percival looks down. I chuck my apple core out of the tent flap.

"A Saxon's word is unbreakable. They would be thrice-cursed by their gods if they renege. No, I believe Framric is thinking very carefully on terms that would be acceptable to us. The Saxons have sustained heavy losses at the end of our swords, and I'll wager he's thinking twice about engaging us in battle once more."

"Good," says Arthur. "Then we might still have the advantage. We look weak without Morgan's men but that's only if we show the Saxons our loss. We can pretend—light extra night fires, patrol the edge of the river with more men than we might normally—and the Saxons will never know the difference."

Heads nod and murmurs of agreement travel around the tent. Arthur nods, satisfied.

"Is there any dissent to the plan?" Silence. "Good. Then the peace talks will continue. Mordred, Vivienne, you may take your lady's men with you when you leave. And you can tell my sister that fighting is not the only way."

CHAPTER XV

It's ten o'clock by the time Anna's movements on the bed jostle me awake. There is something that is supposed to happen this morning—what is it? I don't teach until later.

"Morning," Anna spies my open eyes. "At least, I think it's still morning. I hope you have something good for breakfast. I'm starving."

Oh, well. It can't be that important if I can't remember it.

"I'm sure we can find something. Would pancakes satisfy?"

She runs her hand down my arm, then sits up.

"Sounds perfect." She saunters over to my closet and rifles through my shirts. A white dress shirt evidently passes muster, because she slides it off the hanger, slips her arms into the sleeves, and carefully fastens two well-placed buttons. The shirt tail only just covers her bottom. I hide a smile. Everything Anna does is so artful, perfectly calculated yet with an air of nonchalance. Choosing the revealing shirt is especially amusing, since the housecoat I gave her last night is directly at her feet.

Anna disappears into the bathroom while I pull on jeans and pad to the kitchen. That humming from last night is still here, too low to truly be heard, and yet there it is. I frown.

"Anna? Can you hear that humming? It's still going."

She peeks out and listens with a tilted head.

"No, you're imagining things. How are the pancakes coming?"

She smiles sweetly at me when I raise an eyebrow, and shuts the door. Strange—I wonder where the hum is coming from. It's getting on my nerves.

Back in the kitchen, I gather ingredients. Flour, salt, sugar, baking powder—I love the chemical simplicity of this item—

crack an egg, glug of milk, liberal slab of butter. I pause for a moment to appreciate the grocery store, where all these ingredients are pre-processed, with no work on my part. I have tried my hand at churning butter, and it's a tedious task.

Anna emerges when the first of the batter lands on the frying pan with a sizzle.

"Mmm, I can't wait."

"Syrup or honey?" I hold up a jug of maple syrup in one hand and a ceramic pot of honey in the other, the honey pot covered in sticky drips from frequent use. I enjoy maple syrup, the national pride of my current home country, but honey has always been my first and most beloved sweet.

"Syrup," Anna replies promptly, as expected. When I put the containers down on the counter, my index finger smears a thick blob of honey. I had been trying to avoid that.

"Damn." I show Anna the sticky digit. "I really need to wipe that down."

"Here." She grabs my hand and brings it to her mouth. Her tongue reaches out as her mouth opens to receive my finger. I have no objection, and I'm intrigued enough that I ignore the banging noise from one of my neighbors. We draw closer and her lips close around my finger while her tongue continues to lick the honey. I like where this is going.

"Oh! Sorry, oh—uh—" A voice from the hallway sputters. Anna and I turn to face the voice, and my finger slides out of her mouth. Jen and Alejandro stare back. Alejandro's cheeks are ruddy with embarrassment and Jen clutches her purse tightly. "Sorry, Merry, I didn't—I'm just dropping Alejandro off like I said I would. Remember?"

"Right. Is it that late already? Time flies," I say. Anna gives an amused chuckle. "Come in, both of you. If you were any more embarrassed, I'd mistake you both for tomatoes. Coffee?"

"No, thanks," Jen says. She looks more closely at Anna.

"You look familiar. From Wallerton, right?"

"Good memory," Anna says. She turns to run a hand across my bare chest. "I'll take a shower. Save some pancakes for me."

Anna nods at the other two as she walks unhurriedly to the bathroom. Alejandro leaps out of her way and tries to avoid watching the shirt above her legs wiggle teasingly. Jen waits to speak until the bathroom door closes.

"Are you out of your mind?" she hisses. My shirt from last night is on the floor nearby, and I pull it on while Jen speaks. "That's Anna. The crazy woman who tried to blow up Wallerton. She's part of Potestas. Remember? The people who tried to kill you?"

"I hadn't forgotten. Trust me, all that went through my head when she showed up at my door last night. But you forget that I have some special insight into people's true emotions." I sweep my hand around Jen's head to indicate the lauvan swirling there, invisible to all but me. Jen's lauvan are currently dancing with agitation and fear. Fear for me? I give her a reassuring smile. "Anna's lauvan check out with her story. She left Potestas because I'd been shot—she didn't like their methods."

"But geologic disaster is fine."

I shrug.

"She had a change of heart. It happens—sometimes."

"Or she's a good liar, and you can't keep it in your pants."

I feel my face grow hard. Judgement from Jen, a mere child in the course of my lifetime, is hard to swallow. Jen has no idea what my life is like, can't possibly imagine how I make the choices I do. She doesn't understand, can't understand, the need to pretend for just one night that I'm not alone in the crippling vastness of time.

Although she might have a point—Anna didn't have to try too hard last night. I pass my hand over my face, scrubbing away my expression, but not before I see Jen's face. She knows she went too far.

"What's done is done," I say. "As far as I can tell, she's on board."

Jen sighs explosively and grabs a pancake from the frying pan. She tosses it from one hand to another to cool before she pops it in her mouth.

"I hope you're right. It's just that you said yourself that you can be blind to good judgement when a woman is involved."

My mouth twitches with the hint of a smile.

"I don't believe that's quite the phrasing I used. I promise I'm being careful—she really does appear genuine."

Jen harrumphs but makes no answer. Alejandro points to the pancakes.

"Merlo, they're burning. Can I help?"

"Oops. Please." I pass him the batter and put the kettle under the faucet.

"Merry, that reminds me," Jen says. "I was doing genealogy research for my mother. She's terrible with computers. Anyway, she paid for one of those subscription services for old records: birth, death, parish notes, military, the works. I managed to go back to seventeen fifty on her father's side." She grips the counter. "I tried to look your family up."

I pause to look at her incredulously. She did what? Jen takes a breath and continues.

"I thought you might be interested in your history. But there really aren't many Lyttons in Wales."

Alejandro is frozen behind Jen, a caricature of alarm on his face. I would laugh if the stakes weren't so high. Instead, I finish filling the kettle then put it on the stove to boil. Jen shifts her feet from side to side.

"Then before I searched further, I started thinking—Lytton isn't a Welsh name, is it? And why does Alejandro's family know you as Merlo Nuanez? Are you on the run? What's really going on? What did you lie to me about, your birthplace or your name?" Jen's expression is equal parts fear, anger, and determination.

What do I say?

"Perhaps I wasn't born Merry Lytton." I open a cupboard to take out two coffee cups. "Perhaps I had to change it. Perhaps there's a good reason for that, which I'm not ready to share with you. Yet."

"Are you serious? More than…" She wiggles her fingers in midair. I laugh in spite of everything.

The bathroom door opens, and Jen says, "We're not done this conversation, Merry. I think I've earned your trust after the volcano." Jen marches to the door, and Alejandro hurries after.

"Where are you going, Alejandro?" I call after him.

"There is a café downstairs. I think I will try it this morning."

The door closes, and Anna strolls into the kitchen.

"I think I scared away your guests." She daintily lifts a pancake from the frying pan between her nails. "You're burning them."

I snatch a fork and hastily scoop up burned pancakes. My insides are writhing, and breakfast holds no appeal. What the hell was Jen researching me for? What will I say the next time she brings it up?

"Too bad you burned the pancakes." Anna examines one darkened side then shrugs and pops it in her mouth. "I'm a terrible cook, but I bake the best cakes. I've examined my past lives with hypnosis, and I'm fairly positive I was a baker three lifetimes ago."

I try not to choke on my coffee. Anna doesn't notice.

"What about you, Merry? Have you had any insight into your past lives?"

One ridiculously long lifetime is enough for me.

"Can't say I've undergone much introspection in that direction." Time to change topic. As fascinating as Anna's so-called past lives undoubtedly are, I have a pressing need for information. I carry a plate of salvaged pancakes to the table, followed by Anna with the syrup and honey, before I ask her. "What can you tell me about my shooter? Second rule of battle: know your enemy."

"What's the first rule?"

"Sharpen your sword." I grin at her and she raises an eyebrow.

"Drew is a loose cannon. High as a kite, sometimes—I don't know what he's on, but he can't kick it. That's why he was recruited. He's desperate to quit, but he can't do it on his own. It's a bit sad, really. Mmm," she sips her coffee. "Just what I wanted."

I would chastise her lack of empathy but I'm feeling less than charitable after having been shot.

"Recruited? Why would Potestas want a drug addict who's barely keeping it together? What for?"

"Sure, he's a bit out of control sometimes, but incredibly loyal. He'd do anything for the cause. And the organization is not entirely evil—some of their methods might be questionable, but they do have good intentions."

"And what is the road to hell paved with?" I mutter rhetorically. When Anna looks at me inquisitively, I shake my head. "Nothing. Can anyone join Potestas? Is there an application?"

Anna shrugs and takes a bite of pancake.

"I don't know much. I didn't get very far in. The higher-ups only told us newcomers what we needed to know. What with the secrecy, and the shooting, I had to leave. As far as I know, Drew wasn't acting on Potestas' orders. He went rogue.

But still, there was no action taken against him by the org, none at all. From where I stood, they condoned his actions. And that, I could never agree with." She smiles at me and reaches over to caress the knuckles of my hand.

"Why is Drew so desperate, so loyal? What does he stand to gain?"

"You remember when I told you about the spirits, on the mountain?"

Hard to forget. Her wild exuberance at the coming destruction, the billowing volcano as backdrop—it left an impression. I wonder uneasily what I'm doing sitting across from her at the breakfast table.

"I remember. Something about possession."

"That's right. The disruption of Mt. Linnigan was in preparation to release the elementals, in order for them to share bodies with members of Potestas. In return for allowing possession, the spirits would give us extraordinary skills and abilities."

"And what was Drew so keen to get?"

"He was promised a release from his addiction," Anna says in a hushed voice. "A whole new lease on life. It's all he wants, what he's so desperate to have. And right now, they managed to get him a partial spirit takeover using an amulet of power, so he can see what it would feel like. It's only for a short time, though, and he doesn't want to go back to the way things were. Not at all."

Now the fear and desperation oozing from the glossy gray lauvan finally make sense. But there is one more piece of the puzzle I don't know.

"Why is he after me?"

"You're the one who stopped the plan in Wallerton. You got in the way of his transcendence. To him, you're dangerous, and in the way, and you're at large to defeat Potestas' future plans. He can't let anything else get between him and his goal."

I lean back in my chair to digest this information and stare at Anna while she daintily pours syrup on her last pancake. Now the truth is out. Drew is still after me, armed, dangerous, spirits on his side, and a desperation so intense I can almost smell his fear from here. He won't stop until I am dead.

Good luck with that.

"How did you manage to destroy the necklace, figure out what to do at Mt. Linnigan?" Anna avoids my eyes and takes a nonchalant bite, but her lauvan are tense and waiting. She wants to know, has perhaps been waiting for the right moment to ask. I'm on my guard. Time to think fast.

"You said it had to be destroyed to sever the connection to the spirit world. I ran back to my car, poured my spare can of gasoline onto it, and lit it on fire. I fed the flames with enough dry branches to melt the metal."

There are plenty of holes in my story—there's no way I could have built a hot enough fire to melt metal in the few minutes I had to spare, and I don't carry a spare gas can—but it satisfies Anna, who looks slightly disappointed.

"How did you know what was going on? It's almost like you had some way of knowing things that others don't." She gazes at me searchingly. I give her a disarming smile.

"I'm a good detective. I hate to rush you, but I do have to get to work."

"Of course, I'll leave you in peace." She stands and clears the dishes.

"What's your plan? What will you do now?"

"I don't know if I dare stay in Vancouver. I'm afraid of what the org might do when they realize I've deserted the cause."

"Wallerton?"

"I can't go back there." She grimaces. "Too many bridges

burned, too much like a step backward. Maybe I'll head east, try somewhere new."

I follow her to the door. At the threshold, she turns.

"Thank you for being there for me."

"Take care of yourself, Anna." I kiss her cheek. She smiles and walks down the hall without answering.

I find Alejandro where promised, in the coffee shop on the ground floor of my building. He looks both relieved and disappointed to see me alone.

"I'm heading to the university now," I say without preamble. "Would you like a ride anywhere?"

"I'd like to see the university."

"Need anything upstairs?"

"No, but I was thinking, grandfather's notebook. Is there something in it, some ideas to fight the attacks?"

I nod slowly. My mind searches the memory of those illuminating pages, skimmed briefly during my plane ride home.

"Good thinking. Meet me at the car in five minutes."

Alejandro waits beside my car when I arrive.

"You can get in. It's not locked."

"Merlo. How can you protect yourself with no locks?"

"You sound like Jen. You know, locks on everything are a very modern invention." I reverse quickly out of the parking spot and wheel toward the exit.

Alejandro clears his throat, glances at me sidelong, then

says, "What will you say to Jen the next time she asks difficult questions?"

I exhale forcefully and lean my head against the headrest.

"Secrets were far simpler before the Internet. It was easy to reinvent myself in a new locale. I suppose I'll have to tell Jen at some point. I wish it could have been at my instigation, but I won't be that lucky this time."

I lapse into silence, troubled by thoughts of Jen's investigation. How much does she know? What conclusions is she drawing?

A faint hum, quiet yet distinct, interrupts the quiet. Is that the car? No—it sounds like the hum in my apartment that Anna couldn't hear.

"Do you hear that buzzing sound?" I ask Alejandro. He listens briefly.

"I hear the car, nothing else. Are you losing your hearing in your old age?"

I move to clip his head, and he ducks with a grin.

"I must be. It's been in my ears all morning, and neither you nor Anna can hear it." I signal to turn left and the car behind us, a gray Acura with a scruffy hood, flicks its turn signal on. Nothing is out of the ordinary, yet suddenly I'm uneasy. It could be paranoia, but I have learned to trust my instincts over the years.

I dawdle, taking my time on the approach to the light, and sneak through on the end of the amber. The Acura follows by running the red.

"I don't mean to alarm you, but we might have unwanted company behind us. No, don't look," I say when Alejandro turns. "He might not know that we know, yet. I say he, but I can't tell—the windshield is tinted. Illegal in this province, by the way."

"What do we do?" Alejandro's lauvan are tight and jerky

with apprehension and a touch of excitement. First a shooting, then a car chase—Alejandro must feel like he is in a movie.

"We try to shake the tail, of course. A few red lights ought to do it."

"Have you done this before?"

I grin, momentarily overtaken by a vision of Braulio laughing wildly, turned in his seat to wave at our pursuers, thrown against the door during one of my more erratic turns.

"Once or twice. Remind me to tell you the story another day."

A light changes to amber up ahead. I gear down and hit the gas to make the Lotus leap forward. The Acura barely makes the light—honking follows us on the wind.

"He's tight on our tail now," I say. "If I weren't in the city, his car wouldn't stand a chance."

"Can you pass those cars?" Alejandro points ahead.

In answer, I speed up. A car is headed in our direction but there's enough room to pass—just. The Acura is a car behind until the middle vehicle turns right, and the Acura zooms ahead. There is too much traffic ahead to try again.

"I'm running out of ideas," I say. "I'll try another light, then we might have to get out and confront the driver."

Alejandro's lauvan twitch in anticipation but not much fear. He's turning out to have quite the backbone.

There is one more light before we enter Pacific Spirit Park, the expanse of woodland that separates the university from the city. It's my last chance to shake our follower. I'm not interested in a fight at the moment, not with Alejandro here. Besides, I would be late for work. I doubt I would get a good look at my follower, in any event, since he only deals with me from afar.

The light has been green for a while. Here's my chance. I speed up. The Acura lacks acceleration and falls back briefly.

The light turns amber. I drive even faster and speed through a solid red. Brakes squeal behind me as the Acura stops to avoid crossways traffic.

Alejandro thumps his head back into the headrest and breathes out forcefully.

"We lost him."

"No sweat."

"Come on, Merlo, you weren't even a little nervous?"

"I told you I'd done that before." Alejandro gives me a mildly exasperated look that reminds me of Jen, and I laugh. "Fine, I'll admit it was intense at times. But we're all clear now."

A gust of wind hits the car with gale force. The Lotus swerves wildly before I regain control. Luckily, no other cars are nearby.

"What was that?" I crane my neck backward to see if there is anything on the road. An incredible roaring fills my ears.

"Merlo! Look ahead!" Alejandro points forward, all his lauvan frozen in place. My eyes follow his finger, and I instinctively brake with a tremendous squeal of tires.

A whirling tube of dust and debris spins in the air no more than twenty paces down the road. It's a tornado about to touch down. A tornado, in a region where they are unheard of. It's not a giant, but it's large enough for some small-scale destruction. I don't want to get in its way, but I might not have a choice. Drew is behind this, which means it's coming for me.

Trees whip their branches frantically around us, and whole limbs break and fly through the air. The noise is unbelievable, even more so when the funnel reaches the pavement. Inevitably, the tornado slowly moves in our direction.

"Merlo!" Alejandro screams. I grit my teeth and push the gearshift roughly in reverse. The Lotus shoots backward with a squeal but the tornado picks up pace. We round a corner, and I slam on my brakes. The Acura sits crossways on the road, blocking our path. The door is open, and the front seat is empty.

"Get out of the car!" I shout. Alejandro needs no further encouragement and rolls out promptly. I fling myself out of the door and run sideways onto the median. The tornado shifts to follow me.

"Stay back," I yell at Alejandro from a distance. I don't know if he can hear me over the roar, but he stays where he is. Grit stings my streaming eyes, and dust fills my lungs. I suppress a cough with a gargantuan effort and spread my arms. It's time to see if I can harness the wind myself.

The tornado is a whirling mass of silvery lauvan, and the air between it and me is thick with them. They fling past me with a mild electric sensation every time one contacts my own lauvan. I spread my hands, each finger splayed for maximum coverage, and let the air lauvan run through them.

The tornado is too close, now. With a swift motion, I close my hands and yank the lauvan. The tornado shudders slightly but continues its remorseless advance. My feet back up a few paces involuntarily. That wasn't enough. I need more. Feverishly, I rake through the air and collect fistfuls of lauvan. They are so fragile—no more than a quarter survive my rough handling. The rest break away to fly free. I gather as many as I can before the tornado is upon me and give a great yank.

The tornado wobbles. A mighty quaver reverberates up the column to the pulsating purple clouds above. It spins like an off-balance top, round and round in ever-widening elliptical loops. I watch intently, ready to collect more lauvan if needed or simply run. Finally, the circling column extends too far, and the whole structure disintegrates with dying winds and an explosion of free-floating air lauvan. Almost instantly, the road is quiet once more. Branches lay littered over the pavement, and the poor hail-battered Lotus has a fresh coat of green leaves. A car comes from the other direction, the driver gaping at the foliar carnage.

I calm my breathing on my way to the car. Alejandro slides into the passenger's seat and we both take a silent moment to contemplate. "How's your vacation so far?" I finally ask.

"I think I will need a vacation from my vacation." Alejandro looks at me when I turn the ignition and ease the car forward. "Is your life always this crazy?"

"Not always. Would you believe I once spent ten years in a Buddhist monastery under a vow of silence?"

"No."

"It's true. I tried to find enlightenment. I ended up with a raspy voice and a terrible thirst for beer."

Alejandro begins to laugh, and I join him.

Alejandro wanders off in the direction of the campus biodiversity museum with the promise to meet me after class. I want to speak to Wayne, hear if he has found anything about Drew. I know more after speaking with Anna, but I'm still no closer to finding him. And yet, he is uncannily good at tracking me.

The chatter of students when I walk into the lecture room mercifully drowns out the persistent buzzing that has followed me since last night. I even checked the lauvan around my ears in the mirror in case my hearing was somehow affected, but all looked normal.

"Settle down, everyone," I say mildly, and a hush instantly falls. Years of practice and performance has gifted me with the ability to command a room. I have used that skill for much more critical reasons in the past, but it's handy in any situation.

“We’ll finish our look at Shakespeare’s Tempest today with a discussion about the relationship between Prospero, the magician angling for a dukedom, and Ariel, a spirit of the air whom Prospero controls.” I pause to listen to my own words. I have never given Ariel a serious thought before, but with current events unfolding, I’m intrigued. “Ariel says, ‘All hail, great master! Grave sir, hail! I come to answer thy best pleasure; be’t to fly, to swim, to dive into the fire, to ride on the curl’d clouds, to thy strong bidding task Ariel and all his quality.’ Prospero returns, ‘Hast thou, spirit, perform’d to point the tempest that I bade thee?’”

I stop fully here. Anna spelled it out for me, but I didn’t understand the full import of her words. Drew does nothing, has no special abilities of his own. But what he does do is direct the spirit currently residing in his body. Drew has given it directions to thwart me, and from the attacks to date, it would seem that the spirit is an elemental. The fog, birds, hail, tornado—it’s a spirit of the air.

That changes everything. I was focusing my tactics on finding Drew and protecting myself against a human, even an augmented one. But Drew is not the issue here. I need to prevent a spirit from attacking. My mind whirls and I desperately want to scour Braulio’s notebook for information on elementals. There must be something of use in there. Luckily, Alejandro suggested I bring it today.

“Dr. Lytton? Are you okay?”

I come back to myself to find my students staring at me in curiosity. Whoops. How long did I leave them waiting?

“Apologies. As I was saying…”

My lauvan dance with impatience, but I maintain my composure until class is finished. There are the customary students who like to chat and ask questions after class, but before they can leave their seats, I grab my satchel and dash from the room. I will meet Alejandro, then we can sit and look through the notebook.

"Merry! I've been wanting a word." Wayne sidles up beside me in the hallway. "Although you might want it a private one."

"You found something?" I'm momentarily distracted.

"Sort of."

"Come with me, I'm meeting a friend outside. He knows. We can talk there."

Wayne pushes open the outer glass doors, and I spot Alejandro to my left, leaning against a railing. He is not alone.

"Jen? What are you doing here?"

"I have a few days off until my next job, so I thought I'd come say hi."

"She was worried about you," Alejandro says in a mock-whisper. Jen pushes Alejandro's shoulder in a familiar way. Their lauvan intermingle in a similarly acquainted manner.

"You're not very good at keeping secrets, are you?" She turns to me. "Alejandro told me about this morning. Are you okay?"

"What happened?" Wayne asks. Jen looks flustered. I cover for Jen's slip.

"I wasn't feeling well." A strange feeling passes through me, a rippling sensation across all my lauvan. Hairs rise on the back of my neck, and I scan the sky. For what, I don't know.

"Hi, I'm Jen, Merry's friend, and this is Alejandro, who's visiting Merry from Costa Rica."

The sky above the furthest building shimmers oddly, as if the blue were boiling like water.

"I'm Wayne, instructor for the history department."

The boiling grows larger and spreads across the building as it approaches.

"What courses do you teach?"

It finally makes sense, what I'm seeing. It's a writhing mass of translucent air lauvan coming straight for us. For me.

"Everyone inside!" I yell. I grab Jen's arm and yank the door open, then push her through. Alejandro leaps through after—he is obviously on high alert after this morning. Wayne stares at me, baffled, so I take his forearm and propel his dense frame through the door before I follow and force it shut.

The wind slams into our building like a mighty wave. The doors rattle on their hinges, and the glass of one cracks under the strain. A whirlwind of air lauvan beats against the glass like sand in a desert storm. Even the floor beneath our feet vibrates with the force of the wind that hits the building. The roar fills my head.

Until it stops, abruptly and completely. The frenzy of air lauvan that beats against the doors disappears entirely. The sun continues to shine, unaware of the recent turmoil on the ground.

Jen touches my arm with trembling fingers, and I nod reassurance at her. Alejandro looks pale but resolute. Wayne's brow is furrowed in a perplexed frown.

"What was that? And how did you know it was coming?"

I look at Jen, who shrugs nervously, then at Alejandro, who nods eagerly. I suppose it's time. I hope this goes well.

"Come to my office, everyone. Let's have some privacy."

Once everyone squeezes into my tiny office, I shut the door. Jen perches on the stool I keep for office hours and Alejandro leans against the only wall without bookshelves or window. Wayne sits in the office chair once I wave him toward it, and I balance on my desk with Braulio's notebook in my lap. All three gaze expectantly my way. A thought strikes me.

"Jen, would you like to do the honors? It might sound more sensible explained by someone who isn't so bound up in it."

"In what?" Wayne says.

"Oh!" Jen looks taken aback. "Umm, okay." She thinks for

a minute, and I take the opportunity to flip through the notebook. Time does not appear to be on my side, with attacks occurring as soon as I step foot outdoors.

"Merry is—special," Jen says. I snort and she throws me a dirty look. "Would you rather explain?"

"Sorry, sorry."

Ah ha, the section on air elementals. Does Braulio talk about spirits gone rogue? Are there any protection methods?

"Merry can see things no one else can. There are strands that float around anything with energy, like a bouncing ball or a hot pan or a person. He can grab the strands—he calls them lauvan—and affect the properties of the thing."

The element of air is weakest in the environment of its opposite, the element of earth. How can I use that?

"Okay," Wayne says with an air of patient incredulity. "Assume I understand or believe. Carry on."

Jen gives an exasperated sigh and kicks me gently on the leg.

"Not easy, is it?" I say without looking up from the notebook. "Let me know when you need a demonstration."

"A few weeks ago, Merry got in the way of a shadow organization named Potestas, up a mountain near Wallerton. Did you hear about Mt Linnigan?"

"Yeah, the not-so-dormant volcano."

"Potestas has some connection to the spirit world—"

"What spirit world?"

"We're not sure, it's all new to us too." Jen wrings her hands. "Anyway, they wanted to blow up the mountain for a deal they have with some rogue spirits—oh man, it's complicated. Basically, Merry stopped their plans for world domination, and now they're pissed off. Especially this Drew guy."

"And he is currently possessed by an air elemental, giving

him abilities far beyond his own to hunt me down and take me out." I slam the notebook shut. "But now that I know, I might have a chance at some protection, and hopefully do some fighting back of my own."

"How did you find that out?" Alejandro asks.

"Anna, Braulio's notebook, and my own immense wisdom."

"Wait a minute," Wayne says. He shakes his head. "You two are on board with Merry's invisible strings?"

"I forgot a demonstration. My apologies, Wayne. May I, Alejandro?"

"Okay?" Alejandro's eyes are apprehensive. I wink at him and raise my hands to his head. I work quickly and before many seconds have passed, Alejandro's hair becomes a vibrant shade of tomato red. Wayne's eyebrows rise halfway up his forehead, then he shrugs.

"Now I've seen it all. So, what's the plan?"

"Truly? That's your reaction?" I share a bemused glance with Jen. "You're in a vanishingly small minority."

"'There are more things in heaven and earth, Horatio, than are dreamt of in your philosophy.'" Wayne gives a lopsided grin. "I find it best to roll with the punches and get back in the fight as quickly as possible."

"Spoken like a true warrior." I pat him on the back. "And nicely done, quoting Shakespeare to the literature instructor. As for next steps, Alejandro and I can't stay in my apartment until I find a way to protect it from the elementals."

"Stay at my place," Wayne says. "I have a couple of sofas. It's not the Ritz, but it will do for a few days."

"Thanks, Wayne. Much appreciated. You said you had intel, earlier."

"Yes. I did some digging on Drew Mordecai. I have a friend in the Vancouver police, and she looked him up for me.

Apparently, he's been busted three times for breaking and entering and twice for drug possession. The last conviction was overturned on appeal when he hired one of the top lawyers in the city."

"If he's stealing, where'd he get the money for a good lawyer?" Jen asks.

"Three guesses," I say. "Starts with a 'p.' Thanks, Wayne. It confirms a few rumors. Unfortunately, I'm still no closer to finding him."

"My next stop was to check real estate holdings," Wayne says. "But I doubt anything will come up if he's broke."

"Still, worth ruling out. All right, Alejandro and I need to pick up a few things at the apartment and attempt some protection measures. What's your address, Wayne?"

"I'm coming too," Jen says while Wayne scribbles on scrap paper.

"Are you my bodyguard today?" I don't know what she thinks she'll do, but I appreciate the gesture. Alejandro's lauvan sway at Jen's words. "You're always welcome, but you'll have to take your own car. Mine's full."

"I hate two-seaters."

I don't bother protecting Jen, since Drew has been single-minded in his attack on me thus far. On the way to the parking lot I instruct Alejandro to pick up fist-sized rocks.

"For what?"

"You'll see. Actually, you won't. I'll construct a barrier of lauvan from the rocks for the car. If your grandfather's research is correct, the earth lauvan of the rocks should act as a deterrent to the air lauvan since they are opposite elements."

"Do you think it will work?"

"I have no idea. Are you sure you don't want a ride with Jen?"

"I won't leave you alone."

Those words mean more to me than I can express, so I wordlessly pat him on the shoulder then point at a few likely-looking specimens.

"There are a few rocks. Take as many as you can carry."

When Alejandro lifts a rock in each hand, silvery-brown lauvan form from nothing and coil around each rock.

"Perfect. I'll take these ones."

A few students sitting on the grass nearby look curiously at us, but I ignore them and place rocks in my satchel. When it bulges under the unaccustomed weight, we walk to the car and unload rocks into the trunk.

"Now what?" Alejandro waits expectantly.

"Now I get to work."

I tease the silvery-brown strands from around each rock until I hold a thick bundle of lauvan in my hand. I twist the bundle to ensure each lauvan won't slide back to its rock then wrap the end of each around a different lauvan of the car. Although the car is motionless, there is plenty of potential energy waiting to be unleashed, and the abundance of gray strands reflects that.

It takes a few minutes to complete my lauvan net over the car, especially since I keep checking over my shoulder for incoming gusts of wind. The net stretches over the roof and down the hood, leaving the sides free. Alejandro watches me carefully.

"You don't want to cover the sides?"

"It's a deterrent, not a complete barrier. I don't have enough rocks for that. It's only a test, anyway—if it works, I can get more. Come on, let's go."

All is quiet while we drive. I have one eye on the traffic and one on the skies. Before we leave the park to enter the city proper, there is a disturbance in the air above the car in front. It's a cluster of air lauvan, a gust of wind headed straight for us, and fast. I clench both hands on the wheel.

"Brace yourself."

The lauvan reach us a second later but stop shy of the car. They spread out and slide around us like water against the bow of a ship but avoid touching the net of earth lauvan. They swirl around the car as if hesitant then disperse in a flurry of translucent threads.

"Has it happened yet?" Alejandro peers out the windshield.

"It worked." I don't try to keep the relief out of my voice. Fighting spirits is a whole new world for me, and I'm used to knowing everything. "Good old Braulio. I should have given him more credit."

"He was good at giving himself the credit. You don't need to worry about that."

I laugh out loud.

"He was, wasn't he? Now that this idea worked, I'm eager to try something similar at the apartment. A well-woven earth lauvan barrier at the door should do the trick."

"Don't forget windows, and vents."

"Of course, the vents. Good thinking."

At the apartment, Jen waits for us in the parking lot.

"We need to collect lots of rocks," I say. "Here, we can fill my satchel."

"I have some shopping bags in my trunk. Hold on." Jen rummages in the back then hands Alejandro a bag. Their hands touch briefly, and their lauvan intertwine immediately.

"I like how you didn't even ask why," says Alejandro.

"I'm learning to expect the unexpected with Merry these days," Jen says.

"Less chitchat, more rock collecting," I say. "As many as we can manage. I want this apartment spirit-tight."

"Si, Señor," Alejandro says with a hint of insolence. Jen giggles and I throw up my hands.

"Insubordination in the ranks—I'm on my own."

"Oh, stop being melodramatic. Look, we're getting rocks." Jen bends and selects a few from a nearby path.

Once our bags are filled as full as their straining seams can handle, we traipse inside to the elevator. It stops at the ninth floor and I exit first.

"Stay here. I'll make sure the coast is clear."

"They're after you, not us," Alejandro says. "Let me go first."

"Much appreciated, but you can't see all potential dangers. And I don't want either of you hurt on my account. Don't worry about me—I'm tough."

I flash a grin at Alejandro then walk down the hall before he can argue further. The door is closed but not locked, as usual, and no foreign lauvan are in sight. I cautiously push the door open, ready to spring back if necessary, but only silence and motes of dust linger in the still apartment.

I do a cursory check of each room, but nothing is out of place.

"Come on in," I call out. Jen and Alejandro appear moments later, lugging the bags of rocks.

"Poof!" says Jen. "It's hot in here. Summer heat is nice in moderation. I'd rather be at the beach."

"It's not too late."

"Don't be silly, Merry. Okay, what do we need to do?"

"Spread a row of rocks under any vent or window that might allow air through. Prop them up somewhat precariously on pillows and books—they won't have enough lauvan to work with if they don't have any potential energy. I'll start weaving the door barrier."

They get to work without delay, and I take rocks out of my satchel to spread beside the front door, piled on a stack of papers that I should really mark soon. The hallway is mercifully empty—I don't know what excuse I'd make for my hand waving.

I rake my fingers through the lauvan of the assembled rock pile and tease them gently up. There isn't much to attach them to—the mobile car was easier—but there are a few pale lauvan from the wood of the door that I delicately peel up and twist together with the rock threads. Before long, a fine web of lauvan covers the door. Alejandro appears on the other side then passes through my barrier easily. The lauvan shudder with his passage but remain intact. Alejandro joins me in contemplation of my handiwork.

"I would say it looks good, but I can't see anything," he says. "Are you sure you haven't been relaxing while we've been working?"

"Very funny. No, it's done. Humans can pass through, but air spirits shouldn't be able to. If Braulio was right, that is. Now, I'd better do the windows." I step forward, only to meet a sticky resistance on the threshold.

"What the hell?" I wiggle, but it's like swimming in tar. All the rock lauvan are attached to my lauvan, and it's with great difficulty that I tear myself away.

"Hmm. That's unexpected."

"What happened?"

"Apparently, the barrier works against me, too." I tap my foot, thinking. "It didn't repel me like it did with the air lauvan. Quite the opposite. What does that mean?"

"That it's not a very good door if you can't get through?"

"Damn, that's true. But not quite what I meant."

I ponder what the too-effective barrier says about myself,

but before I can come to any conclusions, the door beyond mine opens and my neighbor Gary Watson walks out.

"Hello, Merry. I thought I heard you. How are you?"

"Been better, thanks, Gary. I had a break-in the other night, and now we're figuring out where I can install a better lock."

Alejandro glances at me but says nothing. Gary's face wrinkles momentarily with uncustomary worry.

"Nothing taken, was there?"

"Nothing important. I believe it was targeted, so I wouldn't worry about you and Mrs. Watson. This is Alejandro, by the way. He's visiting for a few days. And you've met Jen before," I say when Jen peeks through the barrier.

"How d'you do. Merry, I've been meaning to have you over for a game. Mrs. Watson bought me a book of chess openings. There's one, it's called the Two Knights Defense, I'm itching to try. Come and see, all of you, Mrs. Watson baked cookies this morning. She's out now, but she surely won't mind if we eat a few."

I feel satisfied with the barrier I have constructed so far, even though I can't get through myself. It's easy enough for me to pull it to the side when I want to enter, and I'm sure it will deter unwanted spirits. Alejandro looks hungry and Jen seems determined to stick to my side, so I accept for all three of us and we file into Gary's apartment. The floorplan is a mirror image of mine, but there the similarity ends. Where mine is minimal to the point of sparseness, the Watsons have filled every available surface with figurines, photo frames, and knickknacks of every description, lovingly dusted spotless. It's the product of a long life without the frequent need to move.

Gary waves us to the couch and tosses cookies onto a plate with gusto, but without Mrs. Watson's sense of presentation. I flip through Gary's new book while Alejandro discusses games with Gary.

"I've played a little chess," says Alejandro. "But backgammon is what we always played in my family. Sometimes the children had tournaments at family holidays."

"Ah, backgammon," says Gary fondly. "Would you believe, my high school had a backgammon club? I was vice-president, played a few tournaments myself. Long before any of you were born, of course. I forgot about that. What a great game."

"Do you have a board? I could show you my aunt's prize-winning move."

"Gary, you never said," I say. "I didn't realize I had the opportunity to beat you at another game."

"Such a cocky young whippersnapper," Gary says. Alejandro coughs. Jen sniffs and looks around with a frown.

"Do you smell smoke?"

Now that she says it, it's obvious. The smell of burning wood permeates the air.

"Thanks for the cookies, Gary," I say hastily. "I'd better check my place. Must have left the stove on." I leap up and sprint to the hall, where smoke wafts out from my open door. I stop short at the lauvan barrier and hastily rip it to one side. Alejandro and Jen are right behind me, and together we charge into the apartment.

There's a flickering coming from the living room. I burst in and stop, dumbfounded, at the sight of my bookshelf in flames. My bookshelf, which holds the only things that are precious to me. Two birds twitter on the threshold of an open window then take off in a whirl of air lauvan. I hardly notice.

My sketchbook. My sketchbook is burning.

Someone is screaming and it takes me a moment to realize it's me. I reach out wildly, blindly, grabbing every lauvan I can reach, my own lauvan spreading like an electrified cloud around me to pull cushions off the couch and make papers fly around the room. I run to the bookshelf but I'm slow, so slow. The corners of my sketchbook are blackening, curling, disintegrating irretrievably. Heedless of the flames, I snatch the sketchbook and hold it in horror—it's still alight. I can't stop yelling words in Brythonic, Old Dutch, High German, whatever comes to my tongue to express the panic inside.

A blanket falls over the sketchbook. Strong hands rip it from mine and smother the flames. I stop screaming but now I'm hyperventilating, and my lauvan still create havoc around me. Anything lighter than the table whirls in the air. I fling the blanket aside and snatch the smoldering sketchbook from Alejandro.

I rock back and forth on my knees, clutching the sketchbook to my stomach. Its charred edges crumble under my grip but I can't let go. My lauvan spread out from me in a great fan, reaching out to all corners of the room, wreaking havoc. Books fly off shelves, cups smash, pictures crash to the ground. I don't care. My lauvan control themselves in my despair, and I don't bother reining them in. The charred sketchbook fully occupies my attention.

"This is all I have left of them." My words catch in my throat. "The ones I've loved. This is it."

Alejandro kneels in front of me. He peers into my face, his own only concerned, not fearful. My eyes see him, but his face barely registers. He reaches his hand out and presses it to my forehead, then to my chest.

"They're in here, Merlo. And in here."

I grind my teeth in my anguish. He doesn't understand. Given the frailty of human memories, I can't keep a picture in my mind of their faces. Without the sketchbook, I'm sure the fragments of memories will drift away and disappear like wisps of fog in the rising sun.

"I can't picture their faces. They'll disappear. And then I'll be left with nothing. Nothing." My breathing is shallow and rapid. So many years, and I have so little to show for it. Nothing remains. Everyone passes on and leaves nothing behind for me to hold onto.

Alejandro shakes his head and then grips the sides of my head in firm hands, forcing me to look into his eyes.

"Listen to me, Merlo. You don't need pictures in an old musty book. Your loved ones are in your memories, fresh as the day you knew them."

"They're not," I snarl.

"Close your eyes." When I continue to stare at him, my anger and panic likely making my eyes quite terrifying, he gives my head a shake. "Do it."

I oblige. My heart pounds loudly in my ears, and I try desperately to think of some way to restore the lost pages of my sketchbook, even though I know it's impossible. They're lost now, lost forever. I'm adrift on an endless sea with no land in sight and my anchor severed.

"You remember them. You remember all of them. Remember her laugh? Remember when she smiled at you for the first time, and you thought your heart wasn't large enough to hold all the love you had for her? Remember the way her lips pouted when she slept, and you would watch her, trying to memorize every curve of her face? Remember how her hair lifted in the breeze, and the way it felt when you ran your fingers through it?"

Alejandro speaks, and at his words, memories surface. Emmanuelle's infectious laugh and the way her delicate fingers cover her mouth as if she tries to stop the laugh from escaping. Isabella in the market, her arms elbow deep in a barrel of fish and mine wrestling a chicken, and our mutual smiles of embarrassment and humor. Edith sitting in a meadow of wildflowers after our lovemaking, her brown hair loose from its customary braids and flowing in a cascade of chestnut waves over her bare shoulders as we kiss.

I take a deep breath that makes my entire body shudder. They are still there, all of them. I may have lost my physical reminder of their lives, but no one can take them away from my thoughts. My panic drains away from my body in a great rush, and my lauvan release their grip from various objects around the room. I drop my head to Alejandro's shoulder. My erratic breaths take a long time to quiet.

When I'm calm, I lift my head wearily from Alejandro's shoulder and look around. Jen grips the door frame with a cautious look on her face, surrounded by the debris from my loss of control. Papers litter the floor, the contents of Alejandro's duffel bag lie strewn across the room, and lamps are knocked over. I turn my attention back to the sketchbook. Carefully, tenderly, I wrap the blanket around the crumbling edges and tuck the bundle under my arm. Then I stand.

"Drew sent me a message, loud and clear." My voice is hoarse. "This bookshelf contains the only things in the apartment with an obviously sentimental value." I clench my fists and my voice grows louder. "He's trying to fuck with my head. But nobody, nobody does that to me and gets away with it."

"So, what do we do now?" Jen looks scared but determined.

"We go to Wayne's, see if he has any more leads on that whoreson's whereabouts. And close that window—we don't need another possessed bird in here."

"Was that what happened?" Alejandro says while Jen picks her way across the room to the window.

"They were under control, certainly. Why the hell was it open, anyway?"

"I'm so sorry, Merry." Jen holds her hands to her mouth in remorse. "It was me. The apartment was so hot, and I wasn't thinking—I can't believe it, after what happened at the university. I'm so sorry."

"It's done, and now you know better." There is nothing to be gained from berating Jen, although the thought of my charred sketchbook pains me like a spear through my heart. "Give me a few minutes to put barriers over the vents."

My hands tremble slightly as I tease apart rock lauvan, but now it's less from panic and more from anger. Drew is getting too close, pushing too many buttons, crossing too many lines. An attempt on my life is one thing—an attack on my memories is quite another. It's time to end this. I only wish I knew how. It's a strangely impotent feeling to have an enemy at a distance, like swinging at an attacker while blindfolded.

When the vents are covered by a translucent net of silvery-brown lauvan, I gather my essentials—change of clothes, toothbrush, razor, and the like—and go to the door where the others wait silently. Jen puts a tentative hand on my arm, and I squeeze it gently in return. Alejandro has a bag of flour from my kitchen and sprinkles a thin layer over the tiles of the entryway.

"Do you have a plan, or are you simply feeling destructive?" I ask mildly. Alejandro looks up.

"You can stop spirits, but how will you know if a human trespasses? This way, you can see footprints."

"That's clever," Jen says with admiration.

"I have to agree. Nice work. Now, let's go to Wayne's and plan a battle strategy."

CHAPTER XVI

The car is quiet on the short trip to Wayne's in the evening sunset. I mull over today's events—the barrier denying me entry, the burning of my sketchbook—while anger simmers under the surface. That sketchbook is the only possession I own that I care about. I have been carrying around the sketches and paintings in those pages my whole life, in various incarnations. Each depicts a person I have loved in the best artwork I could manage at the time. Some are inked on parchment, some are oils on paper, and the whole collection more closely resembles a portfolio than a book, despite my careful binding along the long edge. Alejandro is right, they are still in my memory, but I can't let go of what's left of this tangible reminder of their short, sweet lives. My anger comes from fear of losing those mementoes. This isn't the first time I've almost lost them, but it's the closest.

And why couldn't I go through the barrier? I know I'm different, but now I wonder in what way.

"Are you okay, Merlo?"

"I'm furious. But I'm not going to melt down again, thanks to you. You knew just what to say. You're turning out to be a true friend. Your grandfather knew what he was doing when he entrusted you with my secrets."

Alejandro flushes with pride and his lauvan squirm happily.

"I brought Drew's gloves with me, from your friend's store. I thought they might be useful to check the lauvan?"

"Alejandro, that was brilliant." I'm genuinely impressed at his foresight, especially since he can't see the lauvan nor fully understand the potential they contain. "I'll certainly have another look, see if I can sense anything that could be helpful."

I pull up in front of Wayne's house, right behind Jen's little

Prius. Jen waits for us next to it. When we join her, she reaches out and hugs me tightly, then holds me at arm's length.

"Are you okay?" She looks at me searchingly. I muster a half-smile for her, although happiness is the last emotion I feel.

"I'll be fine. Once we find Drew."

"What was that book?"

I close my eyes briefly. I don't have spare energy to lie and Jen deserves better. I procrastinate instead.

"I'll show you, but not right now. Now, I need to focus on finding Drew."

She squeezes my arms gently then lets me go.

"Okay, Merry. We'll talk later." She is treating me like a vessel of blown glass, apt to shatter into a million pieces with the wrong provocation.

"Let's see if Wayne has found anything. And I want to examine those gloves."

I stride up the garden path to the front door. The others follow behind more slowly, Jen's murmuring to Alejandro only just audible. I expect they are talking about me, so I ignore it.

"Wayne, hi," I say when Wayne opens the door. "Thanks again for putting us up." After the sketchbook incident, I'm not confident enough in my lauvan barrier to risk staying overnight at the apartment, not until I find Drew.

"No problem. Hey, I might have a lead. Come on in."

Wayne ushers us into his place, which turns out to be the main-floor suite in an old character house. If one hundred years grants a building "character," I wonder what nomenclature I qualify for.

"You remember I was going to check out real estate holdings?" Wayne says. "My sister is an agent, but nothing came up with the regular searches. But she has a friend with a cabin in Hollyburn, up on Cypress Mountain, and there's a Mordecai who owns a cabin nearby. It's not a very common name, is it? I'll have to phone in the morning for more info. But it looks promising."

"Thanks, Wayne. This is really great, what you're doing for me."

He waves off my thanks and points to two couches in the living room.

"There's the luxury suite, all yours. Make yourselves at home. I'll get on the phone and see if anyone is still at work."

Wayne disappears into another room, and I sink onto the nearest couch with a sigh. I'm shaky with the aftermath of my loss of control, although I try not to show it. Jen looks concerned enough as it is.

"Pass me those gloves, Alejandro. Let's see if there is anything new I can glean off them."

Alejandro digs through his bag, and I try to ignore the humming that still rings in my ears, especially noticeable in the quiet house. Alejandro pulls the gloves out gingerly, and the humming changes timbre, as if there are two competing hums. Great—will I end up with a whole symphony of noises?

"Wait—can you take the gloves to the hallway and back again?"

Alejandro looks mystified but complies without question. As I suspected, the hum grows quiet with Alejandro's retreat and increases in volume with his return. I hold my hand out for the gloves.

"What was that about?" Jen says.

"The gloves are humming, in the same way something near me has been humming for the past few days. No, don't bother listening, only I can hear it. Lucky me."

"Why would gloves be humming?"

"They probably wouldn't." I reach in and carefully extract the fragile gray thread of Drew's lauvan. The fear and desperation emanating from it are only a faint echo now. The lauvan won't last much longer.

I have never heard a lauvan hum, but I don't see any other explanation. My eye is drawn to the strange patch of iridescence on the end. I have never seen anything like that, either. I run my thumb and forefinger along the thread until they touch the patch.

A sensation takes over, not unlike the feeling I have when I travel down lauvan cables in my mind. I reflexively close my eyes.

My mind's eye dissolves into a kaleidoscope of color before it settles on a vision of a man lying on the backseat of a small car, its gray seats scuffed and torn in places. He's asleep, his mousy-brown hair untidy. Glossy gray lauvan intermingle with wispy air lauvan around his body. A cheap watch on his wrist indicates the same hour as does Braulio's watch, ticking quietly on my own wrist.

I release the lauvan and come back to my body with a gasp. Jen's consternation is written on her face, and Alejandro leans forward.

"What happened, Merlo?"

"I had a vision. Somehow, touching Drew's lauvan took my mind to where he is right now." I pause and connect the dots. "There's a strange patch of color on his lauvan. It's like nothing I've ever seen."

"What does that mean?" Jen says. She watches my face intently.

"That patch—when I touch it, I can see Drew. And the lauvan hums, which I've never encountered before."

"The humming," Alejandro says. "You said there are two hums now, one from the glove and the one that has been bugging you all day."

"Do you think there's another patchy lauvan?" says Jen. "Wait, does that mean you can see where someone else is?"

"Or can they see where I am?" I say.

"You're being followed," Jen whispers. "You think this is how they know where you are?"

"Only one way to check," I say briskly. I stand and empty my pockets onto the coffee table. Keys, wallet, and phone make a small heap. "See if there is anything odd."

"What do we look for?" Alejandro says.

"Anything that doesn't look like mine. They could have planted an object attached to the doctored lauvan on me, although anything is possible, I suppose. I'll check myself for foreign strands." I run my hands over my lauvan, and Jen bursts into laughter.

"You look like you're feeling yourself up."

I wink at her and continue my examination more suggestively for her amusement. She gives an unladylike snort.

"I think I found something," Alejandro says with repressed excitement. I stop what I'm doing and reach for Alejandro's open hand. In it is a folded piece of paper. On the front is a smudged lipstick kiss, cherry-red. My heart sinks. Suddenly, I have a very good idea of how I came to be tracked.

Inside is a short air lauvan with an iridescent patch on the tip, as well as a handwritten note in violet ink.

Sorry, Merry, but all's fair in love and war. Mixing the two is delicious, isn't it? Anna xo

Wordlessly, I pass the card to Jen, who reads it then tightens her lips.

"You were right," I say. I rub my temples with one hand. "I was suckered in. As she knew I would be. Damn it!" I pound my fist into the arm of the couch. "I hate being wrong."

"But you did check her lauvan," says Jen reasonably. "She managed to hoodwink you, that's all."

"That rarely happens, though. I wonder if lauvan-masking is a new skill provided by their spirits-in-residence. I have no idea what they're capable of, and it's highly disconcerting."

"Does this mean that Potestas is behind Drew's attacks, or are they acting separately, like Anna said?" Alejandro says.

"Can we take anything Anna says at face value?" Jen says.

"Probably not. Either Potestas fully backs Drew's machinations, or they simply want to keep an eye on me, and Drew is exploiting the situation."

"You saw Drew," Jen says. Her eyes widen with excitement. "Did you see where he is?"

"No, only the interior of his car." Hope kindles in my heart, and I sit and pick up the glove again. "Let's see if anything has changed."

Again, the swooping feeling transports my mind's eye to the interior of Drew's car, where he lies sleeping still. I can't change my vantage point to look outside the car.

I open my eyes and rub my face in frustration.

"Do you know how your body reacts when you do that?" Jen says. "It's like you're not there anymore. I can't describe it, but it's not as if you're sleeping or unconscious. You're more absent than that."

"How bizarre," I say, but my mind is still occupied by the conundrum of finding Drew.

"What about this one?" Alejandro holds out Anna's note. The air lauvan sways on its perch. I grasp it eagerly and gain a sensation of flight, dizzying swoops and dives, but without the accompanying vision. I open my eyes again, defeated.

"No use. It's an air lauvan, not one of Drew's. The path leads nowhere useful." I slump back into the couch. "I'm running out of ideas."

We sit in silence for a minute.

"What about that spirituality shop in Steveston?" Jen says. "You said the owner was helpful. Do you think she'd know anything useful?"

"Bethany, Sylvana's aunt," I say reflectively. "Perhaps.

Even a different perspective might help, and it could be she's heard something new about Drew through the grapevine. I'll give her a call."

"Do you have her number?"

"No, damn. I'll drive down when her store opens in the morning."

CHAPTER XVII

Dreaming

"Come, kinsman," says Arthur. "You and your lady have traveled a long way. Share our midday meal before you leave."

Mordred still looks angry at Arthur's refusal to back out of the peace talks with the Saxons, but Vivienne elbows him and answers for them both.

"Thank you. We would be honored to join you."

I duck my head outside the tent and gesture to a slave girl at the opening of a nearby tent. She nods and disappears inside.

"It's not much—supplies are limited—but it will fill you," Arthur says. He waves at woolen blankets strewn on the ground and we make ourselves as comfortable as we can. The slave girl enters with a stack of wooden bowls and a ladle, followed by a boy bearing a cauldron of mutton stew. We all sniff appreciatively.

When Arthur has been served, he turns to Mordred.

"How did you end up as an emissary of my sister, Mordred?"

Mordred scowls but can't seem to find anything to take offense to. He answers begrudgingly.

"She came to my father's funeral, last autumn. You were fighting in the east. She was very kind and offered me a place in her household if I wanted it."

"I suppose favor dries up when the father of a bastard son dies," I say through a mouthful of mutton.

Mordred bristles, but Arthur waves away my comment.

"So, you joined her. She's treated you well?"

"Oh, yes."

"Good. And her policies, do you agree with them? How all

the invaders must leave our lands?"

"I will follow the Lady Morgan wherever she leads."

"That wasn't an answer," I say. "Do you agree, or are you mindlessly loyal?"

"Merlin." Arthur sighs. Surprisingly, my comment does not rile Mordred up.

"Arthur, may I show you something?" Mordred says. "I left it with my horse. I feel it will be illuminating."

Arthur puts down his empty bowl and stands.

"By all means. Lead the way."

Vivienne is silent until they leave. When she speaks, she sounds diffident, unsure of herself, which is most unlike her.

"Merlin."

"Hmm?"

"Can you—can you tell if it's a boy or a girl?"

I look at her in surprise, but she stares into her almost full bowl.

"I'm sorry, Vivienne. I can only see that somebody is in there, not what sort of somebody it is." I think of Mordred's explosive anger. "Are you all right, Vivienne? Is Mordred good to you?"

A flicker of contempt at Mordred's name passes across Vivienne's face.

"We may have shared a bed for a few months, and he may be the father, but I have no intention of marrying him. No, it's kind of you to ask, but Morgan will take care of me and the child. She has already promised."

"Good. I'm not enamored of young Mordred so far." I put my bowl down on the ground and stand. "Speaking of whom, I'd better see what he and Arthur are doing. I don't trust him."

A twitch of Vivienne's lauvan tells me I am right not to. I race out of the tent in the direction of their horses. What is Mordred up to?

My question is quickly answered. Behind a bank of bushes, Mordred and Arthur grapple. They are evenly matched—Arthur has a few more years of experience, but grappling has never been his strength. They lurch back and forth, but it's not clear that either will win. I like to let Arthur fight his own battles, but when Mordred draws a dagger, I step in. I yank a handful of his lauvan upward and Mordred sprawls on the ground, blinking in confusion. Arthur leans over him, his face stern.

"That was an unforgivable breach of my hospitality."

Mordred scrambles up before Arthur can restrain him and runs to his horse. We let him go because there seems to be little to gain from pursuing him.

"This isn't over, Arthur." He spits. "You're a disgrace to your name and your people. One day we will drive the Saxons out of our lands, and on that day, you will beg us for mercy." He kicks his horse and canters away from camp. We are left in stunned silence. At last, Arthur speaks.

"Mordred has taken my sister's desire for a Saxon-free land and spun it into a web of vitriol. I don't believe Morgan is that incensed."

"Although she did order her troops removed."

Arthur does not answer.

After Mordred gallops away, I storm toward the tent, heedless of the rain. Inside, the other men chat languidly, relaxed after their meal. Vivienne picks at her stew.

I bend down and grab her shoulder roughly. She looks alarmed, and her lauvan dance in agitation.

"Did you know?" I growl. "Tell me, was this Morgan's will?"

"Know what?"

I shake her shoulder in frustration. She lifts trembling hands in a gesture of surrender.

"I don't know what you're talking about, Merlin. I

promise."

"What's going on?" Gawaine asks.

"Mordred attempted to kill me," Arthur answers. "He fled when he didn't succeed."

A tumult of chatter breaks out, but my focus is on Vivienne. She wears a disappointed, resigned expression, and her lauvan reflect the same emotions.

"I promise I had no idea of Mordred's plan, nor do I believe it to be Lady Morgan's will. Mordred is hot-headed and very sure of his convictions. It doesn't surprise me that he concocted a foolish scheme like this."

"Well, Merlin?" Arthur says, his eyes narrowed. "Does she speak the truth?"

I remove my hand from Vivienne's shoulder and stand.

"She does. Morgan may have a different vision for the future, but I don't believe fratricide is in her mind."

"The woman must be lying," says Gawaine's brother Gareth. "What shall we do with her?"

Vivienne puts a hand on her stomach in an unconscious gesture to protect her growing baby. Arthur answers before I can.

"She will travel back to her mistress, untouched by us. I will not punish her for her companion's faults, nor risk the wrath of Morgan's forces, which are formidable. Better that they fight for no one than against us." Some of the men look disappointed at the lack of retribution, so Arthur adds, "But should Vivienne or the men she leads attempt any ill while they leave, we will show no mercy."

A cheer erupts. The men are weary of waiting in the rain and I suspect many hope for a skirmish when Morgan's men leave. Vivienne is pale but steady.

"Thank you for your decision, my lord. We will leave peacefully." She stands to depart. Arthur turns to me.

"Accompany her, Merlin. Make sure the departure goes smoothly."

I nod and follow Vivienne out of the tent's opening. She dons her cloak and I pull my hood up.

"I advise you and your mistress to both be careful. Arthur may be young, but he's strong, wise, and has the support of the Gwentish lords."

"And his own personal sorcerer." She eyes me sidelong and my mouth turns up.

"And that."

"Thank you for the advice. I will pass it on. No guarantees it will be followed."

"I suspect as much." We approach the tents of Morgan's men, and a thought strikes me. "One more piece of advice."

"Aren't you full of wisdom today?"

"Don't name the baby after that traitorous bastard."

She sniffs disdainfully.

"Never."

CHAPTER XVIII

The traffic is busy at rush hour. I weave in and out of the highway lanes, lost in thought. Each tantalizing hint of Drew's whereabouts is met by dead end after dead end. My vision from Drew's lauvan this morning showed me only the inside of the car again, with no clue about location. I don't have much hope that Bethany will know any more—if she'd found out anything, I'm sure she would have called—but I'm running out of ideas. I touch the lauvan at my center reflectively, and my fingers find Anna's strand intertwined with mine. That's my next step, my final plan. She is my only link to Potestas. Drew may have gone rogue, but the organization will know how to contact him. My heart races with anger at Anna and annoyance at myself. Why do I keep making the same mistakes? She may have had supernatural help in masking her true intentions, but I still should have been more cautious. It's wearying to not have life under control after so many years of practice.

My eyes flicker to the rear-view mirror frequently but no one matches my pace, which I deliberately increased to watch for followers. Good. Removing the piece of paper that Anna planted worked—I burned it in Wayne's bathroom sink last night and the air lauvan floated away.

I pull into a street-side parking spot just as Bethany arrives at the shop door, keys jingling.

"Bethany." I slam the car door and lope to her side.

"Merry! How nice to see you."

"This isn't a social call, I'm afraid. New developments have me desperate for news. Have you heard anything more about Drew Mordecai or Potestas? Has Anna Green contacted you recently?"

"Anna? No, I haven't heard from her in ages. Come in and

tell me what's happened. I'll see if I can help."

She pulls the door shut behind us and leaves the "closed" sign in the window.

"Drew shot me," I say without preamble. "No lasting damage, but you can imagine that I'm not pleased."

Bethany brings a hand to her mouth in a gesture of dismay then says, "Where is he now?"

"I don't know. He's incredibly difficult to track down, so I'm focusing on defense, with some success. I used earth energies to make a barrier against the air energies he controls. It deflects them well enough but is awkward because I have piles of rocks in my house and car."

Bethany looks thoughtful and traces her hand along the counter absentmindedly.

"Earth is air's opposite—that's sensible. But what if you fought fire with fire, so to speak? Hmm, perhaps not the best idiom to use," Bethany says when I grin. "Use the air energies themselves, if you can."

"What if the spirits use the energies I've collected, and I create a worse problem for myself?"

"That's possible. I suppose it will depend on your strength and abilities. Let's see." She walks around her shop, examining crystals, picking up incense, running fingers over bracelets. She returns with one hand carrying an old-fashioned pendant on a clunky gold chain with the eye of a peacock feather in resin on its face. The other holds a pack of incense. She rummages in her purse and extracts a lighter, then catches my eye.

"Old habits die hard," she says. "Take my lighter and save me from myself."

"Thanks. I assume the incense isn't to make my apartment smell like," I check the package. "Cedar?"

"Cedar is beneficial for balance and grounding, and the pendant has a long history as a traveler's good luck charm. Plus, the feather can't hurt."

I peer at the multicolored lauvan swirling around the pendant.

"There are a few air energies tangled up here. Good find." I look at Bethany's wistful face.

"What a gift." She shakes her head and says more firmly. "One more thing that might help. It just occurred to me." She pulls a leather-bound book off the shelf behind her counter. "This is a copy of an old grimoire smuggled out of Salem during the witch trials. It's a fascinating compendium of early wiccan belief. But what I really wanted to show you was this spell."

She flips through and stops on a page in the center. A stylized north wind blows air through puffed cheeks above a short paragraph of spiky handwriting.

"It's a spell for controlling a storm. I have no idea if there is anything to it, but somebody believed in it enough to risk writing it down in those times."

Bethany has armed me with an odd assortment of weapons. I wonder if there is merit in any of them. My eyes strain to read the unfamiliar writing.

Saye this, the more the strongere the gale.

Festina, o Zephyre! Irascare, Auster dirus! Consurge, o ventus Boreas! Fles violenter, Eurus currens!

"Always with the Latin," I mutter to myself. "Will that language never die?"

"Would you like me to copy it out for you? I don't understand it myself."

"No need. I know Latin, and it's repetitive and easy to memorize. Run, winds of the west! Rage, storm of the south! Rise, tempest of the north! Blow, gusts of the east!"

"Latin too? You are full of surprises, Merry. I'm sorry I don't have any suggestions on how to use these things."

I read the Latin spell once more for good measure then slide the incense and lighter into my pocket. The necklace I drape over my head and tuck into my shirt.

"Just my style. How much do I owe you?"

"Don't worry about it. The incense is cheap and when this has all blown over, you can bring the necklace back."

"Thanks, Bethany."

"Smooth sailing, Merry. May the wind be always at your back."

"I hope not. How would I see it coming?"

She laughs, and I wave as I go. I don't know what use her trinkets will be, but it's warming to have people on my side.

Ten steps around the corner, and a mass of air lauvan descends. It surrounds my head in a tight layer, enveloping my eyes, filling my nose and mouth. A paralyzing sensation of breathlessness takes over—my lungs are empty and nothing I do can fill them with life-sustaining air once again.

My panic lasts only a moment before I remember that I can last for a minute or two without air if I must. I have done it before. A cool head is what is needed to solve this conundrum.

I first grab great handfuls of the lauvan that fill my mouth, but they prove slippery and immovable. It was worth a try. My lungs burn, and I ignore them. Panic won't help.

Next, I pick up a rock from the ground and twist its lauvan into a rope which I wrap around the bundle of lauvan surrounding my mouth. The air lauvan twitch but repel the rock's lauvan.

My chest involuntarily heaves with an unfulfilled breath. I'm running out of time and options. My head is light, but I try to think. What else can I do?

Bethany's weapons spring to mind. Will they work? Do I have any other choice? I jam my hand into my pocket to extract the package of incense. My fingers fumble with the envelope until I remove a stick of incense, and my thumb rasps over the lighter's wheel three times before the damn thing lights. Spots appear in my vision, and I hold the incense in front of my mouth with a fervent hope that this will work. For good measure, I bring the necklace out of my shirt and hold the pendant on my chin.

For a moment, nothing changes. My oxygen-starved brain whirls frantically to find another solution but nothing surfaces. I have emerged victorious from countless battles with humans, but I don't know if I will survive an altercation with the spirit world. I'm out of my league.

My eyes waver in and out of focus, and my body shakes with repressed breaths, but through the incense tiny tendrils of lauvan gather. If lack of air weren't already the problem, I would hold my breath. There are more lauvan than I would expect from such a tiny amount of smoke. What did Bethany say? I can harness the wind, depending on my strength and abilities? Feverishly, I chant the Latin spell in my head, channeling my thoughts toward the steady stream of air lauvan in the smoke. My own strands join and mingle, and with every phrase I utter in my mind, the strands in the smoke grow denser.

They begin to swirl and gather the threads blocking my mouth in a tiny whirlwind that pulses to my rapidly beating heart. I muster all my mental strength into forcing power behind the words in my head. The swirl increases in speed.

Festina, o Zephyre! Irascare, Auster dirus! Consurge, o ventus Boreas! Fles violenter, Eurus currens!

My vision tunnels but before I black out completely, the last of the air lauvan leaves my mouth. Beautiful, delicious, life-saving air pours in, so much that I choke on the plenitude. I drop to my knees and cough uncontrollably. When the coughing stops, I stay on my knees and simply breathe, deeply and laboriously.

Adrenaline still courses through my body, but my mind begins to clear, and I can think about more than my immediate survival. Drew and his spirit are behind this attack, I have no doubt. And Drew is often nearby when his spirit channels the wind. Perhaps they must stay close? I look around from my vantage point on the pavement, but only one curious old man stares at me from a nearby doorway.

"You all right, son?" he calls.

I wave feebly in response, and he nods and continues to push his walker along the sidewalk. How did Drew even find me? He must have followed me in his car, unnoticed even with my diligence. It doesn't matter—how do I find him now? Drew is never in sight. But I know how to see him.

I stagger to my feet and fumble with the door handle of my car. Drew's gloves are on the seat, with his lauvan inside. My fingers tremble when I slip them into the glove—I'm still breathing hard from the lack of air—but they grip the strands firmly. I'm shocked when the thread emerges, almost transparent and limp in the morning sunlight. It won't last much longer. I touch the oily patch and close my eyes. A swirl of color transports me to Drew, who runs along a sidewalk. A black sock flops in his hand, and with a jolt I recognize my own chocolate-brown lauvan waving feebly from it. Is that how he found me? There's a flash of a sign depicting "Art's Bakery." Drew is on the next street.

I jog toward the intersection, but before I take five steps I double over with a fresh bout of coughs. A chase on foot is out. I could massage the twisted brown lauvan around my throat, but Drew would still get away by the time I finish.

I shove my fingers into the glove once more. Perhaps I can

see the direction Drew is moving in, follow with my car. But the frail strand scarcely reaches the light of day before it disappears and disintegrates into wisps of nothing.

"Damn it!" I slam my palm against the hood of my car. It glances off a hailstone dent, and a fresh wave of anger swells on top of the tempest brewing within. Now I have no leads and no way to find Drew.

There is only one course left to follow. I glance down at the single purple lauvan that travels due north from my center, intertwined with a single brown thread of mine. I don't relish this reunion, but I have no other recourse. I must find Anna.

I slam the car door shut with far more force than necessary and shift into gear as if I'm mashing Drew's head with the motion. I think of all the ways I want to make him suffer. My worry is that I won't be able to. Drew's weak vessel houses a powerful force that I'm only beginning to understand. The fact that I have survived this many attacks must be enlightening to Potestas. I wonder what they make of me—if they are keeping as close an eye on Drew as I think they are.

I join the highway to make up time, since Anna's lauvan continue to direct me north. Traffic has eased slightly from the morning rush, and I weave in and out of the lines of cars, desperate to get to Anna and find some answers. I have no idea what I will say. I should be angry at her, but I don't have a lot of energy left over from being angry at myself. I should have known better.

Once I cross the bridge into Vancouver proper, my lauvan swing left. I wait until they are perpendicular, then I signal and turn at the next intersection. Following a lauvan connection is simple, but the best way is to spiral around the person until I reach them, and it always takes more time than I wish.

The lauvan veer left again, and again I wait until they are behind me before I make my turn. The roads are less busy here, and the streets are dim with huge deciduous trees that hang gracefully over the road to form a leafy tunnel. The houses are old and expensive, three floors each and full of ornate details uncommon in today's houses. I doubt Anna has the money to buy anything here—it must be a Potestas house. What sort of scale does this operation run on, and who funds it?

Another left, later than I would have wished due to a one-way road, and then another. I'm very close now. I have narrowed it down to one block—it's time to park and follow my quarry on foot.

Halfway down the block, the fragile purple and brown strands that run from me to Anna point to a white house with dark green trim. It looks innocuous enough. I square my shoulders and ready myself for the confrontation. I need answers, however I have to get them. I hope Anna is forthcoming.

How should I enter? Sneak through the back door? Break the window in a dramatic fashion? I weigh my options, then decide that Anna has no real reason to run nor any expectation that I will show up on her doorstep. I take the steps two at a time and pound on the solid wood door. Even the neighbors would have heard that knock.

Less than a minute passes before the deadbolt slides and the door swings open.

"There you are," Anna says. She's dressed in tightly fitting exercise clothing and wears a smug and satisfied expression. "Took you long enough. Come in." She turns and walks unhurriedly down the wood-floored hallway.

I stand at the threshold for a moment. She was expecting me. How much does she know? I step inside once I realize that I won't get any answers on the front porch and follow Anna into a dimly lit kitchen at the back of the house. Anna stands at the kitchen island, calmly peeling an orange.

"How did you know I was coming?"

"Please. How stupid do you think I am? I know you have some way of tracking me. You found me at Mt. Linnigan multiple times. I was simply waiting for you to realize what I was up to."

"So, leaving Potestas was a complete lie. Something you're uncommonly good at."

"Naturally. I'm still intensely interested in getting my own powers. I have big plans. As for the deception, well, I may have had a little supernatural help." She pops an orange segment in her mouth.

"You came to my place just to plant the note? I didn't realize you were so calculating."

Anna tilts her head and studies me.

"I would feel bad about it, except I get the sense you would do the same."

I have nothing to say to this because she's not wrong. I don't truly feel betrayed, simply angry with myself for being duped so easily.

"Besides," she adds. "It wasn't all work and no play. I do enjoy your company. If you ever want to reconsider your position regarding Potestas, you let me know."

"Yeah. I'll do that." When pigs fly. I won't be deceived by Anna. Never again.

"I'm dying to know your secret, Merry." She rolls an orange across the counter toward me. I make no move to intercept it, and it comes to a halt, wobbling close to the edge. "How do you find me? How can you see spirits?"

"It's almost charming that you think I will tell you anything you can use against me. You'll have to try harder than that."

"Don't say I didn't ask politely." Anna pulls a cell phone toward her from the edge of the island. "The org thought you might need more of an incentive to spill your secrets. Here, look at this." She holds the phone up for me to see.

A picture shows on the screen of an unfinished log-walled room with one tiny window. An old-fashioned wood-burning stove squats in one corner. In the center of the room sits a man bound to a wooden chair and gagged.

"Alejandro," I breathe. "What the hell have you done, Anna?"

"It wasn't me. I'm just the messenger."

"Don't give me that bullshit. You're part of all this—take some responsibility." I rub my hands over my knuckles, itching to take out my anger and fear for Alejandro on someone. Of course Potestas would go after those I care about. If I had thought a little harder, I could have foreseen this. I was too preoccupied with chasing Drew. Where are they holding Alejandro? I look at our connecting lauvan, but they ascend straight into the air. How bizarre—he can't be in an airplane. Then I see tiny wisps of air lauvan wrapped around the connection, pulling, holding it up and away so that I am unable to locate Alejandro. I pluck at an air thread experimentally, but it breaks easily and then reforms around the lauvan. I can't rely on the connection to find him—I need Anna.

"If anything happens to Alejandro, I'm holding you personally responsible. You and anyone I can find in your little cult. You don't want to be on my bad side, trust me."

She doesn't look worried and continues to pop orange segments into her mouth.

"We have no interest in harming him. It's simple, really. We only want information and your promise to desist in searching for Potestas."

"Stop searching—I'm only hunting you down because fucking Drew Mordecai keeps trying to kill me!" I take a deep breath and hold onto the edge of the counter. Keep it together, Merry. It's the only way to help Alejandro.

"Of course, that nonsense will stop immediately. Trying to kill you wasn't on the org's agenda. Drew's primary loyalty is with Potestas, and he will do as he is told."

"I knew Potestas had a hand in Drew's actions. Teasing apart truth and lies from your words isn't easy, Anna. How do you mask your lies so well?"

"How can you see when someone is lying?" Anna leans forward eagerly. I sigh.

"The information you want. What do you want to know?"

"Tell me the truth about yourself. What are you? How do you see what you see, know what you know?" Her eyes open even wider. "Are you sharing your body with a spirit already? Which element chose you?"

I stare at her levelly for a few moments. She gazes back with anticipation, mouth slightly parted, awaiting my response.

I don't handle ultimatums well.

Quicker than Anna can react, I spin around the island and charge toward her. My hands grab each of her wrists and twist her arms behind her back, transferring both wrists into one hand. I slam my body into hers and shove her against the fridge. My hips press into hers to pin her tight, then I twist the strands that surround her head with my free hand.

"You will tell me where Alejandro is," I breathe into her ear. "I'm very persuasive."

Anna simply smiles, an unusual reaction to being forcibly detained. I focus on my task, but her lauvan slip through my fingers. Now that I look more closely, her lauvan are interwoven with translucent orange threads no thicker than the width of a hair. She is joined with a spirit—of fire?

"Just tell me, Merry." Anna leans her head forward and rubs her cheek softly against mine. She whispers in my ear. "Tell me, and your friend will be safe. How do you do what you do?"

I'm tired of playing games with Anna. Giving in to Anna's

threats is not in my nature, and I'm not interested in handing Potestas any information they can use. Their methods are beyond questionable—they have already proven that erupting a volcano above an innocent town is acceptable and killing me unobjectionable. I can't give in, but I can't leave Alejandro at Drew's mercy. Anna has left me only one option I'm willing to use.

With my free hand, I lunge for a large knife that sticks out from a block on the counter. I press the point into Anna's neck before she can move.

"Tell me where Alejandro is, and I won't use the knife."

Finally, for the first time, Anna looks frightened.

"You wouldn't."

"You have no idea what I would do. I've done worse."

Anna's breath comes fast, and her strands dance with agitation and fear. I take no joy in threatening Anna—using physical strength against a woman is unjust, and Anna and I have a history and a lauvan connection—but she made her choices, and innocent Alejandro sits at the mercy of her people. I protect my own.

She holds out for a while, considering the knife. I press it harder to her skin, and she gasps. One more twitch and I will draw blood.

My phone rings. Is it Jen with news? I can answer it. Holding Anna at knifepoint only takes one hand, after all. I fumble with the lauvan behind her back to prevent her hand from moving. That should buy me enough time for a phone call.

I slide my phone out of my pocket with the hand that held Anna's arms.

"What?"

"Merry? It's Wayne. I found the Mordecai log cabin up on Hollyburn."

Alejandro was in a log-lined room with a wood stove.

"Do you have directions?"

"Yes."

"Meet me at your house right away. Quick as you can. Alejandro's a prisoner at the cabin, and we need to regroup to rescue him."

I hang up while Wayne is still sputtering exclamations. He will figure it out. I meet Anna's eyes.

"Luckily for you, I just received the information I need." I step away and slide the knife back into its slot. Anna retreats and rubs her neck where the knife touched her.

"Would you really have cut me?"

"Don't cross me again, Anna." I plant my feet squarely on the floor. "I have a demand of my own. You're not to contact anyone from Potestas until the end of the day, by which time I will have rescued Alejandro."

"You expect me to sit obediently in the house without phoning anyone?"

"Don't worry, you won't have a choice."

She grows pale.

"What are you going to do to me?"

"Nothing you won't recover from. I don't suppose you have any insight as to defeating Drew?"

"Good luck with that," she says with a sneer. "I have a small connection for protection, but Drew is fully connected to his spirit traveler. All powers of the wind are his. Oh, I can't wait—once my ring is fully open, there will be no stopping me."

"Ring? That's how this works? He wears a ring that somehow allows him to be possessed by an elemental?"

I glance at Anna's hand, which sports a ring of fine gold filigree. Anna looks annoyed with herself.

"There's a ceremony. The ring is just symbolic, to show others your connection."

I doubt that. In my experience, lauvan need to be bound to

a physical object. A ring would be a perfect carrier.

"Besides, you'll never defeat him. The spirit traveler is too powerful. You'll never get close enough to Drew to harm him." She laughs. "You'd better bring your windbreaker. I hear there's a storm brewing."

I have had enough of Anna. It's time to rescue Alejandro. I move toward Anna, and a flash of fear ripples across her lauvan.

"I'm not going to hurt you. There's no need, now." I dart forward and snatch her hand before she can resist, and she shrieks momentarily. There is an electrical plug on the island from which lauvan crackle and jump. I swiftly knot her lauvan with the electrical strands, leaving enough leeway for the threads to wiggle out from their bonds by the end of the day.

"You'll stay here until sundown." I move her phone out of reach then lean across and pluck the orange from the other side of the counter. "Here's lunch."

Anna tries to pull away from the plug, but she is too tightly bound. Her lauvan dance with anxiety once more.

"How did you do that?" Her eyes are wide, panicked, but still she wants to know what I am. "What elemental are you bound to?"

I walk away without looking back.

"Goodbye, Anna."

The house where I left Anna is not far from Wayne's. I briefly consider abandoning my car and flying, but I'm too hungry. My bird form would immediately veer off in search of a meal, and I don't have time for that. I assume Drew and his spirit are with Alejandro, but I can't risk being swept away by malevolent winds. A few minutes later, I turn onto Wayne's street. There is no parking, so I pull into the free space in front of a fire hydrant and run to Wayne's door. It's unlocked, and I burst in.

"Merry! There you are." Jen stands up from the couch in the living room, followed closely by Cecil. "You took your time."

"Do you know where Alejandro went?"

"He should be back soon. He just went to the grocery store for some lunch."

I'm intensely happy to see that Jen is still here, but annoyed that Cecil is tagging along. This doesn't concern him, and I don't favor anyone else knowing my business with Potestas.

"What's Cecil doing here?" I say bluntly. I don't have time for niceties. Cecil looks affronted but wisely refrains from speaking. Jen bristles.

"I asked him here. Everyone was gone, and I was sitting here twiddling my thumbs." She turns to Cecil. "Cecil, could you please get my water bottle from the car? I'm really thirsty."

"Sure." He glances between us. "I'll be back in a few minutes."

Jen waits until the front door closes behind Cecil before she speaks again.

"I need to talk to you about something."

"I don't have time for chitchat right now, Jen." I dig in my satchel to find Braulio's notebook and take one last glance to look for anything that might help me in the battle ahead. Perhaps there is something akin to the spell that Bethany gave me. Anything that will give me an edge over this air spirit possessing Drew.

"Make time. I've earned it."

Jen's eyes narrow with resolve. I throw the notebook on the coffee table and lean my forearms over the back of the couch.

"Fine. You have one minute."

"I looked up the name Merlo Nuanez. It's not a common name. Not a lot comes up, until I start searching earlier. There's a marriage certificate in 1951 in Georgia, and a newspaper mention in 1943 in Guatemala."

"They've digitized their old records?" Even through my horror, I'm astonished.

"A few of them. I got lucky. So, that's weird, right?" She stares at me with intensity, as if expecting me to refute this statement. When I don't respond, she continues. "Then I opened my search for Merry Lytton to other places and times. There are plenty of Lyttons in England, including a Merle Lytton in the 1870s."

"Very interesting." I stand up straight. "Your time is up."

"That's it?"

"I don't have time for more. Alejandro is currently a prisoner of Potestas, and I need to gather ammunition to mount a rescue mission. As soon as Wayne gets back, we're heading to Cypress where he's being held."

Jen gasps.

"Why didn't you say so earlier, you idiot?"

I swing around and perch on the edge of the couch to flip through the notebook. Is there anything that can help?

"What can I do?" Jen asks.

"Zip it for two seconds while I find a spell."

"Spell?" Jen murmurs, but I tune her out and focus. Surely, something…

Almost without exception, every polytheistic religion has at least one deity that controls the wind. Where there are gods, there is supplication to the gods. Take Ehecatl, or Ehecatl-Quetzalcoatl as he was often known….

The door opens as Cecil enters, and a car splutters to a halt outside. I read the rest of the paragraph before I slam the notebook shut. That's all I have time for. I hope it's enough.

"Wayne sounds like he's here," Cecil says to Jen.

"Good," I say. "We're going to collect Alejandro."

"I'm coming too," says Jen. She turns to Cecil. "Drew is holding Alejandro hostage."

Cecil's eyes open wide, but before he can speak, I cut in.

"That's not wise. Drew is targeting people I care about, and you certainly qualify. He's desperate, has nothing to lose, and has special abilities that make him extremely dangerous." I glance at Cecil, who looks bewildered and skeptical.

"Give me some defense, and I'll bring up the rear. You might need a decoy, someone to haul Alejandro away—don't argue with me on this."

"Fine. Come. But do what I tell you at all times. Understood?"

Jen nods, but Cecil cuts in.

"You're okay with Jen tagging along to catch some dangerous weirdo who's holding your friend hostage? Why not the police? I don't think you should go, Jen."

Jen picks up her purse and rummages for her keys.

"Thanks for your concern, Cecil, but I'm going."

"Then I'm coming too." Cecil pushes his shoulders back in a confident pose. Jen frowns, and her lauvan sway with hesitation. I grab my own keys and ignore the posturing from this young peacock.

"No," I say with finality. Jen's lauvan freeze with indignation.

"I don't think that's up to you, Merry. Not at this point."

The front door bangs open and Wayne barges in.

"You two work it out," I say to Jen and Cecil. "Just don't let him call the police, Jen."

"What happened?" Wayne asks breathlessly.

"I'll explain in the car. Give Jen the directions, will you? We're having a big jolly outing, apparently." I'm not keen on

Jen joining us, but perhaps it's for the best to have her close. I don't want another kidnapping behind my back. Cecil, I couldn't care less about, except he might slow us down with awkward questions. I wonder what Jen has told him about me. He might be in for a few shocks, and I might have a new initiate—one of the many I have collected over the past few weeks. That is the last thing I want, but Alejandro comes first. I will do my best to hide my abilities. Cecil had better keep up and keep quiet.

As soon as we hop in the car and I turn the key, Wayne speaks.

"What's happening?"

"Drew has Alejandro tied up in a log cabin. I had a vision." I roar out of Wayne's quiet street and onto the main road.

"A vision, hey?" Wayne shakes his head and shrugs. "Sure. Anything else in said vision? You're sure he's at Hollyburn?"

"I only saw the inside, but it's a log cabin with a wood-burning stove, owned by a Mordecai. It's the best lead we've had so far. If he's not there, I'll go back to my source and get more information, however I can."

"Who's your source? I thought we didn't have any leads before."

"A woman I met in Wallerton. She slept over the other night, but she's deep in Potestas, so I'm sure I can uncover what I need to if necessary."

"Not recommended, sleeping with the enemy." Wayne chuckles. "I guess I don't have to tell you that, now. So, what are we up against? We're walking into a hostage situation with no police back up, and our opponent has magic wind powers.

What can I expect?"

I zoom over the Lion's Gate bridge to the North Shore. Sunlight dazzles on the calm bay below.

"Good question. I wish I had a better answer for you. Expect whatever the wind can bring us. I've seen strong pockets of wind, attacking birds, dense fog, a tornado…"

Wayne whistles.

"I appreciate your confidence in me, bringing me along, but how can I help?"

"You'll come in handy. Muscle paired with brains always does."

"And you? Any more tricks up your sleeve?"

"I hope so. I really do."

We are quiet for the rest of the drive. I don't know what Wayne is contemplating, but I'm steeling myself for a fight, and flipping through my memories for anything that will help in the upcoming confrontation. This is it—I need to find Drew and finish this once and for all.

The familiar drive up Cypress Mountain is long and steep, with numerous switchbacks and countless stunning views. The vistas don't draw me in, not with my mind focused on Alejandro. At the parking lot for cross-country skiing, I pull my poor, hail-battered car into a parking space and kill the engine.

"What's the plan?" Wayne says quietly through the stillness after the engine dies.

I ponder the options.

"We wait a few minutes for Jen and Cecil, then we go in on foot with or without them. Hopefully, we can get to the cabin undetected."

Minutes later, Jen's car trundles up the road and pulls in beside the Lotus. I get out to greet Jen.

"You made good time. I thought we'd be waiting a while."

"No one can match your speed, but I did my best, safely."

A thought strikes me. “Jen, do you have any food? I’m starving.”

Cecil looks at me askance, and Jen raises an eyebrow but digs through her purse anyway.

“Is this really the time?” She hands me a granola bar which I tear open and shove into my mouth. I speak through a mouthful of oats.

“It might be necessary, for certain tricks.” If I need to transform into a falcon, I can’t be distracted by my hunger. “Thanks. All right, everyone.” I point to the nearest trailhead. “This is our path. I’ve hiked it before, so follow me and stay quiet. According to Wayne’s directions, Drew’s cabin isn’t far.”

The path twists into a tiny vale, and the forest closes around us. Everything is dim despite the full sun overhead, and the dirt track is dusty and hard after the long stretch of unseasonable sunshine. The glowering trees don’t allow much light through. We pass a ramshackle old cabin on our left held together with nails and twine and a prayer and walk by a few seldom-used trails that branch off the main track. Beyond a massive Douglas fir that leans precariously over our path, I stop and point. A narrow trail disappears over a knoll to some distant unseen cabin. Jen peers after my outstretched finger.

“This is it? What do we do now?”

“Find Alejandro. Keep your eyes peeled and do exactly what I say, no hesitations. Got it?” All nod. I say sharply, “Get down!” Wayne drops to the road, but Jen and Cecil look at me, flummoxed. I shake my head. “Exactly what I say, at all times. Understood?” Jen looks sheepish. Cecil doesn’t say anything, which I take as assent. “Good. Let’s go. Quietly as you can.”

I can be as quiet as a hunting wolf when I want to be. Jen is light on her feet, and Wayne tries as best as he can, but Cecil scuffs and sneezes and steps on the loudest twigs that crack under his feet. I let it slide for half a minute, but when he starts to speak to Jen, it's time to end this. I whirl around and step in close, pressing my face inches from his.

"Cecil. This is not a game. A man's life might end this afternoon. Do you want his death on your conscience? Because it will be if you don't keep quiet. No talking and watch your feet. If you can't, go back to the car. Do I make myself clear?"

Cecil looks mutinous but cowed. I hope that worked. One more peep from him, and I will silence him myself. I should have come alone—but then would Jen have been taken hostage next?

Cecil mercifully steps more cautiously during our approach. There is a small hillock that the path rises to meet. I motion to the others to stop and creep forward myself to peer between trees.

Below me lies a tiny log cabin tucked into the forest. Tree branches brush the walls, and copious moss covers the roof. A metal stovepipe towers, smokeless, above the roofline. Gingham curtains are drawn across two small windows, and no one is in sight. I beckon the others forward.

"Jen, Cecil," I whisper. "You keep a lookout on each side of the cabin's front. Wayne, you walk a perimeter to check for unexpected company. I'll open the door."

"What if we see someone?" Jen whispers back.

"Scream. I'll come running." I grin at her and she smiles wanly. "All right, let's go."

Wayne takes off noiselessly to the right. Jen and Cecil follow me on our approach to the cabin. Even midday, under full summer sun, it's dim and gloomy under the conifers. I point Cecil to the right corner, and he approaches the sawn logs with trepidation. Jen takes the left corner with more aplomb and peers cautiously around it. When she sees me looking, she gives me a thumbs-up.

I give my attention to the door. We are certainly in the right place—Drew's distinctive gray lauvan are draped over the door handle. I listen carefully, but only the twittering of a lonesome bird disturbs the stillness. Time to face my nemesis.

I grasp the doorknob, turn it, and swing the door open all in one swift motion. My other hand is up and ready to wreak havoc with any lauvan that it might find. I whirl to the side of the doorjamb in case Drew still has his gun, then peek my head around the lintel when I hear no commotion. The single room is empty except for Alejandro, bound and gagged. Frightened eyes under tousled hair brighten with relief at my dramatic entrance, and he grunts through the duct tape at his mouth.

I hasten to his side and rip off the tape.

"Merlo! Thank god you're here. Drew, he's crazy, I didn't know what he would do."

"Where is he now?" I say while I rip away Alejandro's bonds. He winces when the tape tears at hair and skin.

"He ran a few minutes ago. He's unpredictable—one minute he boasts about his spirit powers, the next he's terrified of you and what he guesses you can do. He's ready to kill you, absolutely."

"Alejandro! Are you okay?" Jen and Cecil are outlined in the doorway.

"Did I say you could leave your posts?" I snap. "What if Drew were behind you right now?"

They scuttle out of sight. I sigh and shake my head. Alejandro has a smile on his face.

"Jen came to rescue me?"

"Focus, Alejandro. We need to catch this maniac." I help him out of his chair, and he stands with a groan. I say, "Perhaps you should wait in the car. You've been through enough today."

"I'm fine." Alejandro straightens his shirt and stretches his arms. "I want to help."

Privately, I would like Alejandro, Jen, and Cecil to all drive back down the mountain, but outwardly I say, "All right. Do exactly what I say at all times."

"Of course."

"Good man." I pat him on the back then give him a swift, spontaneous hug. "I'm happy to see you in one piece."

Alejandro beams.

"I was so relieved to see you in the doorway, Merlo. Thank you for coming to get me."

"Considering I'm the reason you were taken in the first place, it was the least I could do. Come on, let's catch this *hijueputa*."

Wayne jogs up when we exit the cabin.

"Alejandro, good to see you. Merry, there are signs of fresh passage down an old deer track, over here."

"Let's see it. Come on, everyone." I follow Wayne. Jen's muted greetings trail behind us.

Sure enough, freshly broken twigs at the entrance to a disused track are draped with gray lauvan. They wave gently.

"Drew went this way, for certain."

"The coward didn't want to confront you," Wayne said contemptuously.

"Cowardly? Perhaps. Smart, certainly. Out in the open air he has the advantage. According to Alejandro, Drew is afraid of me, so it makes sense he'd want to confront me at his strongest."

"His spirit-thing's strength, you mean."

"They're currently one and the same, from what I understand. The spirit does Drew's bidding."

"Spirit?" Cecil says. "What are you talking about?"

Damn. How did it come to this? My list of those who know my secrets is expanding at an alarming rate. I know nothing about Cecil, and yet here he stands, learning far too much about my world. I could blame the hostage situation for clouding my mind, but I should have thought Cecil's involvement through to its inevitable conclusion. I turn to Jen.

"Does he truly need to be here?"

She narrows her eyes.

"Yes."

I sigh explosively.

"Fine. Cecil, there is more in this world than you know. Keep your mouth shut and your eyes open. Jen, he's your responsibility."

Cecil opens his mouth indignantly, and I hold up my index finger.

"Mouth shut. There's too much at stake here. Questions will have to wait until later." If all goes well, I can minimize any visible "magic" on my part. Cecil can chalk up the spirits to the religion of his choice.

Wayne crosses his beefy arms.

"What's the plan?"

"We follow and keep an eye out for traps." A thought strikes me, born of my brief, frenzied reading of Braulio's notebook before we left. "Hold on a moment. I have an idea for protection."

I swing around a tree. Behind me, Jen calls out, "Where are you going, Merry?"

I ignore her and swiftly pull the appropriate lauvan to transform into a falcon. I mentally congratulate myself on my foresight—eating Jen's granola bar made this transformation possible without distractions. I tuck my head down and snap my beak until it clasps around a feather. I yank and release a tiny shriek of discomfort before I master myself. Perhaps I will avoid the torso. Wings next.

Once four feathers lie on the dirt before me, I let my lauvan reform and rejoin the others.

"Here." I pass each person a feather. As I do so, I chant a short phrase from Braulio's notebook. It's an Aztec incantation from pre-Columbian Mexico invoking protection from Ehecatl, god of wind. As I do so, I inwardly marvel at Braulio's dedication to his work. Finding all this material about the spirit world was nothing short of miraculous. When the chant is complete, lauvan from the feathers twist tightly with each person's lauvan in a protective shell. I have no idea how strong it is, but anything is better than nothing.

Alejandro receives his feather and chant with a solemn nod. Wayne tries to act nonchalant, and Cecil looks incredulous although wisely refrains from interfering. Let him think me a priest or shaman of sorts—chanting is not proof of anything otherworldly. Jen frowns.

"Where did you find all these feathers?"

"I have my ways." I smile at her impishly. "All right, everyone. Keep a lookout for anything unusual. And eyes to the skies—attacks are likely to come from that direction."

The track is overgrown, so it's easy to see where Drew barged through in his haste to get away. I have the charged feeling of a wolf on the hunt—ears and eyes are open and alert, lauvan are tight and ready, and my whole focus is on my quarry. I only hope I don't turn from predator to prey.

Right on cue, wind rustles the boughs of fir and cedar above us. It starts as a breeze, but swiftly strengthens.

"Merry?" Jen's voice is high. "Is that…"

"I expect so. Eyes peeled, everyone."

The wind picks up further. Birds no longer trill from the canopy. A storm brews, and I know the source. How will Drew's spirit strike first? Not for the first time, I wish I knew more about the spirit world.

Wayne catches up to me when the undergrowth clears slightly.

"I don't want to sound yellow-bellied, but I feel like a third wheel. How can I fight something I can't see? Aren't I just in your way?"

"Don't worry. I expect you'll be useful before long." In an undertone I add, "Probably more than some of my entourage."

We look back at the others. Alejandro pushes along valiantly, but his confinement has taken a toll. Jen glances around nervously, and Cecil looks as if this forest is the last place he wants to be. Wayne shrugs.

"They're here. That's something."

I turn around and immediately cringe. A huge cloud of wind funnels through the trees, visible only to me. The air lauvan writhe and twist, eager to reach us. This is our first trap, our first test.

"Everybody down!" I yell, and everyone drops to the forest floor. I gather what earth lauvan are within my reach and fling them up in a makeshift attempt at a barrier. I crouch down myself and recite the spell I put over each of my companions in the hope of strengthening their protection.

The wind arrives with the roar of a crashing wave. Branches crack and snap around us, and I am bowled off my feet from the force. Shrieks and curses erupt around me which I take as a good sign—at least they are still here and conscious enough to yell.

The gust dies as quickly as it came, but we are left panting in a stiff breeze that remains.

I am the first to stand.

"On your feet, everyone. The quicker we are, the less time Drew has to lay traps."

They all look stunned, but Alejandro gamely pushes to his feet.

"Is everyone okay?" he says. He holds out a hand to Jen, who takes it and gets up shakily. Cecil stands beside her, his face a tableau of fear and outrage.

"Is everyone okay?" Cecil yells. "Am I the only one who felt that? A fucking gale just flattened us." He points at fallen branches that now litter the undergrowth. "And you ask if we're okay?"

"Calm down, Cecil." Jen puts a hand on Cecil's forearm. He doesn't shake it off, but neither does he calm.

"How can I? Seriously, Jen? You're following this freak," finger outstretched in my direction. "With his feathers and spells, hunting a kidnapper? And what the hell are these spirits?" His voice rises a half-octave.

"I don't have time for this," I growl then raise my voice and point back toward the parking lot. "Either shut up or get out."

"Merlo." Alejandro puts up a conciliatory hand. "Let me."

I wave at Cecil with a dismissive gesture and pace over to a nearby tree to keep a watch for signs of trouble. While we bicker and waffle, my enemy plans and plots. And I don't need to see Jen's reproachful face.

"Cecil. I know it's hard to understand what's happening here. I don't know what Jen told you—"

"Not a lot," Jen interjects.

"A man named Drew Mordecai has control over the wind and air—"

"What the hell does that mean?"

"It means we are in danger from the skies. Merlo has abilities that can help us, luckily."

And there it is. No more hiding from Cecil. I clench my fingernails into my palms. Alejandro is well-meaning, but he doesn't yet understand the precarious nature of my hidden self. It doesn't take much to unravel the veneer of my current life and expose the secrets that few want to know.

Too late now. There is a silver lining: I can perform my tricks out in the open.

"I recommend rolling with it," Wayne says. "Don't think too hard about it."

"Drew won't stop until Merlo is dead," Alejandro continues. "I know you don't really know him and maybe would rather leave him to fight his own battles. But Jen will follow him because she is his friend. And if you stay for Jen, the best way to stay safe is to listen to Merlo."

My back is to the rest of the group, and all I hear is silence. Then, a sigh.

"Fine. I'll be quiet and follow orders. I want answers later, though."

"And you'll have them," I say, turning back. "When we have more time. Now, however, I suggest we move. The next attack can't be far away." I beckon to Alejandro while I pace forward. He trots up and the others follow at a small distance.

"Thanks for talking Cecil around, Alejandro. I'm only diplomatic when I have to be."

He smiles, then sobers.

"You never know, we might need him. Extra hands can't hurt."

"Usually."

"Hey, Merry," Jen calls from behind. "I found a feather. Should I keep it? What about collecting rocks?"

"The rocks are a good idea. Keep them in your hands—I don't want anyone weighed down if we need to run."

"Really? We're carrying rocks now?" Cecil mutters, but quietly enough that I can ignore him. He does, however, bend to grab a rock in each hand.

"Is bigger better?" Wayne lifts a particularly hefty stone in his arms.

"Not in this case. I'd rather make good time than lug the heaviest rocks for their minor benefit."

We continue along the track at a decent clip. It worries me

that we haven't been attacked in a while. What is Drew planning?

Two minutes later, my question is answered. Faint cawing reaches my ears.

"Damn it." I whirl around to the others. "Brace yourselves. A murder of crows is on the way. Hopefully not literally." I think for a moment of the best way to protect ourselves. "All right. Huddle together, everyone, and hold those rocks out in a circle around us."

The cacophonous cawing grows ever louder as the group scrambles to follow my instructions. I notice with approval that Wayne has grabbed a sturdy branch and brandishes it in his free hand as a weapon.

"We've got this," Wayne says to me. "This is old hat. Remember the roof? And there's no fog to deal with."

"True." I scan the treetops. "Don't get complacent, though." I grab the rock lauvan from the stone Jen holds in her right hand and tease them upward. I do the same with Cecil's and twist the two bundles together.

"Can't we put the rocks down?" Cecil eyes me with mistrust at my seemingly fruitless handwaving.

"Won't work then. A little trust, please, Cecil. You'll get answers later."

"There they are!" Jen squeaks out. I don't turn but hastily finish weaving my net over the heads of our group. I have always found earth lauvan to be the easiest to work with. My hands now free, I stand in the center of our dome and look up.

The crows are upon us, a black cloud of discordant, overwhelming noise. Wings flap and talons swipe, but all are held back by the net of earth lauvan. The flapping of black wings covers our dome in a feathery blanket and shadows our faces. I sigh in relief.

Until one crow wriggles through. A wing thrashes within

the confines of our net. Then the writhing body, sharp beak, curved talons, and second wing slide through, directly above Alejandro's head. He cringes when the bird plummets onto him like a bomb but holds fast to his rocks. The crow bounces off his back and lands in the center of our circle where it twists to launch itself into the air once more.

"Don't let go of the rocks!" I yell then dive toward the crow. My hands reach to its swirling, enraged lauvan, but they slip through my fingers when it pushes off the ground. It flies like a bullet to my face, cawing madly. I lift my hands to shield my eyes, but before talons reach them, Wayne's club swings in a great arc from overhead and plummets to meet its mark. The crow drops to the forest floor, stunned.

There is no time to thank Wayne because another crow is taking advantage of the breach. Then, above Jen's head, wing feathers emerge through another gap. Our barrier is not dense enough. We need more stones.

I grasp the lauvan of the next crow and manage to entangle them enough to prevent it flying for a few minutes. Another crow immediately wriggles through. Wayne brains the next with his club. The following crow is immobilized by a surprise maneuver from Cecil, who grabs the crow with one hand around the bird's back. The crow's beak stabs cruelly at Cecil's fingers, and he winces but doesn't let go. I spring to his side and twist strands until the crow flops to the ground.

All at once, the black cloud of attacking birds lifts and flies in the direction it came from.

"Why are they leaving?" Jen says, her pale face looking after the retreating birds. "Are they going to get more?"

"They're being directed by another force. No, I think we're finished with birds for the moment. There will be something else shortly, I have no doubt."

"Maybe the crows didn't want any more casualties on their

end." Cecil points to the birds between us, which feebly stir.

"Interesting. Perhaps the spirit can only push them against their natural inclinations for so long. All right, you can put down your rocks now. Let's keep moving."

I stride off without waiting, and the sounds of tromping feet and rustling branches follow me. With every passing moment, Drew could be getting further away or plotting his next attack. I need to find him and end this. I'm sorely tempted to transform into a falcon and swiftly pursue my quarry, but Drew's spirit currently rules the skies.

The trees thin up ahead and the wind is growing stronger. After a small rise, we descend steeply onto a barren plateau. It's a huge slab of speckled granite, flat on top with a hazardous cliff that falls sharply away to trees hundreds of feet below. An equally steep incline soars above us, craggy and impassible. The strait lies beyond our feet, grim and gray under threatening skies, and the usually glittering city is drab.

Wayne strides out confidently, but I grab his arm.

"Take care. We're too exposed here. If I were attacking with wind, this would be the ideal ambush." I look across the plateau, where the faint trace of a trail disappears through the brush a few dozen paces away. A pulsing lauvan cable crosses the plateau on its path down the mountain face, silvery-brown threads gleaming dully in the leaden light.

"We're assuming Drew came this way," says Jen. "Couldn't he have doubled back by now? We could be on a wild goose chase."

"What about this?" Cecil picks up a trucker cap wedged between two rocks at our feet.

"He was wearing that," Alejandro says. "When he tied me up."

"It's covered in his lauvan, too," I say. "Good eye, Cecil. Yes, we're on the right path. Nothing to do but push on, I'm afraid. Everyone still have their feathers? Good. Follow me, close as you can."

I gather them together with a few waves of my hands and hustle them forward. Alejandro trips over a jagged edge of the great rock slab but recovers his footing quickly with a nervous glance upward. I scan the skies, keenly aware that the only warning we might have would be from me. There are no rustling trees to listen to here, no falling branches to warn us.

Before we have traveled ten paces across the slab, clouds billow out of nowhere. Each one is the deep purple of an angry bruise. They pile on top of each other, mounting rapidly.

"Faster," I say, and everyone breaks into a shambling run.

Halfway across, the storm breaks.

"Get down!" I shout and throw myself to the stone surface. My heart beats thunderously in my chest. A monstrous gathering of air lauvan streaks toward our rocky outcrop, boiling in a furious wave of silver strands. The roar reaches us a second before the wind hits. When the force pummels us, my breath is taken away by its ferocity.

My streaming eyes pick out my companions plastered to the surface of the rough granite slab. The blast of wind dies slightly, enough for me to lift my head and shout.

"Everyone all right?"

Heads nod.

"Start crawling forward. We need to get off this rock."

The end of my instructions is swept away by the next fierce gust. Air whistles and roars across my ears and burns my skin with its intensity. The only thing to do is cling to the infuriatingly smooth rock. The wind is so strong that my hands slip, and my body shifts a fraction closer to the edge.

The gust lessens once more.

"Go, go, go!" I scream, and everyone scrambles toward the opposite side. We only make it a few shuffles before the wind returns. I slip further, and even through the roar Jen's shriek reaches my ears. We can't continue like this for much longer, not if the gusts keep getting stronger. A flurry of movement dances in the corner of my eye, and I turn my head. My heart sinks.

Another boiling mass of air lauvan writhes in our direction, peppered with tiny white pebbles. At my strangled shout, Jen's head turns. Her eyes widen, and I know what the pebbles are.

"Hailstorm!" she screams. She drops her head and covers her neck and face with her hands.

An instant after Jen's warning, the hail hits hard enough to bruise. I wince and curl my body into a fetal position to reduce surface area, but the hail still smacks and smarts. My bare arms welt up with red patches from the onslaught.

What can I do? I wrack my brains, but nothing is coming to me. I could try to control the wind that surrounds us, but how can I do that when I can't even stand up, let alone release my grip on the granite? I lift one hand feebly, but the air lauvan whip through my fingers and break the instant I try to grasp them.

A faint shout reaches my wind-deafened ears. Alejandro has lost his grip and rolls toward the edge of the cliff, out of control, past the lauvan cable. My heart stops and I lunge out, heedless of the danger. I can't let Alejandro slide to his death.

His wildly waving foot passes my outstretched hand, too far away for me to reach. I scramble toward the edge. Before I can grab him, Alejandro's body jolts to a stop.

Wayne is stretched out on the granite, one hand firmly surrounding Alejandro's wrist. Both their arms are patchy with red welts from the hail. Alejandro's eyes are wide, and he squeezes Wayne's hand as they both roll closer to the wall.

The hail stops, but the wind remains.

"Keep going," I yell, hoarse from shouting. "That's the

only way to end this."

"Can't you do something?" Cecil shouts back. "They said you had powers."

I don't bother answering, but he's right. I'm overpowered and underprepared and I have no idea what I'm doing. I have led these people to the precipice, with no parachutes to pass out. My blood boils with the indignity of my failure, but I have no object to vent my frustrations on and no energy to spare from survival.

The lauvan cable lies next to Alejandro, a few shuffles away from me. I pull myself over the slab, feeling like a sloth on the ground. As I move, I attempt to formulate a plan. What can I do with the cable?

The wind increases in intensity when I approach the dense mass of earth lauvan, but I find a good grip and plunge my other hand deep into the cable.

My closed eyes roll back with the sensation, but I mentally shake myself and pull out strands handful by handful. It's difficult to reach Alejandro, but I manage to hook some of the earth lauvan to his shoulders. Alejandro's hair begins to tousle gently instead of dancing in a frenzy. He opens his raw, streaming eyes in amazement.

There is no time to communicate. I failed to attach myself first, and now I'm bowled sideways, rolled front over back until I hit another body and then the rock wall. I grab onto the person and discover Jen in the maelstrom. My eyes stream with tears from the blasts of ferocious air, and her long hair flings against my arm in the chaos. She yanks my head toward her mouth with both hands.

"What do we do now?" she screams into my ear. A gust even more powerful than the hurricane we are currently experiencing drags me a few feet away from Jen. I scramble back. What are our options? Harnessing the crazed air lauvan by hand is out of the question, and lighting incense is laughable. The lauvan cable can be a temporary reprieve, but we will never get off this plateau attached to it. What about Bethany's spell?

"*Festina, o Zephyre*," I say as clearly as I can. My words are whipped away from me as soon as they are spoken. "*Irascare, Auster dirus!*"

"What are you doing?" Jen yells. I slip a little further and Wayne's hand tightens like a vise on my ankle.

"Spell. Latin. It worked before. *Consurge, o ventus Boreas! Fles violenter, Eurus currens!*" I pour my whole concentration into the words, willing them to help. I'm out of ideas and out of my depth, high in the sky.

I can hardly see out of my streaming eyes, but is the wind lessening from a hurricane to a gale? Is it my imagination? Jen presses her ear to my mouth and listens intently to my chanting. On the second repeat, she chants the Latin along with me.

"*Festina, o Zephyre…*"

The two voices in tandem accomplish far more than a single voice alone. The wind lessens considerably, enough that we can stand up, albeit still leaning into the wind. The others look to me. I wave them forward impatiently while Jen and I continue to chant.

Alejandro and Wayne reach the trees with Jen not far behind when one more gust appears in a writhing silver cloud heading straight at me. I have no time for a defense, and the power of the gust knocks me off my feet. I roll uncontrollably to the edge of the cliff which is too close at this point. Jen's screaming faintly reaches my ears over the roar of the wind.

My body jolts and comes to a halt. My shoulder wrenches at an uncomfortable angle from a firm grip on my forearm.

"Up, Merry. We've got to get into the trees."

Cecil, you are full of surprises. I stagger to my feet and follow his lead back to the shelter of the forest where the others wait anxiously.

Jen gives me a swift hug then turns to Cecil.

“That was so brave.”

Cecil shrugs nonchalantly, but his lauvan wriggle happily. I put a hand on his shoulder.

“Thank you, Cecil. I am in your debt.” I look at our path and am pleased to see copious amounts of fresh gray lauvan. “I think we’re close. Come on, everyone, follow me.”

I break into a jog, intensely eager to find Drew and finish this battle, face him man on man. I’m tired of dealing with his spirit emissary. I’m the one who’s supposed to have the otherworldly advantage, damn it.

CHAPTER XIX

In the end, it's too easy to find Drew. His lauvan peel off him in clouds like a shedding dog. He hides behind a tree with a view of the plateau, presumably to better witness my demise. Tough luck, Mr. Mordecai.

When he spots our grim-faced group, he takes off in a sprint. Wind swirls frenetically through the fir boughs, directionless.

"There's nowhere to run, Drew Mordecai. Stop and face me like a man."

Drew stops and turns with clear reluctance at the edge of a steep precipice. His eyes dart among us. I'm reminded of a wolverine I cornered, a century ago. It took me hours to heal myself from the wounds.

"Well?" I demand. "No words to defend yourself?"

Alejandro shifts beside me. Drew backs up a step.

"I had to take you out." Drew's voice is raspy. "You stopped the eruption, stopped our plans. I couldn't let that happen."

I put my hand on my chin in a mock show of consideration.

"You couldn't have, I don't know, talked to me? Before trying to kill me? Or worse, those around me?"

"You're too powerful. You even saw the air cluster in your apartment—that was a test, that's when I knew the volcano wasn't a fluke. I have the spirit within me, so I can do Potestas' dirty work."

Drew stands a little straighter at his own words.

"I have the spirit within me," he repeats.

I ignore his posturing. He is feeling in control again, but I want a few answers first.

"How did you find Alejandro?"

“The spirit has many powers. It was simple—I only needed something of his, that ticket stub was perfect—and the spirit twisted his aura to act as a tracking device.”

“The same as Anna put on me.”

My voice is calm, measured, firm. Drew is twitchy and nervous, but when he glances at the swaying tree branches, his shoulders relax. Alejandro steps forward and lays a hand on my shoulder.

“Merlo, let me. Please.”

I look at him in surprise but nod and step aside. Perhaps Alejandro is more diplomatic than I am and can talk Drew down before he attacks again. I would strike first, but I would rather avoid a fight here so there are no innocent casualties. Still, I would like some insurance against Drew escaping, so I catch Wayne’s eye and jerk my head ever-so-slightly. He understands immediately and slides sideways into the trees. To cover him, I cross my arms and pace noisily behind Alejandro. Drew’s eyes track my movements.

“Drew, I know you think you have to kill Merry Lytton to keep your spirit with you. It must be very difficult without the spirit.”

“Difficult?” Drew laughs incredulously. “You have no idea. I can’t go back to that life. This is my only chance. And I can’t have him screw it up.” He points accusingly at me with a shaking finger, and I narrow my eyes. Alejandro continues to speak in a soothing tone.

“You don’t have to kill him. We can talk about this reasonably, come to an agreement. You don’t need to become a murderer.”

Alejandro’s earnest gaze bores into Drew, who stares at him with indecision. I hold my breath. Will Alejandro’s silver tongue win Drew over? If it doesn’t, what do I intend to do with him? Decisions are so much easier in hot-blooded battle than in rational diplomacy. Peace talks were never my forte.

Drew wavers, unsure. A flash of Wayne's black T-shirt appears in the trees behind Drew. Good.

"Come on, Drew," Alejandro says softly. "It doesn't have to be like this."

A heartbeat, two, three…

"There is no other way," Drew spits out, his voice harsh. "Merry Lytton must die. Why am I bothering to talk to you, anyway? I have so much power on my side. You really have no idea." He lifts his arms and tilts his head with closed eyes.

"Now, Wayne!" I shout. Wayne bursts from the trees like a wild boar, and with a mighty yell he tackles the slight Drew to the forest floor.

But Drew has already called upon his spirit. Wind funnels through the trees, breaking branches and tossing fir cones like tiny missiles through the air. I stagger with the force then charge toward Drew. Wayne has him pinned, but a gust full of fir needles smacks Wayne in the face, and he releases Drew involuntarily with a curse. Drew stumbles up and streaks past me. My arm snaps out and snatches a handful of his lauvan. I let go when a huge branch swings toward me, and I leap sideways just in time.

I twist in midair to right myself on contact with the ground. My eyes follow Drew's path. Alejandro and Cecil both charge toward Drew as one, but before they reach him, a dense mass of air lauvan descends from the forest canopy. It splits into two, and each ball streaks toward Drew's attackers. My strangled cry comes too late.

They don't even know what hits them until they are walloped with the force of a speeding car. They both fly through the air with identical expressions of surprise and pain on their faces. Alejandro smacks against the trunk of a large fir and collapses on the ground. Cecil lands on moss but rolls over and over before he stops against a fern-covered rock.

Drew turns to me with a wild light in his eyes.

"Are you ready to die, Merry Lytton?"

"Are you ready to kill, Drew Mordecai? It's both easier and harder than it looks. And I'm more resilient than most."

"I'll take that as a challenge." Drew raises his hands. The air lauvan that usually intertwine with his own now stream out from his fingertips. They plunge toward me as Drew speaks. "I think you're full of hot air. A little more should do the trick."

I attempt a barrier of my own lauvan in the moment before the air lauvan arrive, but the strands dart through mine with ease. They enter my nose and mouth and fill my lungs with a breath I didn't intend to take. At once, my chest feels uncomfortably warm, then hot.

Hot air, indeed. Drew's spirit is cooking me from the inside out.

The burning sensation quickly overwhelms me, but I try to hold onto rational thought. This is a fight against air. Bethany would suggest harnessing the air lauvan myself, but I pull at the lauvan in my mouth without effect. All right, what would Braulio say? The opposite of air is earth. I can't shove rocks down my windpipe…

Or can I? My lungs gasp involuntarily, but I can't expel the burning air. I scramble in the dirt at my feet and scoop a handful of fine dust from the path. Drew's raucous laughter is easy to ignore when my whole being is focused on my burning chest. I close my eyes, throw the dust into the air in front of my face, and breathe in deeply.

I immediately cough as the dust particles irritate my lungs beyond measure, but I don't waste time. I grab any strands I can reach in my mouth, air and earth both, and pull. Whereas before, the spirit-driven air lauvan simply broke between my fingers, now both air and earth threads travel up my throat and bring hot particles of dust out with them. As I hoped, the dust of the earth soaked up heat from the air.

When the burning lessens, I cough up the fine red dust then charge Drew without warning. He staggers backward with a look of panic, and I bowl him over and yank at handfuls of his lauvan. He howls with pain. My fingers close around his neck. Drew's eyes widen in fear.

Silver lauvan spiral up my wrists. Pulses of sharp pain stab deeply into my forearms, and I release Drew with a curse. Drew pushes me off and scrambles up and away. He laughs wildly and runs in Jen's direction—she must have been separated from the others in the chaos. She is near the edge of the precipice.

Drew barrels by, barely noticing her in his haste to escape. Jen—brave, daring girl—grabs his arm. He flails wildly then lowers his shoulder to Jen's chest and checks her.

Time slows. Jen's shocked eyes and open mouth hang, suspended, for too long, yet I can't make my sluggish limbs move fast enough. Her body flies in an arc over the edge.

Jen's scream echoes through the billowing wind until it cuts off, abruptly and completely. My heart drops to my stomach, then rage fills my skull until I can hardly see. I charge toward Drew, heedless of dust devils and falling branches that litter my path. Drew scrambles to get away from my advance. His pitiful efforts are fruitless—I catch up as he attempts to climb over an ancient fallen fir. With a flying leap, I throw my arms around him and we roll to a stop. He wriggles madly, but I press my knee into his chest and he wheezes. I punch him hard in the face, once, and he is stunned enough to stop batting at me with his arms.

One hand wears a silver ring with a small insignia of an arrow. I can only just make it out through the thick air lauvan that cling to it. I rip the ring off Drew and fling it aside where it tumbles into the undergrowth, lost. The silver lauvan intertwined with Drew's own wriggle out and twist into the open air, where they join the dying breezes.

Drew stirs. Hate washes over me, and I want to hurt him. Not for attacking me—I can handle myself. Indeed, it was almost refreshing to have a worthy opponent. But for pushing Jen, that I can't forgive. Small amounts of silver air lauvan drift in and out of Drew's mouth, as they do for everyone. I grasp them in my fist and begin to pull.

Drew's eyes flutter open and he coughs, hacks, tries to draw breath. When it's clear he can't, his hands fly to his throat. I pull the silver threads out of his lungs slowly, inexorably. Our eyes meet. In that moment, he finally knows who he is dealing with. Then his eyes roll back, and he slumps limply to the ground.

I stand and sigh, then turn to where Alejandro and Wayne watch me warily.

"We need to get Jen," I say. "Come on. Drew's not going anywhere soon."

There is no path to the base of the cliff, but we manage to scramble over rocks and past gnarled roots that protrude from the hillside. Jen lies in a small clearing at the bottom of the precipice, its sheer wall looming over her slight body. She is on her side, not moving, with Cecil kneeling beside her. He grasps her hands and speaks quietly near her face. Is she alive? My heart jumps with hope. If she is alive, not all is lost. I leap to Cecil's side.

Jen's eyes, previously locked on Cecil, roll slowly to my face. She is so pale, and her shoulders shudder slightly.

"Jen. You'll be all right. I'll do my best to make it so."

"Merry." Jen's voice is small, wandering. "I can't feel my legs, Merry." She looks surprised to hear her own words, and panic simmers under the surface of her stunned calm. "I can't, I can't—"

"Jen." I smooth her hair away from her face. "Deep breaths. One," I breath in. "Two. And again." She follows my lead. "You trusted me before, now believe me when I say I can help. All right? I will do everything in my power."

She doesn't speak again, just stares at me with her big brown eyes wide. She is on the edge but breathing deeply as I told her to. I turn to Cecil.

"Keep her calm. I'm going to examine her."

"So, what, you're a doctor now?" Cecil snaps.

"Jen needs you, Cecil. Help her."

Cecil glares at me but bends down once again to murmur in Jen's ear. I turn my focus to Jen's body. Beyond a stiffness around her center, likely from her current mental state, the lauvan along her front flow freely. But when I crawl to her other side, the issue is clear. The middle of her back is a tightly bound mess of knots the size of my fist. I carefully lift her shirt, and the bruising has already deepened her skin to a nasty blackish-red.

Wayne has been striding around the clearing for the past minute. He finally stops.

"Ah ha! Reception at last. Now I can call for an ambulance."

He begins to dial, but at a glance from me, Alejandro hits the phone out of his hands.

"Don't dial yet, Wayne." I say. "By the time I'm done, Jen won't need an ambulance."

"What the hell?" Cecil says. "Jen is seriously hurt. She needs a doctor right away."

"I know you have issues with the authorities, Merry,"

Wayne says gravely. “But you can’t decide for others what is best. Jen needs medical attention.”

“Neither of you know exactly what I’m capable of. I understand your hesitation. But you’re right, Wayne, it shouldn’t be up to me. Let Jen decide.” I bend over Jen’s back so she can see my face. “Jen, *carind*, do you remember when your car was totalled, and you woke up and walked away without a scratch?”

“Yes,” she whispers. Her eyes search my face.

“You were hurt in the crash, quite badly. But I healed you then, and I can heal you now, if you’ll let me.”

“Or we can call an ambulance and let the professionals take care of you,” Cecil says loudly.

Jen looks from Cecil to me and back again, then her eyes land on mine.

“How long do you need?”

“Twenty minutes.”

“Okay. Cecil, call for help in twenty minutes if Merry can’t do this.”

I move back to the knot. Jen’s shivering grows to shudders.

“She’s in shock,” Alejandro says. “We need to keep her warm.” He pulls his shirt off and lays it over Jen’s shoulders. We all follow suit. Wayne starts to climb the embankment.

“I’ll keep a lookout for other Potestas members. I know Drew was likely on his own, but it never hurts to be on guard.” He disappears around the cliff side.

I don’t answer. My concentration is focused wholly on the mess of knots before me. Beneath my practiced fingers the threads untangle swiftly, but there are many. Jen continues to shudder, and Cecil murmurs encouraging words while he rubs her hands. Time passes, and my fingers never cease. Alejandro paces, his face pale and strained. Sometimes he watches my hands in their constant motion, sometimes he looks at Cecil with an expression of frustration.

"Five minutes left," Cecil says. He stares at me intensely. I barely glance at him.

"Understood." I'm almost there. It won't be perfect, but Jen will be able to walk again. Perfect can be attained later, without a countdown clock.

I have left the biggest, most important knot until last. It's the final one, the knot that, when unraveled, will snap the vertebrae into place and heal the fractures. Everything else was in preparation for this moment.

"One last thing. I won't lie to you, Jen—it will hurt like nothing else. But then it will all be over."

Jen nods with the smallest inclination of her head.

"All right. One, two…"

I pull the caught lauvan with my fingers, and they spring apart to float freely once more. A crunching, cracking sound emerges from below the former knot and just as quickly ceases. Jen's scream does not. It wrenches out of her throat with an ear-splitting howl, and her body arches. Cecil grasps her arms in shock then glares at me with rage. Alejandro's eyes tell the same story. I raise a hand in conciliation.

"It's done."

Jen's breaths are ragged. I lean over so she can see me. Her eyes flicker up.

"Time to sit up, *carind.*"

"I can't," she whispers. "Not after that. I can't. What if it happens again?"

"It won't. And you don't have to do it alone." I tuck one hand under her waist while the other supports her head and shoulders. "Just relax and let me lift you up. All right?"

Silence, then a slow nod. I tighten my arms and carefully raise her torso. She flinches.

"Relax your body. Let me lift you."

Slowly, eventually, Jen sits upright. I release her but keep a hold on her arms for support. I search her face.

"How do you feel?"

She looks at her legs and wiggles them gently under their shirt blanket.

"They work," she breathes. "I'm okay." Her breath catches in a sob. "I'm okay." Her shoulders shake and her breath comes more and more unevenly. I smooth her hair again and she collapses against me. Her sobs shake her body. Even with her back healed, I'm worried about shock. It's time to calm her down and remind her body that it's not in crisis anymore. I hug her gently and softly sing the first song that surfaces in my mind. It's one of my earliest—a lullaby that my mother sang to me when I was a young child. Jen won't understand the words, but the melody is soothing.

It takes a while for Jen to stop hiccupping. When she is calm enough to speak, she pushes away and looks me squarely in the face.

"I broke my back, and you healed me." She shakes her head and sniffles. "Why you aren't working at the hospital, I'll never know."

"My charity only extends so far." I give her a small smile. "I've never claimed to be a good man—I'll settle for half-decent."

Jen twists experimentally. Her face is expressive with relief at the lack of pain.

"I'll need to readjust you tomorrow. Take it easy until then."

"Thank you, Merry." Jen's smile warms my heart. I help her up, then dig into my pocket and extract my car keys. I toss them to Cecil, who catches them with excellent reflexes considering his startled expression.

"Take Jen home in my car. You've driven stick before,

right?" Cecil nods, and I wiggle my fingers at Jen for her keys. "I would say be careful with the car, but she's so beat up there's not much you can do."

"What about you three?" Jen asks.

"We need to take care of something. I'll bring your car around tomorrow."

Jen nods then accepts Cecil's arm. They hobble up the embankment and disappear. The rest of us shrug our shirts back on.

"You're the real deal," Wayne says. "Fight the wind, heal the sick, can you raise the dead?"

"Sorry, that's not on my list of skills. Not for lack of trying, though."

Wayne lets out a long, low whistle. He looks like he is digesting the new worldview I've exposed him to.

"How about you?" he asks Alejandro. "This doesn't shake you up?"

"I've known for a while." Alejandro give me a half-smile. "Merlo's an old family friend."

"This is too weird," Wayne says. "I'm looking forward to watching TV tonight and thinking about absolutely nothing at all."

"Before we fulfill your wish, I need to take care of a certain someone first." I jerk my thumb up the cliff. Alejandro blanches.

"I forgot about him. What do we do with the body? Will someone start looking for him? What will we say to the police?"

"You think he's dead? God forbid that I should offend modern sensibilities by killing the son of a bitch. Besides, I don't need the hassle. Come on, let's drag his hide back to the car."

The others follow me silently to the top of the hill where Drew's supine body lies in a tangle of Oregon grape bushes. I don't blame Alejandro for wondering. It must have looked like I sucked the life out of him.

"Good, he's still out. I stripped the spirit off him—it must have been a shock to the system. Oh, and when I suffocated him, that likely didn't help."

Alejandro restrains himself from commenting, and says only, "Let's take him to the car." He hoists a leg. Wayne tucks his hands under Drew's arms, and I lift the other leg. We set a good pace, despite our ungainly tromping through undergrowth. The plateau gives me a moment's hesitation, but the only wind is a gentle breeze that cools the back of my neck.

At the car, we unceremoniously fold Drew into the backseat. I hand the keys to Wayne and climb in after Drew.

"You want me to drive?"

"Please. I need to rearrange some of Drew's lauvan." It's necessary for my plan to work.

"And where are we taking 'the body,' after all?"

I quickly search on my phone while I hold up one finger for Wayne to wait. The address I look for appears, and I say it out loud.

"Drew should be out of the way there," I say. "And with any luck, he'll be free of his need to hunt me down."

"That's a good idea," Alejandro says with approval. "See, you're a good guy after all."

"Sure, if I'm allowed to claim decisions made for my own selfish reasons that happen to benefit others. Then, I'm one of the best."

Wayne pulls out of the parking lot, and we cruise down the mountain. I have my hands full with Drew's lauvan, but the job doesn't require a lot of concentration.

"I want to say thank you, Wayne. For your quick thinking and quicker reflexes, for coming along to help, for buying into the madness in the first place."

"No sweat. Thanks for letting me tag along." He grins at me in the rear-view mirror. "It's been a rush."

"And thank you both for coming to save me," Alejandro says with feeling. "Drew was so crazy, I thought I was done."

"Your gratitude is misplaced, on my part," I say, my fingers wrapped in gray threads. "You were only in danger because of me."

"Come on, Merlo, you can't blame yourself for what this lunatic did. If you truly believed that, you wouldn't have any friends."

"I told you I was selfish."

"Well, I'm glad. No one should hide away just to avoid hurt."

I'm attempting that very strategy in my love life, according to Dr. Dilleck, except I'm more worried about my own pain than someone else's.

My thoughts turn to Drew. I had hoped, for one exhilarating moment, that I had found someone like me. Ever since I discovered Potestas, I have been watching carefully for signs. What Drew could do with his spirit companion—it was so like my own powers. Perhaps I'm getting closer to answers, answers about myself that I have been searching for, fruitlessly, for centuries. Perhaps it's time to delve deeper into Potestas.

"How did you let Jen slip into 'just friends,' Merry?" Wayne breaks my reverie. Alejandro glances at him. "You two seem pretty tight, and you aren't the type to let a pretty girl get away. Is it because she was a student?"

"That wouldn't have stopped me. No, she can do better. She has a bright future ahead, and it's not with me. In the meantime, we get on well."

"Fair enough." Wayne eyes me in the mirror. "Do you predict the future, too?"

I laugh and tie the last knot above Drew's left eyebrow.

"No. I know myself, that's all."

"Look, there it is." Alejandro points out the windshield. "Is Drew ready?"

"Yes. I'll wake him up now." One tweak of his lauvan, and Drew sits up groggily. "Nice of you to join us, Drew. I'm Michael, and this is Wilf and Alberto. We're your friends, and we've come to support you as you check yourself into rehab. Understand?"

"Yes," Drew murmurs.

"You will tell the attendant that you wish to stay for the maximum time in order to fully clean up. And not to allow any visitors except for me, Michael Smith. Got it?"

Drew nods blankly.

"Now look lively and go."

Drew snaps to attention and opens the door. He steps out smartly and closes it with a firm hand then marches up the steps.

"Will it work?" Wayne says hesitantly.

"I'm sure it will," Alejandro says confidently. "Merlo is very good at this."

"More stories from your uncle?" I say. He grins back at me. I lean forward. "Let's find a pub. Drinks are on me."

"Now you're talking," Wayne says.

Drinks went a long way toward masking the discomfort of my minor cuts and bruises, but now that I'm back in my own bed, I might as well untangle my lauvan to save myself some pain in the morning when the alcohol wears off. I'm alone with my thoughts. Alejandro's snores from the living room are a gentle backdrop to their meanderings.

My immediate threat is vanquished now that Drew is safely

ensconced in the rehab center. It won't be for long, but perhaps he can shake his addiction and won't need a spirit possessing him. It works for some people.

Potestas, though, is a stickier pot of honey. If they want me alive, why did they support Drew's machinations? If they want me dead, why didn't they try harder? Perhaps they don't care about me one way or another, which my ego rebels against but my head hopes for.

I want to know more about the organization. How do they recruit? My only link is Anna. I glance down at my center. The threads of my connections emerge from it, brightly colored at my center but fading to transparency an arm-span from my body. Alejandro's green shoots in the direction of the living room, and Jen's deep gold travels south. I have a few new ones, interestingly: Wayne's rust-colored lauvan and a midnight blue I recognize as Dr. Dilleck's. I suppose my candid dialog with my therapist went deeper than I thought. Conspicuous in its absence is Anna's purple.

This is worrisome. It was only a few days ago that we slept together, far too soon for a natural fading away. A dramatic cut like that usually indicates death.

What happened to Anna?

I finish up the last of my knots. I shouldn't care, but I can't help wondering if she came to harm during her confinement. A quiet curse escapes my lips, and I rise from my bed.

Alejandro continues his slumber, uninterrupted by my passage. The balcony door slides closed with a soft click, and a gentle breeze lifts my hair. A few pulls of lauvan, and my feathered form soars toward the half-full moon.

The city glows with a thousand twinkling lights gleaming like miniature fires far below my wings. Flying is so refreshing that I have to mentally shake myself to stay on task. There is no lauvan connection to follow, so I'm searching by memory for a house that I've only visited once on the ground.

I circle above the general neighborhood until the streets grow familiar and I can swoop down to the white house, yellow in the dim light of a streetlamp.

All the lights are off. I fly past the kitchen window once, twice, thrice. When I am certain the kitchen is empty, I flap my wings hard to gain altitude for the flight home.

Whatever happened to Anna, it's not likely the result of my actions. That is as much information as I can glean. I hope she isn't dead. Life for mortals is short enough without it ending prematurely, and I wouldn't wish that on her. Besides, she was my only link to Potestas. Now, how do I proceed?

CHAPTER XX

Dreaming

A longhouse emerges though the trees, a rectangular wooden structure with a vast thatched roof. The sun sends dappled patterns on the dead leaves that crunch under our horses' hooves. The air has a scent of decay and approaching autumn. I sigh in discontent.

"I don't know how you talked me into this. Visiting Morgan is a bad idea. For me, at least."

"It's been years, Merlin," says Arthur. "Surely she's forgiven you by now."

"I doubt it. Women have extremely long memories and are highly accomplished at holding grudges. Can you believe I haven't spoken to her since she left your father's house?"

Arthur rubs his chin thoughtfully. A chicken wanders past the longhouse, visible even from this distance.

"I can believe it. She visits only rarely, and you make yourself scarce when she does."

"Avoidance—not the most honorable strategy, but I never claimed to be proud of my dealings with Morgan."

"Whatever did happen?" Arthur eyes me with consideration. "The last time I asked, years ago now, you said I was too young."

"Nothing barbaric. I simply failed to deny certain assumptions she made, namely that I would ask Uther for her hand. When he announced her betrothal to Idris, and I said nothing in return…"

"Ah." Arthur laughs lightly. "I can see why Morgan would take offense. Poor Morgan—she's too proud for that sort of treatment."

"As I said, it wasn't my finest moment. Perhaps she has forgotten by now. Miracles can happen."

"Doubtful. You'd better brace yourself." Arthur slows his horse to a walk as we approach the house. Two figures emerge from the front door at the thud of our hoofbeats on the packed earth. One conceals a rounded stomach under her dress.

"Arthur Pendragon," says Vivienne. "And Merlin. Welcome. My master and mistress are out but will be back shortly. You may wait inside if you wish." She waves at our horses and addresses her companion, an older man with rough spun clothing. "Take their horses to the barn and look after them."

The man nods, and we pass the reins to him.

"It's Vivienne, isn't it?" says Arthur. Vivienne nods and looks surprised that Arthur remembered. "You came to the battle camp a few months ago."

"That's right."

"Hello, Vivienne," I say. "Any sign of Mordred? He wouldn't want to run into me."

Vivienne raises a brow but says only, "He is away."

"Where?"

A shrug, but her lauvan tell me she knows.

"He's likely visiting the other lords," Arthur says. "Trying to turn them against the truce. See, Merlin? This is exactly why we needed to come."

I sigh.

"I fear you're right."

"Can I offer you some refreshments?" Vivienne says. "Come inside, please."

We follow her through the open door, and she directs us to benches by a low fire. Although it's a sunny day, the air has a hint of coolness that makes a fire welcome. Vivienne takes our cloaks and lays them carefully over a chest along one plastered wall. When she turns to us again, the tiny cluster of pale pink lauvan over her stomach wriggle, at odds with the movements of Vivienne's own lauvan. She grimaces momentarily.

"An active little one, I see," I say with a smile. Vivienne purses her lips.

"Always. May I offer you some wine?"

"It pays to be family, Arthur. Breaking open the wine for us? Our lucky day."

"We'll both have some," Arthur answers Vivienne, who disappears through a door in the far wall. I stretch my legs out comfortably. Arthur looks around with interest and notices three sleeping dogs near the fire.

"Morgan's hound must have pupped. Look at those two."

"Very nice," I say with only a cursory glance at the dogs. "Are you ready to speak to Idris? Do you know what you'll say?"

Arthur tightens his lips. He looks older than his twenty-five years in the firelight, grim and resolute.

"I think so. I'm not too hopeful about this meeting, honestly, but we need to try. Their dissonant voices are upsetting our unity. Given a bad harvest, or enough talk, and the other lords may start to listen to Idris."

"There are a few unshakeable loyals on your side. But I agree, men are fickle when they're frightened. Eliminating the temptation is a sound move."

Vivienne returns, bearing two wooden cups half-full of warm wine with an aroma of cinnamon. I sniff appreciatively.

"Many thanks, Vivienne. By the way, you're looking well. Is motherhood suiting you?"

"When I'm not kicked awake by the little monster, yes." Vivienne eases herself onto my bench with a relieved sigh.

"Merlin, tell her what the baby will be like," says Arthur. He takes a sip of wine, then looks alarmed. "You told me she knows, right?"

"Yes, she knows."

Vivienne places a hand on her stomach. She looks wary.

"How?"

I put my hands out toward her stomach but stop short of her lauvan.

"May I?"

"It won't hurt the baby?"

"Not in the slightest."

She removes her hand reluctantly and makes no move to stop my own. Carefully, I pluck one frail pink lauvan from the cluster and close my eyes. My own lauvan gently twist around the baby's lauvan. The connection opens my mind to the baby's personality. In one so small, personality is mostly unformed, but there is a faint echo of the person to come if I concentrate. As I quiet my thoughts, hints of the future person swim into my mind. "Strong-willed," I say at last. "No surprise there. The child will keep you on your toes. But there is a generosity of spirit here that is worth cultivating. This child will make you proud if you allow it to. You won't regret it."

I open my eyes to see Vivienne's moist ones. She dashes tears away with the back of her hand.

"This pregnancy is making me soft."

"I hear that's common." I smile at her, and she returns a reluctant one of her own. "The baby will appreciate it, even if you don't."

Vivienne sniffs and sits up, self-possessed once more.

"Thank you, Merlin." She tilts her head and listens. Voices and the thud of horse hooves drift through the closed door. "My master and mistress are here. I must greet them—please excuse me."

When Vivienne passes through the front door, I turn to Arthur.

"Ready to face your sister?"
Arthur nods, his lips tight.
"Ready as I'll ever be."

CHAPTER XXI

I walk out behind stragglers of my last class the next day to find Jen waiting for me.

"Hi, Jen. I'm glad you're here. Turn around and let me look." She twirls slowly and the reforming knots in the lauvan on her back become evident. "Yes, I need to fix those knots. It's too bad I didn't get them when I picked up my car last night. How are you feeling?"

"A little sore. Can I get a ride to your place? I'm meeting Alejandro there."

"Of course. I'm parked in the north lot."

That's interesting. I wonder why she's meeting Alejandro? His connecting lauvan pull from Jen's center like a taut string in the direction of my apartment.

We keep the conversation light until a few blocks from the apartment. Jen uses a small silence to change the subject.

"It's hard to believe my back was broken yesterday. Have you done that before?"

"Yes." She might feel better about her optimistic prognosis if there is a success story in my past. As predicted, her lauvan ripple with relief.

"What happened then?"

"My friend fell off his horse the wrong way and landed on the side of a stone bridge. He was fine after I'd dealt with him."

"A horse?" Jen raises her eyebrows then shakes her head. "That's good to hear. Do you remember, you sang to me after you healed me? What was the song? I couldn't recognize the language, but it was really beautiful."

Jen's lauvan are tense and waiting, at odds with her casual demeanor. She is onto me. I try to dissemble.

"It was an old lullaby my mother sang to me when I was

small. I don't know what the language is. Nonsense words, I always assumed."

Jen's lauvan grow stiff to match her frustrated voice when she speaks.

"You know as well as I do that's a lie," she says sharply. "Please don't insult my intelligence." When I don't respond, she sighs. "There's something going on, and I wish you would tell me. Your secrets are building a barrier between us. You can tell me anything, you know that, right? There can't be anything weirder than lauvan, and I managed to come to grips with that."

I let out a mirthless chuckle involuntarily. What is stranger, immortality or otherworldly powers? One day, I will let her decide. But not today.

"I don't know what to tell you, except that I'm not ready to share with you yet. Correction, I don't think you are ready to know."

Jen looks out of the front windshield, her jaw tight.

"Then you'd better make me ready if you want to stay friends. Whatever this is, it's getting in the way."

Damn. Has this issue come to a head already? She isn't wrong—I can feel her discontent brewing between us, and she's too inquisitive to let it slide—but I can't tell her yet. It was only a few short weeks ago that I told her about the lauvan, and that was a rocky transition. It will have to be soon, though. I will need to decide on the best approach for Jen, the best way to broach the subject that will not scare her off immediately.

Fortunately, we are close to the apartment building, because the silence in the car is thick and stifling. The elevator ride is no better—Jen is grim and I'm contemplative—and it's a relief to open my door and hear Alejandro's cheery greeting.

"Merlo, Jen, hello. I'm almost ready, Jen." Alejandro disappears into the bathroom, and I wave toward the kitchen.

"Drink?"

"No, thanks," Jen says stiffly. "We're leaving soon."

That was a dismissal, loud and clear. I walk into my bedroom without another word and drop my satchel on the bed. Keys and wallet end up on the dresser. I dither by the window for a moment, then get angry with myself. It's my apartment—I won't be stuck foolishly in here waiting for Jen to leave, like a wayward child. If she doesn't want to talk to me, she can leave.

Jen's back is to me, my sketchbook open on the table in front of her. A flare of annoyance is quickly washed out by a wave of resignation. People are what they are, and Jen isn't one to let a good mystery go unsolved. How can I be angry at her when curiosity is an inborn human trait?

I pace silently across the room until I am behind her. The page is open to Isabella, my sixth wife I met while in what is now Spain during the Umayyad dynasty. She was an outspoken butcher's daughter, and a spark of mischief peeks out through her painted eyes, even through the stiff artistry of the early eleventh century. I always drew the best I could with the most progressive techniques at the time, but this was a long time before the advances of the Renaissance. The parchment is singed from edge to binding, and my heart contracts.

My hand reaches over Jen's shoulder to gently close the charred cover. Jen jumps guiltily.

"That's too far, Jen," I say softly. I can't bring myself to show indignation, and I slide the sketchbook back onto the bookshelf. I turn to face Jen, and her eyes are wary. "I will tell you soon, I promise." Jen's eyebrows twitch in disbelief and hope. "Give me a little time to figure out the best way how. All right?"

Jen nods. I turn her around by her shoulders and sit her on a chair.

"Now, sit still while I fix your lauvan."

There isn't much to tinker with, and I finish just as Alejandro saunters into the room.

"Are you ready, Jen?"

"Yes, she is."

"Oh, that's better." Jen stands up and touches her toes carefully. "Thanks, Merry. Bye." She gives me a small wave.

I nod back and they leave. The apartment is too quiet when they go. If Jen can't accept my truth, it will be this silent for a long while. I will have to leave Vancouver—my comfortable job, my apartment, my new friend Wayne—and find somewhere new to hang my hat. At least I can stay in contact with Alejandro. That's something. I wonder what Tokyo is like these days. I haven't spent enough time in Asia, but now that the world is so cosmopolitan, it's easier to travel to places where I don't visually fit in.

What am I doing? I should be planning how to tell Jen, not plotting my escape.

I should do both.

Dr. Dilleck looks tired. The lauvan covering her eyes are sparse. I wonder again what she is coming to terms with. Whatever it is, she is losing sleep over it. She is silent about our meeting in Steveston, so I follow her cue and don't mention it.

"How are you today, Merry?"

"Fine, thank you."

"That's good to hear. What emotions are surfacing for you today?"

I think carefully. Jen immediately springs to mind.

"Frustration, resignation, fear." I think of Alejandro and Wayne fighting at my side against Drew. "Gratitude, triumph." Then Anna slinks through my thoughts, sexy and duplicitous and missing. "Anger and mistrust."

"That's better. Thank you, Merry. I see we have a lot to discuss today."

She moves suddenly to touch her head with a grimace.

"Are you all right?"

"Yes, thank you." She quickly covers her pain with a forced smile. "Just a headache. Now, you mentioned frustration first. What triggers that emotion for you today?"

"A friend of mine wants me to tell her something I've been carefully hiding for good reason. Honestly, I don't know how she'll react when I tell her—it could be the start of a much closer friendship, or the end of what we have."

"You said 'when' you tell her. Not if?"

"If I don't tell her, she'll drift away. It has to be done."

"Resignation. But you're fearful she'll react badly."

"I don't have enough people in my life that I can afford to lose one."

Dr. Dilleck presses her hand to her temple once more then withdraws it quickly. She looks at her notes to cover her actions, but her lauvan are more conversant. They act oddly—there are spasms of discomfort and some strange behavior toward me. Some twitch sporadically as if nervous of me, and a few twist sinuously in my direction in motions that indicate attraction. It's intriguing, but mystifying. Attraction is well and good, but why the nervousness? I haven't said anything too off-putting in these sessions, have I?

"What about the gratitude and triumph?"

"A few new friends really pulled through for me, and we managed to beat the odds."

"That's wonderful news, Merry. How does it feel that

somebody has your back?"

I smile.

"Pretty good." From the mess of brown lauvan at my center sprouts a cluster of multicolored ones. I'm beginning to amass quite the collection of connections. With interest, I note that the navy-blue strands that connect me to Dr. Dilleck have increased in number. My eyes travel up to hers. Her eyes are even more beautiful now that I can see them better through her lauvan.

"And lastly, the anger and mistrust. What do those spring from?"

Another blue lauvan snakes through the air from Dr. Dilleck's center, and to my surprise is readily met by one of mine. What is going on here? I didn't think we were getting close enough for a rate of connection like this—I'm sharing plenty about myself, but it's entirely one-sided.

"Anger at myself, mainly. You remember I told you about Anna coming to my place? Well, it turns out that she was only there to—well, for purposes other than seeing me." It's getting difficult to remember what I've told Dr. Dilleck and what I want to keep hidden. "Hence the mistrust. It was foolish to let her in again. I knew she was bad news, but she seemed sincere."

"It's not a crime to look for the good in people," she says gently.

"Perhaps. I should have known better, though. I was just—lonely." I smile despite myself. "There's that word again."

Dr. Dilleck smiles back.

"It's good to recognize when it crops up. Nicely done."

It feels strange on one level to discuss my romantic encounters with Dr. Dilleck considering the ever-increasing lauvan strands between us, but entirely natural for the same reason.

"Something else came up this week. A book of pictures, of my wife and others I've lost, was almost destroyed. I lost control. A friend managed to talk me down, but it made me realize how reliant I am on the book to preserve my memories."

"Memories are certainly important. They are how we define ourselves, shape our future. But be cautious about letting your past rule you."

We speak a little more about memories. Near the end of our session, I'm blindsided by Dr. Dilleck's next statement.

"I'm afraid we will have to stop our sessions, Merry. I'm reducing my practice size for personal reasons." Her lauvan squirm with the lie. She is only dropping me. Why? "I can recommend Dr. Simon down the hall. He's a terrific therapist. I can have reception transfer your files if you like."

I don't know what to say. I'm bewildered and a little hurt. Why would she get rid of me, alone? I thought we had a good rapport, and I never got the sense that she felt otherwise. Am I somehow the cause of her anxiety? I have no interest in seeing another therapist—I only started this for fun. I have lasted this long without a shrink; I can manage without one again.

But as I contemplate the future without our meetings, it looks very bleak. I enjoy my time with Dr. Dilleck, speaking freely about the workings of my head without worrying about too much filtering.

All this hits me in an instant, then I smooth my features, paste on a smile, and reach forward to shake Dr. Dilleck's hand.

"Thank you for our sessions. I wish you all the best in the future." I stand. "No need to pass on my files. Goodbye, Dr. Dilleck."

She stands as well, looking taken aback at my alacrity.

"Goodbye, Merry. Be well."

My eyes rake over her face once more. Is this really it? Why do I feel so lost when I imagine my future without her in it? It's likely a common reaction, feeling strangely close to someone to whom you've opened your mind.

I leave quickly. Time to move on. I can handle my own thoughts from hereon out.

CHAPTER XXII

Dreaming

I close the door against the bitterly cold Norwegian night full of blazing stars and turn to face Koll. I push my hood back from my lye-bleached hair so he can see my face. He looks puzzled and takes off his bearskin hat slowly.

"Please sit, Koll. I need to tell you something." I take a deep breath. I have grown close to Koll over the past year. We have worked in the fields together, drank the same mead, even journeyed on a raid to Alban a few months ago. Only one other person in this village knows my whole truth, but it's time to tell Koll. He is too perceptive for me to keep it from him for much longer.

"I'm listening." He remains standing. I brace myself against the cold wooden door.

"I haven't told you the whole truth about myself. I'm much older than I look. Much, much older." I pause to assess Koll's reaction. He looks skeptical, so I plough ahead. "I've lived for hundreds of years, never dying, traveling where no one will recognize me. I don't know how, or why. I was born of a woman, long ago, so I am a man. But more than that, I don't know."

Koll's body and lauvan are both completely still. I can't tell yet what he is truly thinking. I try to soften the news, bring Koll's focus back to our friendship.

"I wanted to tell you because you've been like a brother to me, and I couldn't bear keeping secrets from you."

Koll says nothing for a long moment. His breathing becomes heavier and heavier. Panic flickers in his eyes, which dart to the corner where his sword hangs. I know what he will do a moment before he does it. He lunges sideways to grab his sword and unsheathes it in one smooth motion.

The sword tip lands on my neck. I haven't moved. I'm mourning the loss of our friendship, of my life in this village. I had hoped to remain here for some years to come. I truly thought Koll was ready. How could I be so wrong, yet again? How long will it take before I can predict the outcome of my truth-telling?

"What are you?" he breathes, his eyes wild. "Get away from me. Stay away! I should kill you right now, here where you stand."

I'm suddenly weary, so weary. Why do I try so hard to stay alive? Perhaps I should let Koll slit my throat. It would be a quick death, after all. I have seen it often enough.

But I can't do that. Prophesies and promises swirl in my mind, and I grab a handful of Koll's lauvan before he can react. While he doubles over, wheezing, I twist the sword out of his hands and throw it to the corner of the room.

"I'm sorry you feel this way," I say clearly over Koll's labored breaths. "Know that I always wished you well." I turn and fling the door open to the stars.

Another page turns in the endless book of my life. What's next?

I run to the house of Gunnar, my other friend here. His wooden house is dark and snug against the cold. I knock softly at the threshold. Gunnar appears at the door, his face bleary with sleep.

"It's late, Meldun. My woman and children are sleeping. What is it?"

"I told Koll, and he didn't take it well." I shiver. The night is frigid, and disappointment and fear are getting the better of me. "I need to leave, and quickly. But I didn't want to go without saying farewell."

Gunnar's face drops with sadness.

"You're leaving?"

"For good, I'm afraid. We'll not meet again."

In the distance I hear shouting. Faintly, the word "Meldun" floats on the air. I wince.

"They're after me. We'd best not be seen together."

"Come in for a moment. No one has seen you yet." He pulls me forward and slams the door shut. I hear him fumbling next to the coals of the fire, then he returns with a bundle wrapped in a cloth.

"Bread and meat for your journey, and a flask of mead for warmth." He throws his arms around me in a great bear hug then releases me with moist eyes. "You can be sure I'll give Koll a piece of my mind."

"You'll do no such thing," I say sharply. "You must distance yourself from my memory, for the sake of your life here, you and your family's. In fact, you should take your cloak and go join the manhunt. Please, I want to know you are above suspicion."

Gunnar hesitates but finally nods.

"Where will you go?"

I shrug and try to smile for his sake.

"Wherever the winds take me. Thank you for your friendship, Gunnar. And goodbye."

He raises a hand in farewell. I pull the door open and slip through silently. The bundle tucks into my shirt, then I gather the necessary lauvan for a transformation. I've recently experimented with a new form, a small yet swift falcon, and I find its uses unparalleled. For example, as an escape route.

My wings pull my body powerfully up into the air and through the starlit night. Another false step, another move. I ought to be more judicious in my choice of confidantes, but I was so sure of Koll. My wingbeats thrust me ever forward, onward, to the long future that lies before me. Next time I will be more careful. Next time I will be certain.

The wheelchair squeaks on every rotation, a discordant counterpoint to the chirping of birds flitting above us. Leaves drift down to the asphalt path and crunch beneath my feet.

"I love this time of year," Josephine says dreamily. "The air is crisp, the trees are colorful, and the apples are sweet. Not that I've had any this year, but I'm sure they are."

"They are indeed," I assure her. Josephine's appetite has been minimal in the last few months as her health deteriorates. "I'll buy some when you're up for it."

"That sounds lovely. Stop at the bench—I love this view." Before us lies a garden of roses with a few late bloomers gamely hanging on. Beyond lies a calm, unruffled lake. I wheel the chair to face the garden and sit on the bench with my hand on Josephine's. She squeezes it.

"Do you have to give yourself wrinkles and gray hair?" she says plaintively. "Now that I'm staying in the hospital, I never get to see your true face. We could pretend you're my son."

"I don't fancy the Oedipal connotations. What if we spend some time in your room later? I'll read to you, and we'll tell the nurse to leave you alone."

"It's a deal." Josephine carefully settles deeper in her chair and closes her eyes. The skin under them is a translucent gray and so fragile looking. I rub her knuckles with my thumb. The snarled lauvan at her center draw my eyes involuntarily. I have spent so many hours trying to untangle that mess, but my powers don't work on every ill.

"It's not really fair to you, is it?" Josephine says without opening her eyes.

"What isn't?"

"That you have endless life but marry someone with a shorter one than usual."

"Not fair to me?" I laugh incredulously, then bring her hand to my lips tightly. It's a minute before I can speak. "No. In life, fairness is rarely a factor."

"At least we had a good time, even if it was too short. It was fun, wasn't it? I couldn't imagine spending my life with anyone else."

"It was the best," I agree. "The very best."

"Oh, you. I'll bet you said that to all your wives."

My lips twitch in response to her teasing smile.

"Perhaps, but it doesn't make it any less true."

Josephine opens her eyes and lifts her frail arm to caress my salt-and-pepper hair, carefully constructed this morning in the bathroom mirror of our little bungalow on the lake. Ten years we have lived here—made friends, bought groceries, I even worked as a pastry chef for a hotel in town—and now Josephine's time is almost up.

"Merlo?"

"Hmm?"

"Where do you think you'll go after this?" Her fingernails run the length of my scalp in a hypnotic motion, but not enough to distract me from the pain her question lances through my heart.

"Must we talk about it? Denial is much more comfortable."

"Indulge me. I'd like to imagine you happy and well in the future. Oh, do you think you'll take up with a disco girl, feathered hair, platform shoes and all?" Josephine chuckles, then smooths my hair and looks at me with a critical eye. "I think you could pull off longer hair."

"I'll have you know I'm particularly handsome with

flowing locks. Exactly the right mix of rugged and good-looking." Even as I play along with Josephine's teasing, my mind actively closes off from thoughts of the future. A long span of darkness is all I can see, opaque and complete. I don't need to tell Josephine that, though. Firstly, because she should only have to deal with her own pain. Secondly, because doubtless she already knows.

"I believe it. You'd be my handsome Merlo no matter your hair length." She takes my hand again and we watch geese floating by on the gentle currents. Josephine is due back soon for her pain medications, but we have a little longer. She squeezes my fingers. "Will you visit the Eiffel tower after I'm gone? We never had the chance, and I'd like to think of you up there, in the sky above Paris. I know you've been before, but still."

"Of course, Josie, of course. Anywhere."

"Just there. When you cremate me, you could take some ashes up—no, forget I said that. That sounds far too turbulent. I'd like you to sprinkle me in water. Not the ocean, it's far too big."

"The river?"

"Too fast—it doesn't sound very restful. No, put me in the lake. Borrow the neighbor's dingy and drop the ashes in the middle. Yes, the lake would be lovely."

"The lake it is." I almost welcome the assigned task. At least it is one structured thing I can picture myself doing before the dark void swallows me.

"Good. I'm glad I remembered to mention that." Josephine leans forward with a wince and peers intently out to the water. "Merlo, look. Is that a green kingfisher?"

I follow her gaze. The unmistakable large-beaked profile and white collar of a green kingfisher glides low over the water. It's a rare sighting on this northern lake, although more common in Josephine's hometown in southern Texas.

"Looks like it. It's a long way from home."

"I used to love them as a girl. As comfortable in water as in the air. Oh, look!"

The bird dives gracefully into the lake and disappears. Josephine sighs peacefully.

"A little taste of home. All right, honey, I'm ready to go."

CHAPTER XXIII

Alejandro is peppy this morning at breakfast, spreading jam and crunching toast with gusto. I eye him over my coffee. He finally notices, and hurriedly gulps down his mouthful.

"What?"

"You haven't done much sightseeing on your trip so far. I've monopolized your time with such mundane events as car chases and kidnappings."

"It's been great. No, really," he says when I raise an eyebrow. "It's true. Unconventional, but exciting."

He is telling the truth, amazingly. His lauvan slide slowly in contentedness. He has proven himself to be a worthy companion and a credit to Braulio.

"If you have no plans this morning, perhaps you'd like an aerial tour of the city."

I wait a minute for my meaning to sink in. When it does, Alejandro's lauvan give a tremendous jolt and his eyes widen.

"Do you mean—change? Into a bird?" He grips the side of the table in his excitement.

"It's cheaper than a helicopter."

"Yes! Yes, I'm ready!" He leaps up and nearly knocks over his chair in the process. I laugh loudly and gesture to his food on the table.

"Finish your breakfast. First rule of transformation: only change on a full stomach. It's difficult to fight an animal's survival instincts, and staving off hunger is not natural."

Alejandro sits reluctantly, and his lauvan continue to dance in happy agitation. He crams toast into his mouth as quickly as is decent.

"You're eating like it's going out of fashion. Don't worry, the skies will still be there when you're done. This gives us time to set up a few ground rules."

"Air rules?"

"Just so. Keep a clear idea in your mind of your human self. Perhaps a memory of an activity you enjoy, or a person you love. Refer to it often, to remind yourself to keep the bird at bay." Alejandro looks worried, so I add, "It's more straightforward in the moment. Don't fret, you'll be fine. Stick close to me. Remember, I'm the only one who can release you from your bird form. Still want to do this?"

"Absolutely," Alejandro says, his eyes shining.

"All right. Finished your breakfast? Then come to the balcony."

I move to the glass door, but Alejandro is already ahead of me. He slides the door open and steps into the cool fresh air of an early summer's morning, more typical than the heat streak of late. I follow and position Alejandro to face me.

"Stand still. This will take a few moments. It's been a while."

"Does it hurt?" Alejandro asks with curiosity, not fear. I shake my head and gather the necessary lauvan. I will need to knot Alejandro's strands for him to fly free of me.

"It feels strange, but not painful."

I think for a moment, then twist three strands around my index finger. It's been a very long time since I've recreated this form, but I think I remember.

"What kind of bird will I be? You won't really make me a pigeon, will you?"

I shrug, not willing to spoil the surprise. I have no use for pigeons, brainless flock birds that they are. I have never bothered to learn their form.

"Are you getting picky, now? Flying isn't enough for you?" One last knot, and I straighten up. "One tweak, and you'll transform. Are you ready?"

"Always." Alejandro's lauvan that aren't tied up are tense with anticipation. He has an innate bravery that keeps surprising me.

I pull the lynchpin lauvan, and all the knots I have carefully constructed fall into place. Alejandro dissolves before my eyes and reforms closer to the ground as a large, glossy-feathered golden eagle. I grin when the eagle stretches its wings and peers at them quizzically, then I yank my own lauvan to transform myself into my usual merlin falcon.

I don't waste any time. My beak opens in a shrill cry that clearly says *come*. Alejandro's wings stretch in reply. I thrust my own wings out and down to leap into the sky. A whoosh from behind tells me Alejandro follows.

We catch an updraft and ride it high in the air until the cars shrink to lines of shiny beetles inching along their paths. Alejandro shrieks his excitement. I cut across the wind and clip his wing with mine. When he soars after me, I fold my wings and drop in a heart-stopping dive.

Alejandro is right beside me as if he anticipated my move. We plummet to earth, and I'm overtaken with a fierce joy to share this with someone again.

Wayne and I are on the roof again for lunch. The weather has turned, and our heat streak is over.

"Looks like rain," Wayne says. He points westward at a bank of darker clouds on the horizon. "Hopefully only rain. What do you think, any sign of unseasonable fog or wind?"

"There's been no sign of anything unnatural since we dropped Drew off. Perhaps Potestas has no more interest in me. I believe we'll be able to enjoy our lunch in peace."

Wayne takes a reflective bite of his sandwich.

"No more attacks, hey? That's good news. Although I doubt this organization will ignore you going forward. I did a little digging last night, and I found that all four of those businesses—you know, the cupcake shop, the lawyer—they all have some connection to the same corporation. It's called Feynman Inc."

"Never heard of it."

"No, neither had I. There wasn't much information readily available, but I'll look around a little more. See if we can't track down some names or addresses."

"That would be great." I'm still amazed and gratified by Wayne's speedy acceptance and willingness to jump in feet first. It doesn't happen often.

"So, your powers. You can move things around, change the shape of objects, see the wind."

"Correct."

"And you can mess with people's minds."

Ah, here it is. I'm surprised no one has mentioned it before now.

"In a manner of speaking," I say cautiously. "I can affect a person's mood or emotions. For example, with Drew, I made him very susceptible to suggestion. It doesn't last for long, and it doesn't work on everybody, but I'll admit it is useful at times."

"I'll bet." Wayne looks out over the roof to the empty lawn. The dark clouds loom closer. "What's your take on the ethics of making people do things against their will?"

"It's not great, I'll admit. I only rarely pull it out. But when the choice is death or lauvan, I don't hesitate. Or," I think of the bouncer at the club. "When it truly doesn't affect anyone."

"Murky waters, Merry."

"I know." I grin at him. "You'd better stick around and keep me in line."

Wayne holds up his water bottle in a salute.

"Will do."

The rain starts, a gentle pattering of wetness that brings the promise of fresh coolness, renewal, and change. For the better? I don't know.

"I guess that's lunch." Wayne stands. "Come on, back to the grindstone. Papers don't read themselves. Unless you have a power for that?"

"I wish."

I'm home early and not sure what to do. I wander through the kitchen, but there's no point in cooking if I'm not hungry. In the living room, my fingers pluck the strings of my harp experimentally, but I'm not in the mood to make music. I could go out and do one of the thousands of new and exciting things this modern world has to offer, but at the moment I'm nostalgic for the past.

Where is my sketchbook? I haven't looked through it in ages. I have been afraid of opening it since the fire. I didn't want to see the extent of the damage.

But it's time. My hand reaches down to the shelf where the sketchbook usually lies and grasps empty air instead of the rough edges of bound parchment and paper. My eyes follow, and my heart stutters. The sketchbook isn't there.

"It's here somewhere," I say out loud to reassure myself in the silent apartment. "Perhaps in the bedroom." But even as I move to the hallway, a sinking feeling grows in my stomach. I clearly remember placing the sketchbook on the bookshelf after Jen had glanced through it. A thorough search of my apartment yields the answer I already know.

The sketchbook is gone.

Panic bubbles under the surface even as I try to think. Who would have taken it, and for what purpose this time? I should have protected it, somehow. I was complacent after Drew's incarceration. How many times must I learn the same lesson?

A knock has me sprinting to the door. I fling it open. I must have a wild light in my eyes because Jen looks startled.

"What's wrong, Merry?"

"My sketchbook," I choke out. I take a step into the apartment and rake my hair back through shaking fingers. "It's gone. I know I don't need it, but I can't—I can't..."

"Merry!" Jen looks alarmed and guilty. She comes in and closes the door. "Don't panic. I have it right here." She pulls a package in a plastic bag out of her voluminous purse. "I thought I'd have it back before you noticed. I'm sorry."

My body slumps against the wall with relief, then I snatch the package from Jen's unresisting fingers. My hands shake with anger now instead of fear.

"You had no right."

I march into the living room and sink onto the couch then unwrap the bag with care. I need to see it with my own eyes.

Familiar brown leather with new blackened edges swirls with my own brown lauvan, and I heave a thankful sigh. My fingers run over the charred edge, then catch on something underneath. There is another book there with a laminated red cover and spiral binding. I pull it out. The cover simply states, "Property of Merry Lytton."

I look at Jen with a mute question in my eyes.

"I'm sorry the binding isn't nicer," she says with a wave at the book. "It's all the quick-copy place offered. But I got the sense that the contents were more important to you than the delivery format."

I flip the cover open. The first page of my sketchbook appears. Nimue's gray eyes peek out from the paper with mischief and fun, even through the blocky form and thick lines of my attempt at artistry. It's a high-quality photocopy. I page through the rest, and everyone is there. Perhaps half of the pages are singed at the edges, and a few foreheads and eyes have disappeared into ash, but most pages are intact.

My hands grip the books tightly and my throat closes. Even through her anger and frustration with me, she carried out a plan so thoughtful, so en pointe, so needed. She hasn't given up on me yet, even though I keep giving her reasons to.

"Thank you," I manage to croak out.

"I wasn't trying to be nosy, I swear."

"I know. Oh, I know." I stand and hold the books to my chest. "It's the kindest gesture anyone has done for me in a very long time. And clever—I don't know why I never did it myself."

Jen looks relieved that her gift is well received.

"I don't know either. It was the first thing I thought of when it was on fire. Now you can keep it somewhere safe, and if something happens to your apartment, at least you'll have a copy elsewhere."

Slowly, but without hesitation, I hold the copied book out to Jen. She takes it with a puzzled look.

"Keep it safe for me, please? I want it with someone I trust."

Jen bites her lip then gives me a smile.

"For sure, Merry. I'll keep it safe." She turns to go.

"Jen?"

"Yes?"

"I'm almost ready. Bear with me, all right?"

Jen nods, then closes the door gently. I'm left wondering what she thought of Braulio's photographs tucked into a flap on the last page.

ALSO BY EMMA SHELFORD

ACKNOWLEDGEMENTS

As always, heartfelt thank yous are in order. Gillian and Guy Brownlee, Jude Powell, Kathryn Humphries, and Wendy and Chris Callendar provided outstanding editing and feedback. Maggie Claydon and John-Marc Priest kindly reviewed my manuscript for authenticity in their respective fields (but any mistakes are entirely my own). Dr. Greg Hodges graciously stepped in with his expertise in Latin. Steven Shelford, as always, supports me totally and completely, and never groans when I want to watch *Lord of the Rings* again.

ABOUT THE AUTHOR

Emma Shelford feels that life is only complete with healthy doses of magic, history, and science. Since these aren't often found in the same place, she creates her own worlds where they happily coexist. If you catch her in person, she will eagerly discuss Lord of the Rings ad nauseam, why the ancient Sumerians are so cool, and the important role of phytoplankton in the ocean.

Apart from the Immortal Merlin books, Emma is the author of the Nautilus Legends (a marine biologist discovers that mythical sea creatures are real) and the Breenan Series (a young woman follows a mysterious stranger into an enchanting Otherworld).

Printed in Great Britain
by Amazon